Born in Flames

Candace Knoebel

Thank you, Taylor
You Rock!

a 48fourteen Publishing Trade Paperback

Born in Flames. Copyright © 2012 by Candace Knoebel.

Edited by Kate Wright. Cover by www.ravven.com.

ISBN-13: 978-1-937546-16-8
ISBN-10: 1937546160

Praise for
Born in Flames

~

2012 Turning the Pages Book of the Year Award Winner

"… As a debut novel Knoebel, you hit it out the realm!"

- Autumn at Paperrdolls

"… had me hooked … Who wouldn't want to sink their claws into this book?"

- Jamie Norton at Book Addict

"… fast paced and addicting … A MUST read YA that adults will love to sink their teeth into…"

- Jenny Bynum at Black Words-White Pages

"… a promising start to a new series … intriguing & exciting…"

- Book Passion for Life

"What's not to love? Friendship turning to love, loss, pain, mystery, dragons, magic, unreadable maps, a quest … I couldn't put it down…"

- Sabina of Dangerous Romance

"… I connected with this book immediately… Action, drama, chemistry, and suspense. What more could you ask for?"

- Nicole Tetrev of Book Addicts Not So Anonymous

"… fast paced … enjoyed all the characters …"

- BookNerd Mary

"Knoebel managed to create an amazing fantasy world that you couldn't help but be pulled into …"

- xoBookObsessedxo

"… fresh and original … bound for greatness …"

- Book Pusher

"Knoebel has built a modern, yet fantastical world that leaves one wishing … no not wishing … dying for more!"

- Book Lover 20

For my very best friend, Sonya. Without your unconditional support and talk-me-off-the-ledge ideas, I probably wouldn't have made it. For my wonderful mother and mother-in-law, who have stood by me and supported all my quirks and dreams. And most importantly, for my understanding husband, for having patience and a new joke always on hand.

I love you all with all my heart.

Preface

~

THE CALL OF THE ORB was strong now that it rested in my hands. A song thrummed in my chest as I felt the veins in my neck beating wildly. Looking at it now, the change wasn't as scary as I had thought it would be. Even with knowing that I could be staring my possible death in the face. The question was—would I be strong enough to sustain these powers given to me? Maybe I was just scared of The Fates choosing my destiny, or maybe I was scared that what was about to happen would forever change my life.

Either way, growing up I had always hoped that my life would mean something more than just being a foster child, but this, this was much bigger than anyone could imagine. And what lies ahead? Well if it's anything compared to what I am going through now, then I expect my life to fall into a whole new level of crazy. And I think it may be just what I was looking for.

Chapter 1

~

THE NIGHT WAS STILL AS the pale moon shone through my tiny bedroom window. It was a full moon, one of the largest I had ever seen. Astral said it was a sign of something coming. But what was coming remained unanswered.

All life besides the midnight owl was sleeping—as I should have been—yet I lay there, waiting for the sun to tell me it was time to begin my daily routine.

The owl quivered, shaking off the dewy night as luminescent droplets fell to the mossy earth, then resumed picking at his feathers. We were one and the same, he and I—creatures of the night. Somehow things were easier for me at night, its quiet solitude a balm to my soul. Unfortunately though, I was still part human and expected to be up at the crack of dawn.

I kicked at my wrinkled covers feeling uncomfortably warm. Why did I have to defy the order of things? Wake, eat, school, sleep. That's the way things are supposed to happen. Apparently my restless mind did things a little differently.

If only I had known then how drastically my life was about to change, I may have held onto this moment a bit longer and appreciated the quiet innocence that came with being ten years old. Maybe even appreciated the restlessness that I felt every night. Because even though it may not have been the proper routine to follow, it was my routine. Wake, eat, try to concentrate on learning my powers, and then claw my way to sleep.

But The Fates are funny like that. They don't always wait around for you to decide when things should happen. Sometimes they interfere. At least that's what happened in my case.

I turned from the lonely pallid moon, trying to find the safe haven of sleep by adjusting my rumpled pillow and snuggling up in my blanket in hopes that comfort would help push me into slumber. Of course this attempt didn't prove to be helpful.

A sigh escaped my lips as I propped up onto my elbow in a huff and faced the burning candle resting on the end table next to my bed. The swaying flame always distracted me from my problem with insomnia, the ghostly shadow it cast moving as a pendulum marking the lost hours of sleep. It kept me company when everyone else was fortuned with dreams.

The flame danced for me under my control, a power that I had been blessed with from birth. If I wanted to be pessimistic, I could say the power was more like a curse, considering the destiny The Fates had laid out for me.

I reached out and placed my fingers to the flame, reveling in the feel of the biting tingle to my skin. The tiny flame moved up my arm, warming me through. Fire was the one stable element in my life, a constant burning that ignited my soul.

Another owl hooted in the distance and I smiled as I looked back to the one perched outside my window, returning the hunter's call. *Lucky him*, I thought with a bit of jealously. Even the owl has a friend. If Astral were listening, he would tell me how selfish my thoughts were on such a lovely quiet night. The perks of having a trainer who can read your mind.

As if summoned by my thoughts, my door suddenly burst open. I shot straight up, turning to face the intruder as I pinched the wick to put out the flame and stabled the bouncing pendant on my neck. Astral's glowing blue eyes shone through the darkened hallway, casting a dim glow.

Caught again.

"Aurora, come quick," he urged with an extended hand. I rushed over to the door, noticing a tremble to his hands. Fear snaked its way into the pit of my stomach.

Reaching out, he grasped hold of my wrist and began pulling me down the hall towards the back door. "You must listen to everything I tell you." He rushed on. "This will be our only chance at evading The Fates." He kept his eyes forward, the dim blue glow chasing away the creeping shadows. All his magic was held in the illumination of his eyes—normally he didn't let them glow. So why now?

"Why would we evade The Fates? Why are they here?" I asked, my bare feet slapping against the cold wood floor. I couldn't fathom why we would need to hide from them.

"*We* don't need to hide from them, *you* do," he said with heavy emphasis, tugging harder in his haste. As the hall came to an end he made a sharp left to the back door, already reaching for the doorknob.

The crisp night air bit at my exposed skin when he pulled us outside. I snapped my finger, igniting a tiny flame and touched it to my shoulder. The small flame slid across my skin, instantly warming me and alleviating the gnawing chill.

"Aurora, you're going to bring attention to yourself," he scolded in a stern whisper. "We are trying to hide you from them, not give you away." His ocean deep voice quivered in the silent night air, his words only confusing me more about the sudden urgency of what was happening.

He had always taught me that The Fates were to be respected as Gods. Not to fear them. They gave us the very breath in our lungs, the beating to our hearts. So why should I fear them now? Why would they want me, a mere infant to their existence? I knew I had a small moment of selfish thoughts, but I have lots of those and never before had they come after me for it.

"Where are you taking me?" I asked as his accelerated steps along the damp carpet of grass took us farther and farther away from the comfort of our home. My breath became irregular as my feet padded into the soft ground. Small beads of sweat began to break along my exposed skin, rolling towards the earth.

So much for needing fire for warmth.

He was pulling me towards the woods behind our cottage, the woods that he had specifically told me to stay away from time and time again. I threw a worried glance over my shoulder back to my home. The lights were being turned on one by one, transforming our hidden house into a bright glowing gem in the witching hour. "They're in our house?" I asked, panic rising and cracking my voice. This brought a punch of reality.

"Yes, they're looking for you," he stressed once again, tugging sharply on my arm. The pain from the tugging was hardly noticed due to the rapid fear that now pulsed inside of me.

A painfully loud screeching broke the gasping pants that tugged from my lungs, instantly tucking my curiosities about The Fates at bay as we neared the edge of the woods. It sounded like a thousand people having their souls unwillingly ripped from their bodies. What kind of creature could produce such a horrifying sound?

A line of sweat slid down my face, trailing past my ear. I found myself touching the wetness and using the radiance of the unusually close moon to make sure it wasn't blood.

We were almost to the edge of the forest when the back door to our house slammed shut, echoing off the tree line. Another painful round of screeching followed suit.

Astral's gaze darted behind us, searching for the noisy culprit. "Don't look back," he instructed. Worry clouded the usual strength his eyes held and bit at my composure. He glanced at me apologetically and said, "I should've seen this coming. I should've answered their summons. Your dragon form is a magnet for trouble."

I didn't know how to respond as we entered the inky darkness of the woods quietly, careful not to rouse the lurking shadows. The autumn leaves clung to my damp feet and calves, but the reassuring crunch of broken twigs that normally followed my step was gone. Astral was going through great lengths to keep us hidden by removing the sound of our steps. Even the beautiful radiance of his eyes had disappeared.

I shivered.

A sudden blast of white light illuminated the night behind us like an explosion of fireworks. Their voices—which Astral had described but I had never heard before tonight—once again shrieked loudly. Like jagged metal scraping along another piece of metal, exactly as he had said. I pictured the gates of hell opening up to swallow us whole.

I stumbled and grabbed onto a tree trunk to brace myself, fighting my body against the need to freeze in fear. A fit of shivers began as my hands defensively shot up to protect my abused ears. I silently prayed that my eardrums wouldn't burst, my eyes pooling in pain from the torment.

Astral abruptly stopped and crouched down. He then spoke telepathically, "Get on my back. My enchantments won't hold them off for long."

I did as he said, thankful that he could speak inside my mind. Clinging to his neck, I held my breath as he ran at a supernatural speed, gliding through the misty night.

"Try not to make out the screeching sounds, Aurora, it's not meant for such fragile ears," he continued in my mind. I felt choked in fear by the idea of them catching up to us. Never before had I seen Astral so shaken. He was an Ancient, one who worked for The Fates, and wasn't scared of anything. I just couldn't imagine why The Fates would be so angry with me. Or even why they would want me to begin with.

The moonlight peeked through the thinning tree line like gleaming, hungry fingers anticipating their prey. Peering back, all I could see was the distant glowing house, a mere star in the vast gloomy night. Hope kicked in. Maybe we would get away.

"We're here," said Astral, jarring us to a stop. He let out a pent-up breath and then looked back to the forest, probing for The Fates.

I climbed off his back and found myself standing in a clearing, spinning in a slow circle to quickly survey my surroundings. I had never been on this side of the forest before. Massive black, mirrored stones, immense in their girth, made me feel like a speck in the crowded area. The shadows that preyed over us from the sneaky moon's light only increased my discomfort.

I glanced around one last time, as if that might change the circumstance I was in, and then focused on something simple—the cold leaves still clinging to my feet.

I reached down to brush the leaves off, taking what sliver of control I could over the situation. "Where exactly is here?" I asked through short breaths. Dirt and rotted leaves stuck to my hands. I transferred the slimy mess to my pajama pants as an unstoppable shudder broke.

A swift wind carried the sound of limbs cracking and breaking under great strain from behind us. The familiar vibration of Astral's deep voice began, chanting the ancient magic used for spells as his eyes illuminated brightly. "...Protegum...destructum..." My ears picked up bits and pieces of the old language he quickly weaved.

I turned, seeking out what he could be protecting us from. My heart raced wildly once again as a fresh dose of adrenaline shot through me. The thought of The Fates catching up to us, had frozen my body in place.

The trees began to move under Astral's control, ready to punish whatever was coming. They weaved together to form a barricade, but it was short-lived as Gabe broke through it.

Sword at the ready, he was panting harder than my own anxious heart and covered in a mess of leaves. He sheathed his sword when he saw us, leather hissing as it accepted the blade. Placing both his hands on his knees, he took a moment to catch his breath, green eyes darting from Astral, to the forest behind him, and then to me.

"Sorry," he spoke in between gasping breaths, "I didn't mean to startle you, but your trees almost ate me. I thought you wanted me to get here as quickly as I could." A wry smile appeared on his lips.

Astral's eyes narrowed, his lips forming into a thin line.

Gabe's smile vanished. He cleared his throat and said, "They're closer than we'd like, but everything's in place, sir. The full moon is almost at its peak." He ran his hand through his golden hair. "Eve sent the boy over and is awaiting my arrival with word. I didn't realize the corruption had gone this far. How many are involved?"

"Two out of the four Fates. I received word of their plan to take her life from an inside source just before they showed up. Without the other two stepping in, we can't stop this."

Gabe's shoulders slumped over. "There's no time to enlist their help now, is there?"

"They won't interfere, Gabe," Astral answered helplessly.

"They, unlike their deceitful brothers, uphold the laws of our realm."

I felt my stomach churn as Astral's words sank in. He said they wanted to end my life. He couldn't have meant that.

Astral's hand rested on my shoulder with a gentle, reassuring squeeze. With a protective growl he spoke, emphasizing each word carefully. "When it comes to her, I will do *anything* to protect her. The Fates be damned." I'd never heard him say anything negative about The Fates before.

Gabe's hand shot out to Astral's shoulder, head bowing to the ground. "I understand, old friend. That's why we are doing everything we can to keep her safe. She is our salvation." His voice was so gentle and understanding, it broke the tension of Astral's grip on my shoulder.

"You're right," Astral admitted with a sigh. "My need to protect overwhelms me at times. Everything will be fine. As planned, we will give the Seer her pendant once she ports." He sounded so sure, but his body language was all wrong. He was still standing protectively around me, almost crouching like a cat waiting to pounce. His eyes continued to pierce the forest line.

"They're gaining ground quickly so time is of the essence. You should say your goodbyes now," Gabe said grimly. He glanced back towards the forest. "I hope this works. It's such a shame, both so young. I thought we would've had more time. I thought The Fates would've let the prophecy play itself out. The way it should be."

"I feel they would have, but hunger for power broke two of The Fates. Sending her away will set the prophecy back on course."

My scattered mind was scrambling to catch up. I felt nonexistent as they talked about me, shuddering underneath Astral's steadied hands.

"Gabe said both? I thought they were only after me," I said, pulling on Astral's arm for attention.

"They are only after you. Not to worry. We've got it under control, little one," Gabe answered for Astral.

Everything was happening so fast, too fast. I glanced back up at the bitter moon, the same moon that only a few moments before felt so serene. Now it watched as the rug was yanked out from under me, probably laughing at me for defying life's routine.

We all flinched in alarm at the distant sound of movement disturbing the quiet forest life. "Get the portal ready, now!" Astral barked at Gabe, and then he turned towards me, facing the woods and bending down on one knee. Both his hands were planted on my shoulders as he spoke. "It will be a while before we meet again, my Little Flame. We have but moments left so listen closely. You are going to another realm of time. When you cross over, you will forget everything, but trust in me. When the time comes for you to return, if you choose, you will remember again."

The urgency picked up as his words tumbled over one another in a rush to leave his lips. They were getting close, close enough to light up the darkened woods.

"What do you mean?" I asked, the familiar wetness brimming my eyes. "I want to stay and fight with you. You taught me not to run from fear. Not to be afraid of anything." I spoke fiercely, but my body began to shake against my will as the sinking feeling in my stomach bottomed out. I paused, trying to gather myself, and then asked, "Why are they after me?" I didn't know what to think or feel or even believe anymore.

Reading my mind like he so often had, he tried to justify his actions. "How could I expect you to understand? You're but ten years old, and I am a fool for thinking that by ignoring The Fates, they would go away."

He leaned in closer, madness lacing his sincerity.

"They want to take you away from me. They want to take away

your right to follow your path. I can't let that happen. I must protect you. You *must* remain hidden."

His eyes wove around me and back to the forest. I saw the reflection of the white light inside the pupils of his glowing eyes. They were close behind me now, about to break the tree line.

Gabe's apprehensive cough grabbed our attention. I hadn't noticed him opening a portal, but there it sat in the middle of the clearing, whirling like a black hole.

Astral stood, moving one arm around to clasp firmly on my shoulder, and walked me towards it. "You promise I will see you again?" I asked. Many questions buzzed in my mind, but that was the most important.

"Sooner than later, Little Flame." He pulled me close in a one-armed hug and winked. The screeching that I had heard earlier reverberated through the tree line, echoing in the night air and piercing my already wounded ears. Again my hands sought to cover them in protection.

Astral's eyes lit up to their brilliant blue glow as they filled with sudden fear, his face paling to an opaque white offsetting the brilliance. "You'll be safe, don't worry. You have to go now," he said, pushing me towards the portal.

Gabe was already moving towards the screeching as tree limbs cracked and the ground rumbled. A rush of sleepy animals bolted past me, running for their lives. Shouldn't we follow? I tried to glance around Astral's protective stance, but he prohibited me from seeing the action as Gabe's cry of pain punctured what little bit of composure I had left.

Astral bent down and smiled a ghostly smile and then shoved me through. "Find the keys to return," was the last thing I heard as the pendant on my neck shot to his hands, ripping the connection to my power.

Chapter 2

~

Life in General

FLAMES CONSUMED ME AS I stood in a clearing. I should have been screaming in agony—I could feel my mind doing just that—but then I realized that the flames felt delicious along my skin. I spun in circles, arms stretched out, smiling towards the starry night sky. Somehow I felt at home inside these flames.

In the distance a pair of glowing blue eyes peeked out through the trees. I started to move towards them but then felt shaken. Something was pushing me. I turned, trying to find what was moving my body, but saw nothing. I heard a male voice. "Aurora," it called, the tone ocean deep. I knew the voice, I just didn't know how.

I woke to the incessant buzzing of the alarm clock. A listless glance at the time told me I'd hit the snooze button one too many times, leaving me with only a few minutes to get ready. *Great*, I thought as I rolled my face into the pillow.

The faucet was running in the bathroom, and I could hear the back and forth scrubbing of a toothbrush. Fenn was up, which meant it was almost time to catch the bus.

I kicked at the wrinkled covers and started my ritual of rubbing at my neck in an effort to ease the ache that ran along it. The constant dreams of fire seemed to be the cause of my chronic tension.

I looked over at the clock again and grimaced. If I was going to make it to work on time I really needed to get up and get going. Fenn poked his head from around the bathroom door and said, "Morning, Sunshine," with his toothbrush tucked neatly into the side of his cheek. It was cute, the way the frothy bubbles slid down the side of his toothy grin.

I frowned at him as I walked over to the bathroom, pushing him out of the way and closing the door in his face. I heard him say, "Hey, I wasn't done," but ignored him as I turned the shower on. With a smile, I might add. He could finish up at the kitchen sink.

For some reason this dream made me think of Mily, my foster mom. She did her best to take care of Fenn and me. She was supportive of us, even of the strange occurrences that always seemed to happen when I was around.

As strange and as sad as it sounds, I didn't have any memory of the time before I ended up in the foster home. I was ten, as was Fenn who was dropped off the very same day. From there, well, life just went on. We grew up, graduated, and now the two of us are on our own, trying to scrape by.

Kauai, Hawaii, in the small town of Kapaa, is where amnesia chose to sink in. Rays of sunshine and seas of coconut trees helped to ease the despair that could have easily been my childhood.

Fenn shouted from outside the bathroom door, "Come on Rory! We're gonna be late…again."

I smiled. Fenn had been the one who helped me get through the worst of not knowing who I was. He was in the same boat as far as not remembering anything before the day we were dropped off—it was easily an instant connection. So when it came time to graduate and move out of Mily's, deciding to be roommates was a no-brainer.

Scalding hot water steamed the mirrors and soothed my aching skin. I focused in on the rushing sound coming from the faucet, letting it soothe my rapid mind. Somewhere between the steam and the scented bath soap, I finally found my morning peace.

With a speck of discouragement, I forced myself to shut the water off. It was already my fault we were running late.

I side-eyed the straightener. I guess it would be another humid-air-curled hair day for me. My hair was long and layered, and I certainly didn't have enough time to mess with it.

I took a quick glance in the mirror, rubbing some lip gloss in. My lips were of average size, not too full but not too thin. They suited my oval-shaped face. Freckles danced on both my cheeks just below my eyes.

I threw on the diner's t-shirt and a pair of worn-in jeans and felt ready to embrace the day.

My real parents were out there somewhere, waiting for me to come and find them. Or at least I hoped they were. My plan was to find them whether they liked it or not. What else does an ordinary foster child have to hope for? I say foster child because I refuse to believe that I was abandoned. They simply must have forgotten where they put me.

After shutting and locking the front door, I hurried down the stairs, my footsteps alerting Fenn that I was coming.

"So glad you could bless me with your presence, Oh Late

One," he joked, briskly moving forward. Fenn hated being late for anything.

"No one told you to wait," I answered with a smirk as he took a deep gulp of his on-the-go morning brew. He pulled off the diner's t-shirt and well-worn jeans so much better than I did. His hair however was still in sleep mode, disheveled and out of place which wasn't uncommon for him. And yet, somehow it added to his blue-eyed charming dreaminess.

I don't know why he was in a rush; he was scheduled for a double today, on a Sunday of all days. That meant that I would most likely pick up an extra shift. We were trying to scrape up as much money as we could before making our first attempt at finding each other's birth parents.

For the time being, our money came from a little diner called Paradise Diner where tourists and local blue-collar workers supported us. The constant traffic had landed the local fish fry a feature on TV. I was nothing but grateful for the funds that rolled in with the Diner's fame.

"Hi-ho, hi-ho, it's off to work we go," I chanted sarcastically, squinting into the morning sun.

We took the local bus to and from everywhere in town. It was the perfect means of transportation for us. A car would have been nice, but we were fostered, working on minimum wage and living in a small town. We couldn't really hold our expectations too high. The town was small enough that the commute only lasted between twenty and thirty minutes.

It beat walking.

We reached the bus stop underneath the clear morning sky and I slumped into the far end of the bench, trying to ignore the fidgety man waiting next to me. He clutched an old faded denim backpack to his chest in a death grip.

Sheesh, I thought.

I pulled my tattered baseball cap out of my purse and pushed my hair inside it. I liked to keep my hair tucked away when I was in the general public since it was ruby red and stood out against my pale skin. It helped lessen the curious stares.

I noticed the man next to me, side-eyeing me through my peripheral vision. He had blotchy skin, and smelled of rubbing alcohol. A tuft of milky-white hair sat atop his head and swayed in the breeze. I wondered if the breeze picked up, would the feathery tuft float away like the seeds of a dandelion?

Fenn looked back at the two of us. He shook his head, suppressing a chuckle as he watched the fidgety man squirm next to me. Strange things always seemed to occur around me. This creep was proof of that.

The guy cleared his throat and straightened his back, tightening his grip on the pack, knuckles paling from skin stretched thin. There must be something important inside there.

Fenn casually backed up a couple of steps to be closer to me, whistling and keeping his hands in his pocket, ever the silent protector. It was a job he had always done well. Living on this island, the locals found it hard to adjust to the trouble I unintentionally brought.

I've kind of been responsible for a few accidental fires (started by my thoughts though I never told anyone except Fenn). The fires have only started when I felt angry, but things have definitely exploded into flames around me—things like a bookshelf in a library that took a while to douse out.

Now the town simply looked at me as a freak of sorts, some

religious people even crossing themselves because they believed I could actually hurt them.

So yeah, Fenn was always there to defend me. Just in case.

I glanced at my watch, thinking the bus should be here any minute and that I'd be glad to get away from this freak next to me. His constant squirming didn't sit well with me.

Then I heard the awful screeching of the brakes as the bus came barreling into view a few seconds later. The front wheel plowed over the curb before it came to a thud on the street. The exhaust made a wheezy sound, probably fatigued from the driver's mistreatment, and the hinges squealed as the old doors swung open, inviting us in.

I have told the driver many times that he should probably get the brakes changed, but he always just looked at me and laughed in an idiotic way. Sort of a mix between a cackling witch and a hyena. Visions of sticking my foot in his mouth always came to mind. If only I could set this bus on fire, but then I guess I'd be out of transportation.

"Hit any tourists today?" I asked casually as I stepped onto the bus. His usual smirk instantly pointed south. I kept moving, not giving him a chance to respond, as I pulled my hat down as low as it could go and took my seat near the back. The creepy guy from the bench took a seat directly across from me, continuing to side-eye me.

"Great," I mumbled.

Fenn slid in next to me, and the doors swung shut. The driver pulled out, never checking traffic to ensure the road was clear. All I can say is that we haven't been in an accident yet…and I stress the yet.

We rode in silence for a while as the powerful hum of the engine sang a poor man's lullaby. I could still feel the creepy guy's burning gaze on the side of my face. *What is it with this guy*, I thought. I was tempted to say something, but a large pothole stopped me.

Everything went flying, including Fenn's coffee. Of course it decided to find a dry place to land on, like my shirt. Agitated chatter began as everyone reached for the items that had flown from their laps into the aisle.

"Dang it," I groaned, trying to blot the lukewarm wetness off my white shirt now stained coffee brown. I'd have to change into a new shirt when I got to work. Another small dent in my paycheck.

"Sorry," Fenn said, picking his music player up off the floor. "He's such a douche. When you gonna learn to stop egging him on? You know he did that on purpose." The bus driver's demonic smile peered at me through the rear view mirror. I exhaled sharply, glaring back at him.

A sparkle caught the corner of my eye. In the aisle sat a pendant, right next to the creepy guy's bookbag. He was rubbing his head, probably from smacking it against the window, not paying attention. I leaned over to grab it, arousing his awareness.

Our heads collided on the way down, but my hands were the quickest of the pair. As my fingers touched the pendant, an instantaneous flash of a clearing under an unusually large full moon ran through my mind along with a haunting pair of glowing blue eyes. Then a rush of power, tingling like electricity, spiked up my arm, throwing me backwards and into Fenn's lap with a blast of light. The pendant was seared into my grip, the energy still coursing up my arm and throughout my body.

"Rory, are you okay?" Fenn asked immediately, his worried hands running all over me, checking for any sign of damage.

I looked up at him and said, "Fenn, I'm fi-" but was cut off by the frightened look upon his face. "What?" I asked hesitantly.

"Your eyes, Rory...wait...is that blood?" he asked, panicked. His thumbs pulled at my lower lids as his eyes widened in horror.

"Wha-what?" I stammered, feeling my own panic rise as I pulled my phone out of my pocket and held it up to my face to see my reflection.

My irises were ruby red like my hair. They glistened as they caught the sun's light. I moved to touch them but felt a foreign hand on my shoulder stop me.

"The pendant, girl, give me the pendant," said the creepy man, loud enough for only me to hear.

A low growl built deep within, the pendant warming in my hand as if awakening something in me that had always been there.

"Why do YOU have this?" I gritted through clenched teeth. Something foreign stirred inside me, overtaking my reasoning. Something powerful that longed to break free.

He yanked the pendant from my hand and then placed his hand and face mere inches from my own, a white glow radiating from his palm.

"Silly girl, the bus is no place for your change," he said in a whisper as the blinding glow encompassed my face. I felt the heat kiss my eyes and then it all disappeared.

"Stop it," Fenn commanded, pulling me into him as he shoved the creepy guy off. I shook my head, dizzy from the cloudiness that instantly fogged my brain. Fenn squeezed my shoulder.

"Your eyes…they're, they're normal, but how?" Fenn's concerned face made me turn towards the man who was still staring directly at me, etching this weird moment deep inside my brain. "What did he just do?" whispered Fenn.

My cheeks ran red as I held my gaze with the creep, ignoring the onlookers and their curious stares, and asked, "What did you mean by 'change'?"

The answer never came. He continued to stare a minute more until the screeching brakes told us we had made it to the next stop.

Still staring at me, he grabbed his bag and shoved the pendant inside it, once again clutching it to his chest. He headed off the bus, the white glow on his hand touching each of the passengers as he walked by. Their heads slumped over as the white glow enshrouded them, and then they each shook their heads, dazed, as if trying to remember where they were.

"Did that really just happen?" Fenn asked, muddled.

I blinked, my mind going blank. I wish I could have answered him, but I had no idea what had just happened. My head was still foggy and aching.

"Maybe it was just another strange occurrence?" I suggested, skeptical. I faced him with a forced smile.

"What'd he whisper to you?" His hands were still bracing my shoulders.

"Something about a change…I don't know…it was hard to make out because he was talking so low. Weird, right?"

"Weird is definitely right." His eyebrows knit together, forming a perfect V. "I should follow him and demand an answer." Anger flashed in his eyes. I felt him move like he was about to follow through with that plan so I placed my hand on his chest.

"No, it won't do any good now. He'll be long gone. Let's just forget it, okay? Pretend it never happened and focus on finding my parents." I searched his eyes, waiting for his usual give.

He sighed heavily. "Yeah, you're right. I'm just glad you're okay," he replied, putting his earphones back in and then after a brief smile, turning back to the window.

We still had three more stops to go. Three more chances for me to get a grip on myself before I had to face a restaurant full of curious faces. I sighed and leaned back, putting in my own earphones. I closed my eyes and tried to let what just happened slip away. No use trying to decipher it, I would get nowhere like always. I just knew that finding my birth parents would resolve so many questions. Unfortunately, the beginning of that search was still paychecks away from happening.

Chapter 3

~

Wuik, Oh Joy

THE SHORT RIDE WAS FILLED with nervous tension from everyone praying that we didn't wind up in an accident. My mind was still racing as I tried to forget everything that had just happened. With any luck, I'd never have to see that guy again, but the horrible image of my blood red eyes played back, bringing a shudder along with it. I wasn't ready to face what lurked within me.

The doors rasped open, as a soft gust of tropic air greeted me, calming my frantic nerves. It was one of the few things that I enjoyed most about living here. Salty ocean water mixed with the sweet tang from the local fruit stands always helped dampen my anxiety before work.

For now I'd have to tuck away the incident on the bus and focus. The parking lot was already buzzing with the morning crowd as cars pulled in, drivers anxiously awaiting the famed breakfast. This place never seemed to rest, now more than ever since its fifteen minutes of fame on a food network.

I glanced up at the old wooden dockside house and huffed at the sign that read Paradise Diner. A picture of a mahi-mahi, painted along the front side of the building in bright fluorescent colors, greeted the guests as they walked in. As always, the angry fish stared at me—I guess it was just as happy to be there as I was.

Fenn held the door open for me. We were instantly greeted with the sounds of early bird chatter and the smells of freshly brewed coffee mixed with French toast and sausage. The servers already on the floor glanced up at us with pleading eyes. *Here we go*, I thought glumly.

Fenn put his hand on the small of my back and pecked the side of my hair, whispering, "Catch ya later," as he hurried to the kitchen. He was one of the three chefs and would clock me in, as usual.

"I didn't think you guys would ever get here. Over slept again, didn't you?" asked Susan, the shift leader, as she marched up to me smacking her bubble gum. She could have been plucked straight from the eighties with her side ponytail and pink lipstick. A little over the top if you ask me.

"You know how I do," I responded lightly, straightening my ball cap and pulling my shirt out to show the stains.

"I was going to ask you," she said, pointing at my newly dyed shirt, "what did you do?"

"Not what *I* did, it's what the bus driver did." I rolled my eyes at the memory and then felt a wave of nausea. I shook it off, not willing to let the strange occurrence ruin my day.

"Ah, I see, I see," she said, pulling me out of my thoughts, "yes that explains it. Well, go ahead and grab a new one and then meet me back here." She patted my arm and then, swiping up a few menus, turned to some customers who had just walked through the door.

A box in the back of the diner was packed with extra shirts, adorned with the infamous mahi-mahi. "Oh how I love to wear him day after day, greeting my potential paychecks with a chest full of ugly fish," I said out loud with a giggle.

The morning went by quickly and led straight into the hurried and moody lunch crowd. Susan moved me from hosting to waiting tables for the lunch hour so she could take a break. It was the distraction I needed to keep me from continually revisiting the bus incident.

"Please," she said, bracing my shoulders as she pleaded without dignity, "I *need* a smoke."

She needed *not* to smoke, but I wouldn't tell her that. I figured her blood-shot eyes and washed out brown skin spoke for themselves. It's not that I didn't like Susan—I didn't like to be touched by anyone that I wasn't close to. So that narrowed it down to just about no one, except Fenn.

"It's cool, I've got it under control," I reassured her, politely removing her wrinkly, sun-damaged hands from my shoulders.

"Good 'cause look what the cat just drug in, or threw up," she shuddered, motioning her head to the front door.

Time stopped for a moment as dread spread throughout my body like a rapid disease.

"This can't be happening," I said under my breath. It was the creepy guy from the bus. Was he following me?

He seated himself in my section without waiting for a hostess to show him to a table. As soon as he sat down, his eyes shot to mine, the intensity of his gaze freezing my train of thought.

Stop it, I thought to myself, trying to regain my composure, to not let fear dictate me. I straightened my apron and put confidence in my stride as I approached his table.

"Good afternoon, sir, can I get you something to drink?" I asked, noticing the slight quiver to my voice.

He opened his menu and took his time to glance over everything, never acknowledging my presence or the fact that I had just asked him a question. Rude, but somehow expected coming from him. A foreign burning rage began to build deep inside of me.

"Would you like some coffee, water, maybe a glass of soda?" I gritted out, adding in my head, *maybe a lobotomy?* I squashed the smile that tried to form on my lips.

He huffed at my suggestions with an air of smugness and flipped to the back of the menu. I rolled my eyes and saw the jean bookbag sitting on the floor next to his chair. The amulet popped into my head along with an urge to take the bag and run.

I was just about to act when he looked up from the menu and said, "I'll have a cup of coffee and some toast," in a deep, almost philosophical voice. The one good attribute he seemed to have. His face looked unnerved as I blushed. I hoped I wasn't as readable as I felt.

Fenn always told me that I couldn't hide my emotions, that everything I felt seemed to be written on my face. Apparently that was why I could never lie to him.

"I'll be right back with that," I mumbled as I quickly walked away. I could feel his gaze searing my back.

"Fenn, that guy from the bus is here," I announced as I busted through the kitchen door.

"Really? I guess he needs me to show him that he's not going to play games with you," he declared, untying his apron and heading towards the door.

"No," I rushed to him, handing him back his apron, even helping him tie it. "Maybe," I paused, trying to decide if I really wanted to go there, "maybe it's just a coincidence he's here. And if it's not a coincidence, then maybe I need to hear what Mr. Creepy has to say? I mean, I could be like," I leaned in to whisper, "a demon or something." I finished tying his apron and stepped back to face him.

He laughed. "Rory, if you're a demon then I'm rich and famous. Oh wait, that's right…I'm not. And you're not a demon. But I don't think looking to 'Mr. Creepy' for answers is a good tactic. It's dangerous and I don't like it one bit. After the bus and your eyes… what if he hurts you? I will kill him if he lays one finger on you."

"Fenn," I said condescendingly, trying to dissuade his intent, "reason with me…if he tries anything, anything at all, you're within shouting distance. Okay?"

He nodded in agreement as Susan burst through the door, bumping into me and knocking the prepared salad over.

"Oh, sorry, Rory," she said quickly, bending over and tossing the wasted lettuce into the garbage can. "I need you to pick up my shift tonight, if you don't mind." She looked panicked. The same look she always wore when she was thrown off her daily schedule.

"Okay," I said, suddenly seeing my way out of dealing with Mr. Creepy. She pulled me into a tight hug as I looked back at Fenn and smiled. He smiled back.

"The babysitter, she's…"

"Sick again," I said, finishing her sentence as relief washed over me.

"Yes. I'll cover for you right now so you can have a break before I leave." Exactly what I wanted to happen. I told her every table's order and pummeled out the back door. Fresh air never felt so good.

Fenn and I spent most of our breaks out back sitting on upside down buckets. A lot of good theories and ideas were sprung here while looking at the distant ocean.

I was relieved to not have to go back and face Mr. Creepy. Facing him meant facing whatever was wrong with me. What else, besides a demon or some kind of devil, could have red eyes like that? From touching a necklace?

I picked up a dry twig that rested on the gravel and stared at it. I wanted to try and set it on fire with my mind, like I had so many times before. Too many times to count on my hands.

But nothing happened as expected. It only worked when I was really angry, which was not convenient. I lost track of time as I sat there trying and trying again with nothing to show for.

Fenn poked his head out the back door. "Break's up, Rory." I glanced down at my watch.

"Dang it," I muttered, snapping the twig in half and tossing it. I'd been out here for a good 45 minutes wasting time on a solitary dead limb. Thank goodness nobody was here to witness my futile attempts.

Then my stomach went sour. Hopefully Mr. Creepy would be long gone by now. He certainly had plenty of time for coffee and toast.

Susan was sitting on a crate, impatiently tapping her foot when I came back inside. "Sorry." I shrugged as I took the orders from her and left the kitchen.

I stumbled forward when I saw Mr. Creepy still sitting at the table. Our eyes met and then I looked away.

Oh well, if he wants to hang here, so be it. I would just give that table to someone else. And with coming to that decision, the afternoon rolled into the bustling night smoothly. He stayed at his table, watching me. I could feel his gaze on my every move, but I did my best to ignore him.

Fenn periodically poked his head out through the kitchen doors, checking on me, and giving me some reassurance. Before I knew it, we were locking the doors. Closing was the easiest part of the job.

But not tonight.

As I walked Mr. Creepy to the door and went to lock it behind him, his arm shot out and grabbed onto my wrist in a sumo death grip. The pupils to his eyes went white, churning the building fear in my stomach. His grip tightened. And then he spoke: "Of dragon born, a conqueror prevails. The chosen one fated to protect the dying race. Third of three deemed protector to the Progeny. The other marked for revenge. The book of life pages turn yet unwritten. The canvas to your mortal soul. The connection to your immortal enemy. A death will come to He that breaks the barrier."

A flash of white so bright it nearly blinded me shone through his eyes while he spoke, and then he blinked them back to normal. That sound of his voice, the sound of a thousand voices speaking through one, resounded in my head.

"Let GO of me!" I yelled. Fenn was already behind me, circling his arm around my waist and yanking the guys grip off of me. He shoved the guy back, moving to close the door, but I stopped him, my heart beating wildly against my chest.

"Don't," I cried out, shoving Fenn out of the way as I rushed to face Mr. Creepy again. A better time to get answers couldn't have slapped me in the face any harder.

"Who are you?" I asked, breath rushing out of me while holding the door open. Mr. Creepy stood still, eyes unmoving.

"Rory, get back, he's dangerous. Didn't you see what just happened? Don't do this," Fenn pleaded. I jerked my head around to face him, scrunching my eyes in annoyance, and said, "Just give me a minute."

He huffed and then stepped back, clearly angry with me.

I turned to Mr. Creepy. "You can't just waltz in here, stalk me all day, then go all prophet on me and not explain who you are and why you are doing this to me." I grabbed his pasty arm and pulled him back into the restaurant. Everyone had left so I figured this was the best place to confront him. "So again I ask, who are you?"

I crossed my arms and waited, impatiently tapping my foot as the silent seconds seemed to drag on forever.

His chest puffed up. "I am the answer to your questions." He stuck his chin out. "And here you stand so defiant and demanding answers while you should be questioning who *you* are."

I stepped back towards Fenn, seeking that protected feeling he always gave off, as the reality of what Mr. Creepy had said hit home.

"Why do you think I stopped you?" My eyes fell to the floor. "Obviously because I *do* question who I am," I rushed out. "Instead of mocking me, why don't you try explaining? The pendant...your eyes...my eyes...my strange abilities with fire. Why is all of this happening?" I asked boldly.

"Because you are the Progeny, the chosen one," he answered, pausing to let it sink in.

I took a step back.

"The Progeny? To what? What am I chosen for?"

"Did you not hear a word I said to you, girl?" he asked, annoyed. "I foretold the prophecy to you. Did you not listen?"

I frowned. "I did listen. It sounded like a lot of mumbo jumbo to me," I mumbled.

His face distorted as if I had insulted him. "Mumbo jumbo?" he repeated, sounding as if the words he had just said were curses. "I foretell a prophecy that declares you as a savior, and you insult me in return?"

"Look, I'm not trying to insult you, I'm just trying to understand," I admitted, hoping that he'd show some sympathy.

He huffed and then rolled his eyes. "First, you have to find the keys in order to return home. The rest of the answers lie within the prophecy."

It was like hearing Pig Latin. "What keys? This can't be real. This can't be happening," I said under my breath. I suddenly felt my world shifting and crumbling beneath me. Everything that I have ever known…

Fenn tugged on my hand, startling me. "The chosen one? Really? What kind of rubbish is this? Aurora, seriously, you're really going to listen to this guy?" His voice was disapproving.

A low-bellied laugh came from Mr. Creepy. "You think you are excluded from this boy? Have you not also questioned who you are? How naïve." He looked Fenn over with a patronizing stare.

Fenn's fists clenched as his eyes narrowed into slits. "What are you even talking about?" The confidence in his voice was gone.

I looked at my friend through new eyes. All these years, I had only thought of me and my weirdness. We had only discussed my incidents. Stuff was happening to him too? I didn't know if I should be hurt that he didn't confide in me or pleased that I wasn't alone.

"Fenn?" I asked, disbelief coloring my tone.

"Ahhh…so you haven't told the Progeny then, have you?" Mr. Creepy asked smugly.

"That's none of your business," Fenn retorted. "And since you think you know so much then tell me who I am." He ignored my stare and the fact that he had just been called out.

Mr. Creepy didn't hesitate. "You are third of three deemed protector to the Progeny. Do not look at me and tell me you have not felt your magic stir within you."

Fenn shook his head as if trying to take it all in. I just continued staring at him open-mouthed.

"What? You both have nothing more to say? No smart remarks? And to think I gave everything up for this. For a Progeny who doesn't even believe in her own destiny? For a boy who dares to question me? He told me you would know, assured me that my sacrifice would be worth the price," Mr. Creepy ranted, anger rising in his voice. "You are mere children. You know nothing. Instead you cower at the truth. How can you save us when you can't even accept what has always been right in front of you?" He was now yelling at the top of his lungs while pacing to and fro. Crackles of bright white energy popped around him sporadically.

"But you can help us, right?" I spoke up, so shaken by everything that I felt obligated to try and accept what he was saying.

He stopped mid-stride and said, "Only if you are ready to accept the truth." The sparks fizzled out like a sparkler.

Fenn's head was still shaking as if trying to undo all that had been said. I laid my hand on his chest.

"Fenn?" He looked down at me, eyes intently searching mine. "I know finding each other's parents was the plan, but what if this is the right way to go?"

He looked away, his lips forming into a hard line. He didn't want me to push the issue. But I kept on. "My 'incidents' can't be coincidence. And you…he said you're a part of this too." I leaned in to him, catching his gaze. "As much as I want to deny this, it feels right. You know?"

I felt Fenn give in to me. A smile formed at the corner of my lips. He leaned his head forward, resting it against mine.

Then, out of the corner of my eye I saw Mr. Creepy move, his hands once again glowing that eerie white glow as they moved towards where Fenn and I stood.

"He said to let you choose, but you have no choice," he began, his voice low and cold. "You need to know the truth. This should've been done long ago." Fenn shoved me out of the way and tackled Mr. Creepy, slamming his body onto a table.

"I may be a freak like you and have whatever that," Fenn pointed to Mr. Creepy's glowing hand, "is, but I bet I'm much stronger than you." His hand was around Mr. Creepy's throat, pinning him against the table. He held him there for a moment, daring him to try something else. Mr. Creepy didn't fight back.

When Fenn let up, Mr. Creepy stood and straightened his clothes. He went to take a step in my direction, but Fenn pushed him back once again. His face was rigid. "Don't try it, buddy," he threatened, his tone livid.

Mr. Creepy shook his head. "Fools. You are both fools and will die fools," he declared, and then stalked off towards the door.

"Wait," I called out, but Fenn stopped me, pulling me back and walking me away from the door.

I needed to see, needed to watch the answer to all my questions walk away. I peered over Fenn's shoulder and found the eyes of the man searing into mine.

I tightened my grip around Fenn, pushing a little harder on my tip-toes to get a better view as Mr. Creepy backed up slowly, shadows creeping up from the ground to his feet. They moved up his legs and then covered his chest, leaving the whites of his eyes as the last image I had of him burned into my brain.

"A death will come to He that breaks the barrier." The last line of the prophecy Mr. Creepy just gave replayed through my mind like a haunting tune as he disappeared.

If any of what he had said was true…I shook my head. It wouldn't help to worry, it's not like I'd ever get a chance to find a way to keep death away now that Mr. Creepy was gone.

I laid my head on Fenn's shoulder, scared. Scared of what was to come. Scared of what he had said and what he had done and, most of all, scared of what I was.

"Hopefully we'll never see him again," Fenn said curtly. He slowly let go of me, moving to stack the rest of the chairs.

"Hopefully?" I asked severely. "Fenn, you just ruined any chance we had at finding out exactly what *we* are. You know, since you conveniently forgot to clue me in on the energy you feel flowing through you," I said in a disparaging tone. I wanted him to hear the hurt in my voice.

He stiffened, keeping his back to me as he spoke through a low voice. "You don't know what you're talking about and neither did he." He turned to face me. "I don't feel anything," he finished with heavy emphasis.

But he didn't look at me when he said it, something he only does when he's lying.

I felt my face go hot with fury. He still chooses to lie to me? My palms tingled with an urge to slap him.

"Well, whether you lie to me and yourself or not, it's real, and it was right there, in our faces, and you ruined it." I looked away, deliberately.

"No, Rory, you're wrong. I saved us," he said firmly, his eyes blazing. "We don't even know who that lunatic is. I mean, if you want to believe him so bad, then did you ever consider that he could be from the wrong side of wherever we're from? He could've killed you." He slammed the chairs as he stacked them, struggling to control his anger.

"Well, I guess we'll never find out now, will we? Thanks for that," I threw back at him sarcastically.

"You're welcome," he replied bitterly, untying his apron and throwing it in a bundle on the ground. He stormed off towards the kitchen, probably to clock us out.

I watched him through a haze, seeing him but not really watching him as my mind began to tumble in what had just happened.

I inhaled, dragging in a deep breath, pulling the air through my body as if it would wash away the fear and uncertainty of the situation. It felt good, that deep breath, but it didn't change anything.

I knew Fenn didn't want to take any serious thought to that guy's words, but something in me couldn't ignore them. They related to all the other crazy things that had happened to me. And the magic that guy used was undeniable.

I repeated what he had said over and over inside my head, trying to sear it deep into my memory. The word, dragon, sent a jolt through me. He said I needed to find the keys in order to return home. I wouldn't even know where to begin without his help.

With more questions than answers, I picked up Fenn's apron and counted my tips, separating out the house money. Fenn returned moments later and flipped the lights off. He broke the silence by saying, "I don't want to argue with you. Let's go home." He sounded sincere.

I rolled my eyes as an answer and followed suit as he threw his arm over my shoulder.

Chapter 4

~

The Truth Will Set You Free

ON THE BUS, I YAWNED as the streetlights lit up the empty vessel, small blips of light peeking in and out as we rumbled down the quiet streets. The driver's usual arrogance was gone, maybe with the late hour. Does he ever take a break from driving? The thought came and went. I didn't care, I was tired and just wanted to be home.

Fenn pulled out one of my earphones and whispered, "Tomorrow will be a better day, I promise." Then he gently leaned his head against mine.

"Yeah," I replied monotonously.

The screeching of the obnoxious brakes told us that we had made our destination. I took Fenn's offered hand and pulled my aching body out of the seat.

A lit sign announced M tel 6 right above a man dressed in rags holding onto a rusted shopping cart full of knotted plastic bags. I looked up to the second floor of the motel where our room was. *Yep, this is my life*, I thought with a sigh as we walked across the desolate, fissured parking lot.

I trudged up the stairs, anxious to be in the comfort of my home. Fenn and I shared a cheap room with a queen-sized mattress on the floor in the middle of the room. A TV rested on a cheap old end table we found at a yard sale. In the far corner was our tiny, run-down bathroom, the chipped tile and rotting paint still waiting for the manager to fix. The kitchen consisted of a stove, a refrigerator, and a sink along the back wall. A couch, doubling as Fenn's bed, sat along the front window next to a dresser that we shared.

The pink and green striped wallpaper peeled off in various places revealing the cold, hard concrete walls. I was tempted to rip all the wallpaper away and be done with it. At one time, I'm certain the wallpaper meshed with the hunter green carpet.

I quickly changed and got situated before letting the bed engulf me. Falling onto my bed after a long day was a feeling that I always looked forward to.

Fenn pulled out the couch. I watched him through dreary eyes as he put his sheet on and threw his pillows to the end. My comforter did its intended job of being very comforting, like a mother's love. In my case, it was Mily, my foster mother's smiling face that had always comforted me.

Instead of throwing himself into his own bed of comfort, Fenn walked over to me and said, "Can we talk for a sec?"

"Sure," I replied, scooting over so he had room to sit.

The nervousness that lingered in the air reminded me of standing on Mily's doorstep at the age of ten, unsure of where I was or how I'd gotten there. When she opened the door, Fenn was standing behind her, and somehow by seeing him, well, I just knew that I'd be okay.

"I want to talk to you about something." He spoke softly and stared at the floor, his shoulders slouched over, both hands gripping the bed. Whatever it was, it was serious.

"Okay," I eased.

"What that man said was true…I have felt something inside

me before. But never like how you've described it. And I've never actually *done* anything, like with fire or whatever. I've just always felt...different." He didn't look at me, which was what he often did when he was uncomfortable.

I felt a rush of excitement as I asked, "But different how?"

He shifted and said, "Like whenever you seem in danger or something, this rush of strength surges through me. I can lift things that are at least four times my weight. And I heal quickly. Any cut that I've ever had has always healed hours after." He finally looked at me, his eyes full of uncertainty.

I laid my hand on his back. "It's okay, Fenn. Maybe this is why we don't remember our childhood. You don't have to be scared," I said, trying to help him along.

"I'm not scared," he said defensively. "I've just never said anything because there was already so much going on with you. I didn't want you to worry." He paused a moment, as if deliberating, and then finished, "I think I just didn't want to come to terms with it. I just want to be normal." He leaned into me, resting his head against mine like he always does when needing relief.

"Well, it seems like we don't have much of a choice. We are what we are," I said softly.

"We *do* have a choice, Rory." He sat up. "Avoid it and continue living normally. Just the little bit that we've experienced so far has been too dangerous for you, and I can't let anything happen to you. You have to trust me," he urged.

I felt the threat of a smile and tried to tuck it away. "That sounds a lot like what Mr. Creepy said. You're my protector, remember? And you're not fighting that instinct," I teased.

There was an immediate awareness in his eyes as my words hit home. He knew I was right.

"I do trust you, Fenn, and I'm really glad you decided to tell me the truth. Let's just take it one day at a time. See what happens, okay?"

He nodded and kissed my forehead.

A soft, very faint melody sounded in my mind as the kiss to my head lingered on a moment longer. It was the oddest, most hauntingly beautiful sound I'd ever heard. A tingly feeling awoke in the pit of my stomach from the warmth of his breath against my face.

My cheeks were instantly red. "Good night," I said with as much indifference as I could muster, turning away from him.

I slumped back into my bed where I could hopefully rest for the night, pulling the sheet up to cover my nose. I rolled over and shut my eyes as tight as they would go.

Something happened when he kissed me so softly, something I wasn't ready to acknowledge. *Ignore it*, I thought as the soft whirl of the fan pushed me into sleep.

I woke only a few hours later from the confusion of a dream and found myself curled into Fenn. My hand was resting across his chest, as if we'd slept this way a thousand times.

When the haze of sleep wore off, it hit me. I slowly eased myself off of him and onto my side hoping that he wouldn't wake to find me there. I didn't want him to get the wrong idea. We were just friends...right?

Get up, I told myself. *Just get up and go back to your own bed.* But I didn't want to. It felt right to be next to him. "At four o'clock in the morning?" I whispered as I glanced at the clock. What was I thinking?

"Alright," I mouthed to myself, and slowly tried to ease up on one arm. But just as I pushed up, his arms locked around me, and he said, "Stay just a little while longer." He gently pulled me back to his chest.

I lay there wide-eyed and caught.

"Huh?" I asked, holding my breath as I waited to see if he was actually awake. But he wasn't.

I wonder if he was thinking of me when he said that. Maybe I should just stay. No, that would be stupid. He would get the wrong idea.

He began to say something else so I leaned in to listen, not following my own advice. "No, the bumblebees are coming," he muttered. His words were so jumbled, it was almost impossible to make them out.

I silently laughed, letting the moment pass, and eased out of his bed, heading back to my own. Huffing at my insanity, I pulled the blankets up over my head. This is ridiculous. Every night I wish for peaceful sleep, and every night I'm still lying here, waiting for sleep to come.

Waking up in a good mood would be completely out of the question come morning. "Let's try this again," I whispered to myself and closed my eyes. Maybe this time the dream gods would leave me alone so I could actually sleep.

Chapter 5

~

The Surprise!

I WOKE THE NEXT MORNING greeting the ceiling with a blank stare. I rolled over and then grimaced at Fenn. His intruding smile illuminated his face.

"Well, good morning to you too, Sunshine," he taunted as he got up from the couch and headed to the bathroom.

"How long have you been sitting there?" I called out, rubbing the sleep from my eyes.

"Long enough to hear all your secrets," he replied with a wry smile before he shut the bathroom door.

I rolled my eyes. Mr. Creepy's eyes suddenly popped into my head—flashing a white so bright it had burned into my retina. I needed to find him and learn more. But how could I do that with both Fenn and me having the day off?

"You okay?" Fenn asked as he came out of the bathroom. "You have that serious plotting look written all over your face."

"No, I don't," I replied a little too hastily. "Are *you* okay?" I tried to sound inconspicuous.

"Uh, no," he said as he moved to the couch.

That's when I noticed my bookbag by the door. I'd put that

away on the highest shelf in the closet after graduating, glad to never have to use it again. Why was it out?

I crept over to it and rummaged through its contents. An extra pair of clothes, a sheet, my phone...

"Okay? What's this?" I asked with a grin.

He was sitting on the couch flipping through channels on the TV, all casual-like.

"What's what?" he asked innocently. His lips twitched, fighting back a smile.

I sat down next to him and noticed that he smelled like a fresh bar of soap. I looked swiftly away, my face instantly flushed. What is wrong with me? That tingly ache resurfaced over my skin.

I recovered my composure and said, "What do you mean, 'what's what?' You know what I'm talking about. Where are we going?"

"That is for me to know and for you to find out, little lady. A little normalcy for a change might do us some good." A smug grin stretched across his face.

"Is that what you think?" I retorted, trying to hide my elation.

"Yep, so you need to get ready. We are on *my* time today, which means *on time*, something I know you're not used to," he finished with a laugh. He looked satisfied.

"We're on *my* time," I mimicked as I headed to the bathroom, blissfully smiling.

I took a quick shower, pulled on a pair of torn jean shorts and a hot pink cami, and threw my damp hair into a sloppy ponytail. I really couldn't have moved any faster.

Locking up, I rushed to meet Fenn downstairs, my footsteps bouncing with giddiness. Although it was a detour from what I had initially wanted to do, it was something he had planned, exclusively for us, which was not typical for him. Acknowledging that idea awoke many butterflies.

I stopped when I saw what Fenn was standing next to. Mily's car was parked in the first parking spot. "Pretty courageous," I commented, impressed.

"She let us borrow her car. She must be losing it." Fenn smiled. I hopped in and noticed he had a CD of my choice playing. Indie Rock.

"Awwww," I stretched out. "I'd be so lost without you," I quickly looked to the window as crimson once again marked my cheeks. I could have said it before and it wouldn't have embarrassed me, but now... I let the thought disappear as quickly as it had surfaced.

His hand touched my knee. I jumped. Then his fingers brushed under my chin, turning my face to him. "I feel the same," he replied, keeping his smoldering eyes locked with mine. My breath caught and then he looked away, easing the intensity of the moment.

For a moment, I couldn't speak. There was no denying what he meant. The music filled the ticking seconds as I tried to erase the shock from my face.

"So...where to, Oh Mysterious One?" I finally managed.

With a secretive smile, he threw the car in drive and peeled out of the parking lot.

"Put this on," he said, tossing me a bandana.

"For what? And could you please slow down a bit? That was a little dramatic, don't you think?" I asked, tightening my seatbelt for effect.

"Just put it over your eyes until I tell you to take it off," he instructed, curbing the lead in his foot.

"Is this some sort of fantasy that you've always dreamed about? Having me blindfolded?" I wrapped it tight around my eyes.

"You know it," he confirmed with a chuckle as I relaxed back into the seat and let the morning glide past. The mid-June breeze drifted through the car, the sweet hint of blossoming fruit mixing with the scent of the ocean. My sense of smell was heightened from my closed eyes. It was a heavenly morning, relaxing my soul.

Just as I began to nod off Fenn said excitedly, "Okay Rory, take it off."

I hurriedly untied it and found myself staring at The Grand Palms of Lihue, a hotel built to house the rich tourists that stimulate our tiny economy. We never had a reason to come out this far. Commercial restaurants and fancy hotels didn't really appeal to me.

"What are we doing here?" I asked in dismay.

He turned the car off and slid out, lightly jogging over to my side of the car and opening the door.

"Don't be such a pansy, Rory. We're going into that hotel and having a nice breakfast like normal people would do. And you are not going to fight me on this. Today is going to be one hundred percent normal," he said as he tugged my arm.

"But that's a five star restaurant, Fenn. We can't afford that." I yanked my arm back and pouted. "Just what I need…an opportunity for more people to stare at my hair."

"No one will stare at you," he said, tilting my chin up. My eyes lifted to his. "I've got this under control so get your butt out of this car." His eyebrows grazed his hairline in expectation.

"Whatever you say, Fenn." I gave up. Only because he had planned this and I didn't want to ruin it.

As we walked up to the sliding doors, I took a deep breath, preparing myself for all the stares. But once inside the lobby all of that worry disappeared. I paused in awe, letting the surrounding beauty soak into me.

The crystal chandelier swayed slightly from the breeze as the door opened and closed. Red carpet lay effortlessly against the tile flooring and played off the white pillars that lined either side of the lobby leading up to the massive center staircase.

Fenn had already moved up to the front desk and was looking back at me, waving his hand to hurry me along.

I slid my arm through his as he led me to the lounge area where we were met by a hostess who quickly showed us to a table for two.

I nudged him and said, "Thanks, Fenn, this really means a lot. I guess your sweeter side isn't as dusty as I thought."

"Oh, does this come across as sweet? It's all just a part of my master plan to make you fall for me..." He broke off with his quirky smile as I poked him teasingly.

I rolled my eyes and said, "Ha ha...you. You're just *so* funny."

He pretended to wipe laughing tears from his eyes. "I try, I try."

A blur of black and white caught my eye as the waiter approached the table.

I ordered what Fenn was having, trusting that he had already looked over the menu. My appetite was usually one with the birds.

"So, what do *normal* people talk about? Hmm," I teased. "Are you happy with the way your life is turning out?"

He shook his head with a smile and said, "Yeah, of course, I hadn't imagined it any other way. Being with you and on our own, well, it's perfect right now." He was stacking the coffee creamers.

"I'm just glad that I have a roommate, one that I can trust and feel comfortable around. Even though he's not normal," I played, continuing to hint at what he was trying to avoid today.

He narrowed his eyes at me. "Come on, Aurora. Just one day. Is that so much to ask?"

"Sorry," I said, fidgeting with my silverware.

"Oh look, food." He smiled.

The waiter brought us our orange juice and some biscuits, and I watched as Fenn smothered his in honey. I giggled when the napkin he picked up stuck to his fingers. His agitated state was amusing to me, like a monkey banging the keyboard on a desk because he can't figure out how to use it.

I dipped the tip of my napkin in my water and handed it to him. "Here use this to wipe it off, goof ball," I said, smiling.

This really was pleasant, a feeling I hadn't experienced in a long time. "You're the Yin to my Yang," I blurted out, hoping he wouldn't catch the real meaning.

"Oh yeah?" he said, picking up on our old little game. "You're the pen to my paper," he retaliated.

I smiled and shot back, "You're the music to my I-pod." I got him good with that one.

He snickered in response. "Puh-lease, you are the lyrics to my heart song."

I rolled my eyes. Crap. "You're the cheese to my macaroni?" I knew I had been defeated.

"Seriously?" he asked, strained in laughter. "You're going to pull the same line you used when we were like what, fourteen? Smooth," he joked.

The waiter walked up balancing a tray filled with our breakfast. He laid it out, the smell tantalizing our taste buds.

"My kind of breakfast," I mumbled as I dug into the delicious sausage. We ate in silence. After the waiter took our plates away, Fenn decided to pick up the conversation where it had left off.

"So about the Yin and Yang thing, I've always felt that way about you. You're my perfect balance. That's why I set this whole thing up. And I was thinking, recently that is…" His face went red as I coughed a little. I didn't want to go there because going there would mean a change in our already perfect relationship.

"I was only playing," I said quickly before he could finish that thought. "People like us don't find a perfect balance, realistically I

mean. We're lucky enough if we can live our lives coming to terms
with who we are. Why add something as complicated as a relationship with someone else's feelings to the picture?"

He stared at me in disbelief. "Who said anything about a relationship?" He pulled his napkin off his lap and bunched it up a little
aggressively before throwing it on the table. "I was just gonna say
we should maybe invest in a car together or something because I
trust you and I know how much you hate the bus."

My face flushed.

"Gosh, Rory, you really thought I was gonna say something as
crazy as I have feelings for you or something like that? That would
be way too *normal*," he said bitterly, turning to stare out the window.

Okay, so that hurt. It shouldn't have, but it did. "I'm sorry," I
said lamely. "Excuse me." I quickly stood and headed to the bathroom.

Standing in front of the gilded mirror, I asked myself, "What is
wrong with you?"

Fenn would be a perfect balance if I chose to let myself go,
which for a moment back there I had. I let him know that when I had
unintentionally said the yin-yang thing out loud. He thought it was
a game I was initiating, but was it really? I just couldn't bear messing up with him and losing his friendship. He was my best and only
friend in the whole world.

"Get it together," I said as I splashed water over my face.

A few minutes later I left the bathroom, only to find an empty
table. Fenn's chair was flipped over, and there were people gathered
at the window, occasionally glancing back at our table.

Uh-oh, I thought as I stepped through the automatic doors.

There he was walking out to the parking lot. But he wasn't alone. In front of him was Mr. Creepy. Fenn was following him. No, not following him—he had one hand around the guy's arm, pushing him forward and shouting at the top of his lungs. This couldn't be good.

I hurried over to the car and waited, watching as they yelled at each other. Then, as if he felt my presence, Mr. Creepy's eyes shot to mine, burning through my core. My brows furrowed as Fenn yanked the guy's chin away from me and back to his face.

"You don't look at her, you hear me? You don't touch her, you don't follow her." He leaned into the guy's face a little closer, crowding him, and finished, "and you NEVER go near her again or you will have to deal with me." He shoved him hard against Mily's car.

I winced. Mr. Creepy straightened himself out, defiantly sticking his chin up at Fenn. I could feel the burning desire, the anger, and the hatred emanating off of both of them.

"You will do this alone then. And when *she*," he pointed toward me, "is harmed by your ignorance, don't come looking for me," he snapped, his tone cutting. His eyes lit up as he scowled, and then he turned his back on me and walked away.

I was stunned silent. Harmed? Panic flooded my veins as I moved to plead for an explanation. But he was already gone.

Fenn appeared in my line of vision. "Ready to go?" he asked tightly, forcing a smile.

"Again? Really? You blew our only source at finding things out again? Fenn, he said I would be harmed!" I glared at him.

"He-he's full of it, Rory," he said skeptically. "I wouldn't let anything happen to you. Remember? Super strength? And what happened to having a normal day? We can't very well do that with him tagging along, ranting some crap about lightning and fire and the initiation to your change happening tonight. He's crazy and likes to ramble a bunch of nonsense."

He opened my door, indicating with his hand that he wanted me to get in. Sucks to be him because I wasn't moving.

"You mean to tell me," I said under my breath, poking his chest as my temper flared, "that he told you something would happen tonight? Information coming from a man who obviously knows things about us. Things we've never disclosed to anyone besides each other. And you pushed him away...again?" My voice rose with anger and I felt my blood boiling. A small wisp of smoke left my nose.

I ignored it, swatting it away.

"Look, Rory, that guy..." he paused, the words seeming to struggle their way out, "there's something not right with him, okay? And you agreed to a day of normalcy. Nothing will happen to you. The forecast said clear skies all day. There's proof that the man is a lunatic."

I shook my head in disbelief, looking to the skies for some patience as I grit my teeth.

"All right, Fenn, you get one day of normalcy and then it's my turn. I will flip this island over until I find him." He moved to disagree but I stopped him. "No. I will find him and get the answers I need, and if after that, if he turns out to be a crazy, then you will have your way. Agreed?"

He paused to consider, a tinge of humor playing on his lips, and then nodded in agreement. "Please get in," he coaxed.

I huffed as I sat down, my legs still resting on the pavement outside the car, and impatiently waited for his answer.

He reached over and grabbed the handkerchief, gently wrapping it around my eyes once again. "Agreed," he answered as his fingers brushed my cheek softly, a thrilling burn left in its place.

Stop it, I told myself.

I should have stayed mad at him, but all I could feel was the blood rushing to my cheeks as I stumbled upon what my heart was feeling. There had to be a logical explanation. Fenn was my best friend. I had known him for, well, ever since I can remember…literally. There was no way that I, Aurora Jay Megalos, had feelings for Fenn Aiden Lovick.

But I had to resist the insane urge to grab his hand as he pulled away from my face. I tried to steady my racing heart as he picked my legs up and gently laid them into the car. The butterflies couldn't help but roar to life at such innocent contact, but the slam of the car door quickly jolted them away, back to their hiding place.

"So…umm…where to now?" I stammered, coughing to hide the slight tremble to my voice. I hoped he didn't pick up on it, but I couldn't see his face so there was no way to tell.

"Like I've said before, you'll see when we get there." His own voice sounded rough, like something strange had come over him.

He turned the radio up and put the car into drive. The hum of the engine calmed me, quieting my thoughts for a bit. I wanted this, I wanted something exciting to happen. But I certainly hadn't predicted this intense attraction to be the something that appeased my boredom.

Chapter 6

❧

The Storm

WE DROVE FOR A SHORT while and listened to the ocean breeze. I had no idea where Fenn was taking me, but I liked the silence between us. I tried to relax and push away the thought of what Mr. Creepy had said about the harm I could be facing.

Clear skies, I kept repeating inside my head.

"Okay, Rory, we're here."

I leaned forward and untied the back of the handkerchief, anxious to finally see something other than the back of my eyelids.

Following the blinding light of the sun, valleys filled with lush trees covered the expanse before me. I felt like I was staring at a green sea where the blue heavens met, lightly kissing the treetops.

I hadn't been to this side of the island before but had always dreamed of going. It was as close to the Garden of Eden as you could get. Horses grazed the rich grasses, and I knew right away what he had set up for me.

"You're taking me horseback riding?" I guessed, noting the smell of hay and the sound of the neighing horses.

"I wanted you to try something you've never done before so I pulled a couple of strings and managed to get us two horses for the day." His face was bursting with excitement. I'd seen that face before—when we got our driver's licenses, and at every shared birthday, right before we blew out the candles to make a wish. So why did I have the sudden urge to grip his face and kiss the smile into my soul?

"Lucky for you," he continued, pulling me out of my sudden daydream, "I already know how to ride so you're in good hands." He opened his door and got out.

I frowned.

"Rub it in. You got lessons and I didn't," I said after he opened my door for me.

"It was the only thing I asked for that Christmas."

We were both fourteen. I wanted make-up, and he wanted to learn how to ride a horse. He helped me out and then walked off in the direction of the house.

"Whose house is this?" I asked as I jogged to catch up with him. His pace didn't hide his excitement.

"That would be John Stark's house." He didn't turn to face me—he knew I'd be baffled.

"A couple of strings, huh? How the hell did you manage to get the quarterback from high school to lend you two horses for the day?" He headed towards the back of the tropical colored house, away from the front door. I weaved around the random pineapple plants, trying to keep up with him.

"Are we stealing these horses?" I whispered. "I'm down for something I haven't done before, but that doesn't include visiting the inside of a jail cell, Fenn Aiden," I called out after him.

"It's not stealing, per se...John is simply letting us borrow them," he answered confidently. "He sat next to me in Calculus so he owes me one. Besides," he added, "he was all for it when I told him who I was planning this for."

I contained my gag. I had a few dealings with John Stark, none of them good. Let's just say I didn't care for his lewd demeanor and grabby hands.

We strolled around to the back of the two-story house and came upon a path that curved like a ribbon, leading to a barn. The yard stretched out ahead like a never-ending carpet of green as we moved along the well-worn path. Solitary palms dotted the landscape, swaying their massive leaves in the slight breeze. There was no doubt about it, this was a beautiful day.

The barn doors were wide open, inviting the sultry breeze to flow through, perfuming the air with the scent of hay.

Once inside, I instantly fell in love with the horse closest to me. The sun's rays filtered through the barred windows, accenting the floating dust that shimmered like stars around the ivory horse. The nameplate on the stall door read Snow Lily. *A perfect name*, I thought as I hesitantly rubbed her velvety soft nose.

"Is that the one you want to ride?" Fenn asked. I nodded as I heard the creaking of a stall door opening. Fenn led his caramel-colored horse out and tied it off. I moved out of the way so he could get Snow out of the stall. I was of no use so I walked over to the other horse and waited, rubbing the suede-like fur.

I watched as he placed the saddle with ease on his horse. It looked simple enough so I decided to give it a try with Snow. As soon as I picked up Snow's saddle, my arms started aching against the strain, and a bubble of embarrassing laughter popped out. Maybe I should have tried harder in Physical Education.

"Weakling," Fenn teased as he grabbed the saddle and placed it on Snow's back for me. I watched him feed the leather strap under the horse and tighten the girth.

"Psh, weak, as if. I'm not weak, I just wanted my man servant to do it for me." I reached up for the saddle harness but he grabbed my arm, stopping me.

"You sure you want to try getting on her alone? It's not as easy as it looks, especially for a shorty like you."

I shoved him back and out of my way. "I'll show you," I said, reaching again for the saddle horn. I stuck my foot into the stirrup, testing its sturdiness. A smile crossed my face with my ever-growing confidence. I braced my foot in the stirrup and pulled with all my might, surprised to find myself actually moving upward.

"Eat your words," I said presumptuously. But just as I went to throw my leg over, my hand slipped on the saddle horn as the horse shifted.

In the flash of me falling, Fenn was there, holding me in his arms as if I was as light as a feather. He seemed to know what was about to happen before it even happened. "Guess you weren't lying about your strength," I commented weakly.

The corner of his mouth turned up as his amused eyes only made those nervous butterflies twirl like a twister.

He set me on the ground, gripping my waist, the heat of his gaze piercing my resolve.

"Is that a blush I see, Aurora Jay?" he asked softly as he tucked a strand of hair behind my ear.

I gulped.

"Let's try this again, together," he instructed lightly. I had to tame the thoughts that instantly flooded my mind. "Ready?"

I reached for the saddle horn again, holding onto it securely as I put my foot in the stirrup. Fenn's hand was there to hold it in place. "Now pull yourself up. Don't worry, I got you," he added as I felt his hand move from my foot up my leg, settling on my inner thigh, bracing me as I pulled my body up to throw my leg over the horse's back.

A broad smile rested on my face. I was on a horse.

With a knowing nod, Fenn cocked his head up at me and winked before he turned to his horse. "Ready for this?" he asked as we took off at a walking pace. The clip-clop of the horse's hooves was curiously comfortable. It felt easy being on top of the horse, unlike the mounting. That was not easy.

"Actually I think I am," I replied, grabbing the reins from Fenn's grip. I lightly kicked Snow in the flanks as he had instructed me to do earlier. It seemed to do the trick. She took off at a fast clip. "Whoa," I yelped, gripping her with my thighs and praying that I wouldn't bounce off my precarious perch. After all, it was a long way down with no Fenn to catch me.

After a few moments of bouncing around, the ride grew effortless. I let my body ease into the horse's gait as the wind flew through my hair. This was better than I could have ever imagined. Fenn was right in thinking that this would be something that I would absolutely enjoy. Then again, he was my best friend.

We rode through the sunny afternoon, changing pace here and there, talking and bantering back and forth. The temperature was perfect. Everything felt right. There were no worries to clog our afternoon, just me, him, and the beautiful, lush world.

I led the way taking paths that had us winding up through the hills and into the forest. We were close to the botanical gardens, the so-called Eden that I had always been so eager to see.

Somehow, I managed to worm our way into an area just beyond the entrance to the forest that was full of beautiful flowers collected from different parts of the world. A sacred garden. I wasn't sure if we were allowed here, but I wanted to see it and it seemed like we were the only two people around.

The sun shined through, illuminating the field to sparkle and taunt us, urging us to take a break from riding. Every flower seemed to dance beneath the rays, enchanting the moment, while the moss-laden trees hugged around us, hiding this spot from prying eyes. I could see the comparison to Eden.

I hopped off Snow and took a moment to steady myself. Although it was amazingly fun to ride, my legs weren't so keen. I could feel the tension building up into my thighs. It felt like my body was stuck in the riding position, my legs wouldn't straighten themselves out. Fenn chuckled at me so I stuck my tongue out at him. I tried to walk around for a few minutes and eventually found a semi-normal walk that worked for the time being.

"This place is amazing," Fenn surveyed in awe. A little stream gently rushed over jagged rocks not too far from where we stood, melodically nourishing the supple earth. A picture-perfect moment.

I waddled over to Fenn's horse, my muscles still protesting, and rummaged through his bookbag to see if he had packed a camera. He had, thank God.

"Smile," I said, catching him off guard and getting a great picture in return. His stunned face gleamed in the sunlight as the water ran behind him. "My turn," I said, tossing the camera to him. I walked over to where he stood and posed, hands on my hips, cheesing as hard as possible. He laughed and shook his head before snapping the picture. Then he jogged over to me and took one of both of us, poking me in the side right as our images were captured.

I took random pictures of various exotic plants as he tied both our horses by the stream. Then he pulled out a pack of sandwiches from the saddlebag of his horse.

"Wow, you really thought this through, didn't you, Bear Grylls?"

He paused and placed both hands on his hips, looking like Peter Pan as he said, "Now I'm going to show you how to survive the wild Botanical Garden."

"You're such a goof," I replied, brushing him off with laughter. He bent over to continue setting up our picnic. Laying the sheet in the very middle of the field where the sun shone the brightest, he gestured for me to rest. So I sat down while he gave each of the horses an apple. A moment later he sat next to me, his smile laced with satisfaction.

He handed me a sandwich and then cleared his throat. "I wanted to give you a normal day. This is your perfect day, Aurora Jay, all joking aside."

My face flushed once again, my blushes beginning to blend together.

"It is perfect," I said softly, avoiding his gaze. I could feel his eyes searching the side of my face, waiting for something.

"Normal's not so bad, is it?" he continued.

"I suppose not."

"So you admit that I was right then?" he said confidently.

I could hear the smile in his voice. I turned sharply towards him. "Absolutely not!" I answered, disbelief coloring my tone.

He chuckled. "I'm just messing with you," he mused.

I nudged him playfully, glad that the mood had shifted. He took another bite from his sandwich and then leaned back onto his elbows.

I looked down at his adorable face and giggled. His puzzled expression, particularly with mustard staining the corner of his mouth, made me laugh even harder.

"What?" he asked, letting his curiosity get the better of him.

"Nothing," I answered, touching the corner of my mouth. He caught the hint, quickly wiping the mustard away and turned his head to the sky.

We sat there for a while, looking around at the flowers and then back at each other, delight lingering in the air. He started humming a tune he often played on his guitar absent-mindedly. I wriggled my toes to the beat, a feeling of bliss bubbling up inside me. I watched him as he hummed merrily, admiring the features of his face. His smile held such peace as he took another bite from his sandwich.

He finished the last bite of his sandwich and then dusted his hands off. I don't think the day could've been any better. He had to have felt the same. That is, until things suddenly took a turn for the worst.

He looked up and then all of a sudden his face paled to a ghostly white. My eyes followed his stare and then my stomach twisted in terror. The sun's rays began to disappear upon the horizon and our new special spot turned grayish and shadowed. A dark cloud was forming above us.

Oh my god.

"It's not supposed to rain today," he said, suddenly worried. His eyes grew in horror, pleading for it to be untrue. I felt a drop of water land on top of my head and then another on my forearm so I quickly put my half-eaten sandwich back into its baggie and signaled for Fenn to get off the sheet.

Mr. Creepy's words replayed, "And when she's harmed by your ignorance…" I shouldn't have listened to Fenn. I should have followed my gut and chased Mr. Creepy down. The fear of the unknown was like a crushing weight.

"We need to hurry before the rain breaks," I rushed, trying to steady my trembling hands as I threw everything back into his pack. Thunder barreled off the hillsides in the distance.

"It's going to be okay, Rory," Fenn said, remorse shading his tone as he moved to help me up onto the horse. I waited for him to mount and then took off for the barn. Not even ten minutes into the ride, clouds opened up and let us have it. I looked back to see worry written all over his face. I don't know if I was trying to assure her or myself, but I leaned into Snow, whispering to her that everything was okay.

We were racing time, trying to beat the inevitability of lightning that Mr. Creepy had predicted. If only we had just listened to him. Just as I glanced back for comfort, a lightning bolt landed about twenty feet in front of us, thunder echoing off the hillside, amplifying the horrifying sound.

Snow reared back, and it took everything in me to keep a hold of her reigns. The fear-filled neigh pierced my heart as Fenn cried, "Rory, hang on!"

"I'm trying," I yelled back, doing everything in my power to regain control of her. I didn't have time to panic. She was still jumping and weaving her head to and fro, my hand full of her mane. I whispered soothing sounds into her ear, trying to calm her and my frantic heart. With a jarring thud, her hooves slammed to the ground.

Snow skittered right to left in a dance of nervousness. It was as if she didn't know which way to run. The rain fell harder, distant thunder still echoing through the darkened sky. I tried with all my might to hang on, but my grip was slipping from the rain. Then another lightning bolt sounded, cracking off to my left, lighting up the darkened sky in a brief burst. Flames shot out of the tree it struck like an inferno brought to life.

I couldn't take my eyes off the fire as Snow screamed and reared again, this time throwing me onto my back and knocking the breath out of me as I slammed onto the ground. Massive hooves plunged towards me, and even though I tried to roll away in time, I got nicked in the forehead.

"Snow," I moaned as stars danced in front of me. It did no

good. She had taken off in her panic, racing away as fast as she could. Pain lanced my forehead, and I reached up to find a line of blood wetting my fingertips.

I heard an awful lot of hissing and popping behind me so I glanced back over to the fire and turned to it, enthralled by the orange familiar. The flames felt alive, burning through my core and I wanted more.

Forgotten was the horse that ran away, forgotten was the blood sliding down my face, and forgotten was Mr. Creepy's warning.

I should have felt panicked because Fenn had dismounted his horse and was crouched down beside me, saying my name over and over and touching my head, apologizing incessantly. But panic didn't set in. Instead something else stirred to life, waiting to seek its moment.

I wobbled forward and tried to sit up out of Fenn's grasp. I wanted those flames. They roared again, as if acknowledging my desire, the burnt orange color lighting up around us.

Suddenly, as if my will became reality, the ground rippled in a wave, and as the wave rolled past me, Fenn was thrown backwards, away from my side.

The moment I felt the earth shudder beneath me, something changed. I stood as a line of flames raced towards me along the grass, breaking right before they touched me and looping around me in a large circle. The rain-drenched hair that was stuck to my face magically dried. All of me was dry, like it had never even rained to begin with.

I stood slowly, hearing Fenn's footfalls as he yelled out my name, running to where the circle was still open. I needed to get back to him before things got out of control like before, before I blew something up. Something like me.

But I could control these flames. It was an irresistible urge, one that I didn't want to ignore. As the realization sank in, the flames roared to life again, as if agreeing with me. They danced in a perfect circle, untouched by the falling rain.

A smile painted my lips as I reached out and brushed them with my fingertips. As soon as my fingers touched the flames, a pulsing energy awoke within me. My eyes closed in bliss as I tilted my head to the sky. Pure energy raced through my veins, sparking out of the palms of my hands. It was a rush unlike anything I had ever felt. When I finally opened my eyes, I imagined the flames growing higher and watched in awe as they did.

"Aurora!" Fenn shouted in desperation. He darted across the field towards the circle and skidded to a stop just as he neared the flames. His face was frightened. "Aurora, you have to jump!" He wanted to pull me away from the flames.

I couldn't let this happen.

Blankly, I turned to face him, and as he tried to throw his arms around me my hand shot out. "No," I commanded as flames swayed across the tips of my fingers.

Before he could make it into the circle, the force of the energy pulsing through me had Fenn flying backwards as the flames closed up around me. Their tall warmth now comfortably enshrouded me. I didn't care to figure out how I was able to do any of it. It didn't matter. All that mattered was that I wasn't crazy, that what I could do was real.

I touched the flames once again, and my blood shot through my veins with the newly charged energy that yearned to be used.

"Aurora!" Fenn shouted weakly, "I won't let anything happen to you!" The flames shot upward, reaching for the sky, challenging him. And then he appeared as he jumped through the wall of fire, the flames licking his skin.

It was this moment of horror that brought me to my senses.

He had been burned. I had burned him. He swatted at his skin in panic, trying to douse the flames that ran along his arms and legs. *What am I doing?* I thought in a cloudy haze.

I looked to the flames and lowered my hands, magically pushing them into the ground. They followed my command, rushing towards me and running up my legs, tracing the lines of my body. I absorbed the fire, taking in the last of the flames as they burned out with a pop of smoke.

He rushed over to me, pulling me into him. "Are you okay? Are you hurt?" His voice cracked as he trembled limb to limb. I watched in profound relief as his skin that had been harmed healed almost instantaneously.

"I'm fine," I replied hoarsely, hugging him back.

"I should have listened. I shouldn't have been so stubborn in thinking that we could force normal." His voice burned with regret. "Oh my god, Rory," he said, shamefaced with realization. "I ruined any chance we had at finding out the truth." He looked away, deflated.

Mr. Creepy had been right. Something in me did change. And he'd made it clear we were not to come looking for him.

I grabbed Fenn's face and made him look at me. "We'll find him and we'll make it right, Fenn. He has to help," I insisted, trying to make my smile warm and full of hope.

But what if he meant what he said, I thought as I bit my lip. My head was pounding. "I wish I had your healing ability," I said, attempting to lighten the mood as I rubbed the pained spot.

Fenn lightly kissed my wound and said, "I'm such a jerk. Sorry won't change it, but I am sorry for not listening. We will look for him tomorrow, and I will apologize to him. Come on, let's get back before something worse happens."

With my horse gone, I had no choice but to ride back with him.

He had been smart enough to tie up his horse even in the midst of the chaos. He threw his hand out to help me up behind him and we took off, heading for the barn.

Back in the barn, we found a drenched Snow happily munching hay and watching us from her stall. Someone must have put her away.

I shivered as I watched Fenn quickly brush his horse down and throw a chunk of hay into the stall. "Okay, let's go," he beckoned, grabbing my arm and pulling me out of the barn.

We had parked on the shoulder of the road so getting to the car meant another jog in the rain. We darted across the yard and practically threw ourselves into the car, anxious for shelter.

The slam of the car doors brought reality crashing back in. And after a brief moment of staring off into the storm, Fenn broke the silence.

"You hungry?" he asked, shifting his weight in the seat. *Not really*, I thought to myself. *Not after all of that.*

"A little, I guess," I said instead. "Do you think it's safe to drive in this weather?"

"Sure it is," he replied as he reached in the back for my bookbag. "Here, dry off with this." He handed me a towel as he started the car and turned the heater on. I did my best to dry my hair and pat my clothes down before handing the towel to him.

The air outside had dropped a few degrees as the already setting sun was covered by blackish clouds. I was too tired to change into the extra clothes he had packed.

We both remained silent as he pulled out and onto the road. I think we were still trying to absorb what had just happened. My eyes weighed heavy and a yawn escaped my lips.

The vibration of the engine tested my sleepiness along with the pitter-patter of the rain and the swishing of the windshield wipers. The strain of the day along with the riding and the accident wore on my body.

Leaning back, I closed my eyes and felt myself drift off into a comfortable rest. My head throbbed a little where the horse's hoof had connected with it, but I was suddenly too tired to care.

Don't fall asleep, I kept telling myself, but time seemed to weave in and out. The last thing I heard was, "We're almost there, Rory."

"Okay," I answered groggily.

Chapter 7

~

Say What?

I WOKE UP IN MY bed. My legs felt like they had been put through hell, and my first attempt at sitting up didn't go so well. I laughed at myself for being so out of shape and tried again. Success. I sat up and looked over to the clock, rubbing the ache from my muscles.

What had happened with the fire played itself over and over again in my mind. I was secretly glad it had happened because it proved to my sanity that I hadn't made up my abilities. I really could control fire. I just wished I had control over *when* I could do it.

I huffed and stood, swallowing the first bit of soreness in my legs. *Today is going to be fun*, I thought with a snort. I started stretching my hamstrings then reached up to the cut on my head when a small wave of dizziness came over me. No wonder my head was throbbing, I'd been horse-punched. I felt a band-aid covering the wound.

I walked over to our dresser and looked in the mirror. My fingertip ran over a Strawberry Shortcake band-aid. *Fenn*, I thought with an eye roll, *always the prankster.*

My head was slightly purple and tender to the touch. I grabbed two aspirin and swallowed them quickly, downing the glass of water

Fenn must have left out for me. He was passed out on the couch.

I remembered bits and pieces of him carrying me into our room, but that was about it. I didn't even think I had dreamed. At least there was no ache to my skin. I wondered if it had anything to do with the fact that I was able to actually connect with the fire. *Mr. Creepy would know*, I thought with a jolt of excitement. Hopefully he would give us the time of day.

I crept over to the couch and kneeled on the floor in front of Fenn. One arm and one leg were hanging off the side. He must have been as exhausted as I was.

A part of me felt bad. He had worked so hard to plan a "normal" day out for us and then reality cruelly crushed his dreams.

He rolled towards the wall.

Quietly, I got up and went to grab some O.J. from out of the refrigerator. My throat felt like my own personal desert. I threw on a pot of coffee for Fenn and even went as far as putting cinnamon rolls in the oven. It was the least I could do.

The delicious smells played their part well, waking Fenn and coaxing him into the kitchen.

"Mornin'," he rasped groggily with a half-hearted smile. He stretched his arms above his head, and then let out a huff as he sat at the table. My brain was scrambling, trying to think of the right way to remind him about last night.

"So…we're going to stick to the game plan and find Mr. Creepy today, right?" It was the best I could come up with.

He paused as if I had just cursed at him, and then his shoulders slumped over. "Yeah, Rory. Like he said, we have no choice."

My face softened. "I don't want to ruin your mood, Fenn. I just…I think it's for the best," I tried to convince, hoping that he wasn't too upset with me for bringing it up first thing in the morning.

He sighed. "It is for the best, and you could never ruin anything for me." He ran his thumb over my chin as the lullaby I heard the night before last spun through my head. Our eyes met. "Remember that, okay? You are perfect in your own dysfunctional way. And it's exactly what I want." With that, he let my face go, breaking our eye contact.

His admittance to his feelings sank in. I looked back up at him, on the verge of saying to hell with it and stealing that kiss I had been drooling over when, of course, there was a knock at the door.

Opportunity missed.

I took a quick second to gather myself and waited as Fenn answered the door. It was a UPS man.

After Fenn signed for the package, he shut the door and tossed it on the table. "It's for you," he said curiously.

"For me? What is it?" I asked, puzzled.

"I might be strong but I don't have x-ray vision, Rory." The two of us chuckled as I handed him his coffee and a roll and then took a bite of my own. Tasty, yummy, cinnamon-y goodness swarmed my taste buds.

We ate in silence as I stared down the package. It was small, only the size of a letter, and I had no clue what was inside.

"How's your head? Let me take a look at it again," he asked, gently moving a piece of hair that was covering it. "You got a nice bruise there. Very purple, but the knick isn't that bad. I don't think it's going to leave a scar. Your head hurt?"

"I took two aspirin so ask me again in about thirty minutes," I replied. I took a quick sip of my orange juice. "I'll just keep Neosporin on it and maybe sizzle me some Alka-Seltzer."

He grinned, stuffing the rest of his roll into his mouth. After swallowing he asked, "You going to open it?" He hinted to the package with his eyes.

I pulled it towards me, nervousness coating the freshly eaten cinnamon roll in my stomach. What could it possibly be? I anxiously tore it open and pulled out a folded up piece of parchment.

"My dearest Aurora," I read out loud, running my fingers over the indented calligraphy.

I turned it over and questioned how old it must have been. The parchment was stiff, the color of creamed caramel, and sealed by wax. So strange, it was the prettiest red color—like the color of drying blood—and had intertwining dragons. They crossed at the tail and neck with mouths wide open revealing two gleaming sets of teeth. In between them was a round object, a stone maybe? My thoughts flew to my dreams and the glowing blue eyes.

I hated to break the seal, but couldn't contain myself any longer. When I pulled the paper out, a key clanged on the table. It was gold and had a three-digit number on it.

I looked up at Fenn who took it from me and began inspecting it. As I unfolded the letter, careful not to rip the fragile parchment, I read aloud:

My dearest Aurora,

Your destiny is not as far off as you think. After all, you were named after the goddess of morning—a new dawn is what you are. You will bring change to many a life.

The key that is enclosed is for a security deposit box. In that box lie clues to your return home. It's the beginning to finding out who you really are. And what you're capable of.

No matter what, I want you to have a choice. Remember that you can choose your own destiny, no matter the cost. That is why I sent you to where you are now-to escape those who disagree. No one can take that from you.

My love and protection is always with you...

As my lips read the last word out loud, a tiny fire started at the corner of the paper. I reacted by letting go, but before it could hit the table, the paper singed completely, the faint ashes drifting off as if the letter never was.

Wow.

I looked up at Fenn and for once I had nothing to say. Could this be from my birth mother? Why would she wait so long to give this to me? What was I escaping? So someone else knows about my powers? My mind was racing with the possibilities of finding my birth parents.

"Well, I know what's next," he said eagerly.

"What?" I asked cheerfully.

"Get dressed. We're going to the bank." I quickly did as he said.

Bank on Third was the only bank we had in this small town which goes to show how confining and suffocating it was here. I had no idea this place even held security deposit boxes. Then again, I never paid much attention to my banking options besides depositing my check and keeping up my account.

We rounded the corner of our motel and crossed the street. It was early enough that the traffic was far and few between. Fenn grabbed my hand once we were on the sidewalk and pulled me the whole two blocks it took to get to the bank.

Once inside, I jumped in the short line, anxious to find what was waiting for me. Fenn threw his arm around me and pulled me into a bear hug. I leaned into the scent of his cologne and took a deep whiff. My eyes drifted around the room, and I noticed a couple sitting in two comfy chairs watching me as I smelled Fenn.

I jerked my head forward, trying to remain inconspicuous and nonchalant as my cheeks reddened.

A clerk appeared from out of her windowed office and beckoned for the next customer. The man in front of us stepped towards the clerk, making us the next in line. I was nauseatingly anxious and ready to get this over with. I had never been good at waiting, and it wasn't proving helpful at this moment in my life.

"You're so close yet so far away," said Fenn, matching my thoughts and playing with my hair at the ends, weaving them in and around his fingers. He often played with my hair in this manner. It was comforting at times and annoying at others. I leaned back letting him do as he pleased. This was a comforting time.

A man who looked to be in his mid-twenties with a Guido hairdo and bronzed muscles motioned for the next in line.

"Let's go," I said grabbing Fenn's hand. Now more than ever I would need support.

The agent smiled at me and recited lines that I'm sure he's said on more than one occasion.

"Aloha, welcome to Bank on Third. My name is Joey, how may I help you today?"

So polite he was, I thought in my Yoda voice.

The smell of warmed paper and orange blossom cleaners wafted through the air as I handed Joey the key and said, "I'm here to access my security deposit box."

"Okay, we can surely do that," he said, his fingers moving a mile a minute on his keyboard, a skill that I had yet to acquire even in this day of technology.

"And what's your name, Miss?" he asked, never looking up from the computer.

"Aurora, Aurora Megalos," I said, trying my best not to fidget. I slid my ID towards him and waited as he glanced at it. He typed some more, making me spell my last name out loud even though he had my license in front of him. He looked up at me as his fingers stopped their dance.

"This was set up for you in December of 2000 and hasn't been touched since, correct?" he asked, handing me back the key. That was the month and year I was dropped off at Mily's. Fenn and I both looked to each other.

"I'm sorry," I said, shaking off the brief moment that I spaced out. "Yes, correct. Umm, do you have a name of who set it up?" I asked, hoping that I didn't sound suspicious.

"Actually, yes, one second," he replied as he went back to typing. "It says here, Soothe, no last name. That's odd, right?" He looked up at us with a smile.

"Soothe?" I mouthed to Fenn. He shrugged.

"If you'll follow me, I'll take you to the back room where you can wait for your security deposit box." He came around the counter and took the lead. Fenn put his arm around my shoulder as we followed, giving me the extra support to face what was up ahead.

The hall we walked down was very narrow and led to a door that required a card swipe to pass through. Joey took the badge from around his neck, and we soon heard the approving beep as the little light turned green.

I leaned into Fenn and whispered, "Who do you think Soothe is?"

He shrugged and said, "Maybe whatever's in the box will say."

The space we now stood in was like a massive closet with three potential doors. Joey unlocked our door with another swipe of his badge. The room itself had to be the size of a broom closet. There was just enough space for two chairs. Fenn and I took a seat as Joey explained that a box would slide through the opening in the wall—a wall covered in poker green velvet. I ran my hands along it, enjoying its textured smoothness.

"When you're finished, just push this button and push the box back through the hole, Miss Megalos." I nodded and he shut the door behind him, leaving us alone.

"Boy, this just keeps getting crazier by the minute," Fenn mused. The level of my anxiety had skyrocketed and the muscles in my legs started to quake, making it hard for me to sit still.

I sighed. "Tell me about it. I just hope this is the beginning of figuring things out," I replied nervously. A clicking sound caught our attention and then a small door opened up in front of us.

Chapter 8

~

The Ring

MOMENTS LATER, A SMALL BOX appeared through the opening. I sort of felt like Alice deep inside Wonderland, only without the rabbit. Maybe Fenn could be my rabbit?

We both popped upright in our seats. I put the key into the lock and looked over at Fenn in anticipation. The sound of the key clicking through was music to my ears. Fenn leaned in, putting his arm around my chair, and we both held our breath as I slowly opened the lid.

Another aged piece of parchment with my name on it was the first thing I saw. I lifted it up and found a tri-folded, faded piece of hide. Handling it very carefully so as not to damage it, I was about to open it when I noticed a silver ring on the purple suede at the bottom of the box. The ring caught the overhead light, glinting and sparking my curiosity. "Cool," said Fenn in a daze, the light reflecting off his eyes.

My hands shook as I picked the ring up. The stone set inside it was as blue as the infinite sea with specks of white and gold streaking through it. Like seagulls flying above the sun-kissed ocean. Three tiny symbols wrapped around the band: a swirling infinity sign, a five-pointed star, and a crescent moon with a small circle just off the right side.

"Maybe this is like a family heirloom. I bet we could google this, or maybe even visit the historian in town to see if we can get a time period on it. He'd probably know about this," Fenn said, taking the ring out of my hands. How was his head already full of ideas? He was the energizer bunny reincarnated.

"Something's inscribed inside the ring. Third of three, protector to the Progeny," he read looking up from the ring.

"Maybe it's yours," I guessed.

"But this box was set up for you," he pointed out.

"Yea but Mr. Creepy said…"

"I know, I know, just keep it for now until we find out for sure." Fenn handed the ring back to me as if it were a poisonous snake.

"Okay." I grabbed the letter, hoping that it would give me some sort of understanding. I coughed to clear my throat and unfolded it as carefully as I had with the first letter.

Aurora,

Of dragon born a conqueror prevails—words of a prophecy set in motion. You shall come to understand soon enough.

The ring I have enclosed will help unlock what is deep inside your heart and is a source to one of the keys.

You will also find a map that will guide you to the hidden keys. You must find the portal in which you crossed over in order to undo the spell that has been cast to protect you. The locations will be found under the light from the second sun.

Now the hard part—you must choose. For your protection, the keys have been placed in three different locations on this is-

*land. If you choose to return home, you will find the scattered
pieces using the map.*

*There is a catch. The spell will seal the portal off forever
should you choose not to pursue the keys. Your time is limited.
You have until the coming full moon. Once the portal is shut, it
must stay closed. The choice is yours. I trust you will make the best
choice for you.*

*I'm sorry I cannot explain more. My words are crucial to
your fate. As before, I am with you and send my protection.*

May love and protection guide you...

Just as before, the tiny flame lit up on the corner of the paper
and within seconds, had completely ignited, ashes littering my legs.

"I guess this creates a slight detour from your plan of finding
Mr. Creepy. The full moon is like a week away, or maybe less," said
Fenn.

I frowned.

"That's an understatement," I replied with a sigh. Then I looked
at him, realizing something. "Fenn, the letter mentioned you by
name. You really are a part of this, like Mr. Creepy said."

"I figured as much, considering my strange abilities." His tone
fell flat.

"And...?" I let hang.

"And what?"

"How does that make you feel?"

He huffed. "Well if you must know," he said in a rush, "then I
guess I feel reassured."

He avoided my gaze. I'm sure he could feel the smug smile that
beamed on my face.

"Told you," I declared. I couldn't help myself.

His face darkened. "To be honest, I definitely would feel crappy if I wasn't a part of your life in some aspect." He looked up at me, a smile forming at the corner of his mouth. "So I guess it feels good to know that we can continue on together."

"Definitely so. I wouldn't have it any other way."

We both smiled as I picked up the map, rubbing the texture of the grainy hide, feeling a faint hum of magic.

"This map is practically unreadable," I commented as I handed it to Fenn. I leaned over him to point out the problem. "It looks like a treasure map, but the outline of the island is off, like the lines are overlapped or something. Or like the person who drew it was drunk or had unsteady hands."

He nodded, turning the map in his hands to see if we were looking at it wrong. No matter the direction he turned it, it still was unreadable. "Why would whoever gave you this letter, give you a map that's unreadable?" He scratched his head, still turning it every which way.

I huffed. "We'd probably understand it a little better had Mr. Creepy been able to tell us what he wanted to say," I said, my tone full of accusations.

Fenn's back stiffened. He put the map down on the table, shoulders slouched over in guilt.

I threw my hands up, shaking my head in dismay. "Maybe he would have explained all of this. I mean, besides following the instructions here, we really have nothing to go off of," I admitted blatantly.

He grabbed my hand, his eyes pleading. "I know, Rory. I messed up. But at least we're back on track, right? We know we have a time limit and we know that we have to use this map to find three keys. It's a start." I sighed, knowing he was right. He leaned forward, his tone gentle. "And we can still look for him. This is just like an added bonus or something." His eyes searched my face, waiting for me to fold.

"Yeah, I guess so. This is all so much to take in. I think I may be leaning toward your desire to be normal now." I rubbed my temples in angst.

"Explain?"

"I mean, I just feel like there's something I need to live up to. Like I'm supposed to be doing something with whatever my 'powers' are, and I'm severely failing. And now we have this map that we can't read. I just feel like it's one step forward, six steps back."

His lips turned up as he tucked a fallen strand of hair behind my ear. "Well, before you go into freak-out mode, let's finish up here. This tiny box of a room is suffocating me."

"Sure," I managed, sounding pitiful.

Defeat poured out of me as I closed the lid on the box then slid it back through the hole and pushed the button. Fenn rubbed my back in an attempt to soothe my current frustration. It was appreciated.

I slid the ring on my middle finger and noticed that it fit a little loose. Sighing with discontent, I took the letter and the map and offered Fenn a thankful smile.

He kept that "I don't know what to say" look on his face as we both stood up. Then he said, "Just remember, we don't have to make any decisions tonight." I nodded and followed him out.

Chapter 9

~

Name Calling is Not Nice

STEPPING OUTSIDE UNDER THE HAWAIIAN sun, I let out a pent-up breath and watched everything around me. People walked to and fro, in and out of shops, naively going about their lives. And there I stood, confused and oh so doubtful.

"So matey," Fenn jested in a pirate voice, "we best be on our treasure hunt." He laughed and finished with an "ARGGG!!"

I frowned. "I have to make a decision, Fenn," I replied, ignoring his joke. "And I don't know if I should be mad, or sad, or happy, or confused. I just don't know anymore. I mean I don't even know what these keys look like and who has hid them. What would you do?"

He shrugged his shoulders as we started walking back towards our motel. "I don't know, Rory. I mean, I'd want to know who my parents are and more importantly where my abilities come from. But in the same breath, to live a *normal* life without any worries, I just don't know what I'd choose." He looked over at me. "What if they aren't what you expected?"

I shrugged dismissively. "I expect anything with the hand I've been dealt so far," I replied, slumping along the way. "Seriously though, this is so ridiculous. The more I think about it, the angrier I get. I'm not sure if *I'm* crazy or whoever is writing this stuff is crazy!" I could feel the anger brewing within.

Fenn was trailing behind me, head down as he listened.

"This is getting weirder and weirder by the minute. Not only do I control fire and you heal at super speed, but we have some crazy guy following us around, speaking of dragons and prophecies, and then this," I groaned, holding up the letter, "this comes and adds another iron to the fire."

"Aurora," I heard faintly, but I was too far in my vent to stop and ask Fenn what he wanted.

"Not to mention that we have to figure out who Soothe is. What kind of a name is Soothe anyway?" I looked back at him. He kept quiet. "And," I indicated with a finger, "and now we have to go on a hunt with a map that's practically unreadable and we have to find these hidden objects within the week or making a choice won't even matter. Pinch me, Fenn, please, because I must be sleeping."

"Aurora," I heard again, as soft as a whisper. *Well if he's going to whisper to cut me off then whatever*, I thought.

My hands were flying at this point. I was spewing my every thought, determined to rid myself of this confusion. "I mean come on…who gives someone a map and tells them they have until the next full moon to find everything? No pressure, right?" I sneered.

I heard Fenn chuckle behind me.

I groaned and continued, "I just wish someone would give me some sort of answer. Like someone would help me out a little bit and not make this so complicat-"

"Aurora," my name came again, interrupting me mid-thought.

I quickly spun around. "WHAT?!"

Fenn's brow furrowed as he innocently replied, "What?"

"What do you mean 'what?' You've called my name like three

times now, and I'm trying to vent to you to find some sort of peace of mind. What? What is so important?"

He started laughing. "I never called your name, Rory," he said sincerely.

"Okay then who-" I began.

"Aurora," the voice called again. This time it was a distinct female's voice.

"You had to have heard that, it was plain as day," I insisted, glancing around.

His brows knit in confusion. "Rory, really, I don't hear a thing," he tried to assure me.

"Aurora, come," the voice commanded. I turned in the direction it came from. No one was there. "Aurora," it said a bit louder.

"Someone's messing with me, Fenn. Are you in on this?" I started walking in the direction the voice came from, not waiting for his answer.

"Aurora, come here," it said again. I glanced back at Fenn, eyebrows up, asking if he heard it yet. He shook his head no. I let out a stifled moan.

"Yes, come here, Aurora." The voice got louder in my head. It was an older woman's voice, a stern sounding voice.

Fenn was jogging to match my pace. "Rory, seriously, I don't hear anything. Are you absolutely positive it's your name?" I stopped dead in my tracks and turned to him, putting my finger in his face.

"Do not call me a liar. Someone is calling my name, okay? If you don't hear it, well I'm so sorry. Maybe you need to get your ears checked with as loud as you blast your I-Pod."

He was dumbfounded.

I turned from him and continued on my quest. I was going to find that voice and ring her neck.

We passed shop after shop, my name coming quicker and more

prominent until we reached the end of the sidewalk.

"Almost here, Aurora, I have something for you," she teased once more. I knew where it was coming from now. The light-pink, wooden house was in plain sight, and although no one was on the porch, I knew that was where the voice wanted me to be. It was pulling me towards it, urging me on.

Crossing the street, we paused in the middle to let a car go past, and then ran across, stopping in front of the grungy, blue steps to glance up at the illuminated sign on the front of the building.

"Really, Rory, Madam Pomphry's Palm Reading? You could have just said 'Hey, Fenn, why don't we go check out a psychic?' You don't have to pretend to hear voices." He was laughing now, so sure of himself. I let my elbow fly backwards right into his stomach.

"Hey," he exhaled sharply, his laugh ending abruptly.

"I thought this place was on the market," I commented, whispering. "I didn't know someone had opened up a new business."

"You want to check out the new business? That's your excuse?" He snickered.

I rolled my eyes and started up the creaking steps. As soon as my foot touched the first step, the sound of my name swarmed my mind. "Aurora, Aurora, come…yes, Aurora, Aurora, AURORA!" it yelled. My hands went to my ears defensively, but the voice didn't disappear.

I reached out and touched the brass doorknob. Instantly, the door opened and an older woman appeared in my direct line of sight.

"Hello, Aurora, we finally meet."

The voices ended.

Chapter 10

~

Psychics are for Believers Only

THE HOUSE WAS MADE OF weathered, pink-paneled wood. In the front window a neon light hung in the shape of a hand. All five purple fingers lit up separately, creating the illusion that they were moving. Next to it sat an OPEN sign in red, blinking rapidly.

Typical, I thought cynically.

"Come in," the woman summoned, stepping out of the way for Fenn and me. I looked back to him and then at her. Her face seemed to tense at the sight of him. When she looked at me, the tension left, replaced by a stern smile.

Weirdo, I thought to myself.

We followed her into a dimly lit room, a majestic energy pulsing through the air. Black and white pictures of women adorned the sparkling gold walls. Some of the photos looked old enough to have been taken when they had to use a light bulb every time they took a picture.

Scarves hung over the deep scarlet and exotic purple lamps stationed throughout the room. She had Victorian style furniture— love seats with floral print outlined in mahogany wood and a chaise lounge sitting underneath a window with a black silk curtain.

"When did you settle in?" I asked, guarded.

She didn't miss a beat. "Yesterday," she said in a tone that implied it should be obvious. "I saw this place and I just knew it was perfect. It's almost like fate wanted me here." Her gaze pierced right through me, like there was a deeper meaning hidden behind those words.

"Oh," I said solemnly.

She forced a smile. "I am Lady Eve, the person you have called upon for help."

Lady Eve had short black hair that angled around her face. Emerald-covered hairpins—the same color as my eyes—held back her hair on the left side. Her eyes held lines of knowledge in each corner and were the color of trees–a deep brown with green freckles like falling leaves. She had thin lips that had probably whispered many a fate. I felt intimidated by all of her.

Naturally, she reached for my hands, holding them weakly with the tips of her fingers. When we locked eyes a funny feeling lingered in my stomach, kind of like déjà vu, then she said, "I've been waiting to meet you for a long time, Aurora." Something about her was oddly familiar, her voice, her look. It was like we had met before.

She let my fingers go and continued, "Let's get started. Follow me and I will help with the questions you have come here seeking answers for." Fenn once again placed his hand on the small of my back, ensuring my comfort.

We headed towards a sheer purple curtain that hung in the doorway. Pulling it aside, she waited as we walked through and then followed behind.

"Please, have a seat," she instructed as she pulled her chair up to the round wooden table dominating the center of the quaint room. The single light that hovered over the table wasn't enough to illuminate the entire space. Shadows lurked, obscuring the corners from sight. To be honest, it unsettled the thinly-veiled courage I had summoned just to come here.

On the center of the table was a crystal ball. *But of course, standard protocol*, I thought with a sneer. I slid my hand into Fenn's.

"Aurora," she charged, extending her graceful hand across the table. "Don't be afraid as your fate shall be revealed." Again the connection of our hands meeting sent chills down my spine. I shifted in my seat.

"Of dragon born a conqueror prevails, the words of a prophecy set in motion before your time," she chanted as her eyes began to cloud over. Mr. Creepy's eyes came to mind.

Okay, this was definitely beginning to spook me. How did she know that? I looked over at Fenn who was just as intrigued as I was.

"You have a big decision to make and choices that will affect the fate of many. You must use the map—it will lead you to the keys needed for your return. Let me see the ring," she requested, opening her refined hand.

I paused a moment, trying to gather my rapid thoughts. I felt panicked. How did she know all this stuff? I mean, sure, she's a so-called psychic so she's supposed to know, right?

I looked to Fenn, asking with my eyes what I should do. He lifted his eyebrows upward and towards her so I quickly slid the ring off and placed it in her expectant hands. The light above us flickered as a small gust of wind blew past my face. I turned to Fenn, whose hair had been disheveled.

"There is a lot of magic in this ring, ancient magic. See the symbols around the stone? They are symbols of a higher power. Symbols that you will find on the keys." She brought it closer to her eyes, twirling it and then studying the inside. "Third of three, protection to the Progeny. You'll need this in the near future, but this ring is not meant for you," she revealed, her eyes meeting mine.

I was hoping to get the name of who she thought it belonged to, but nothing came. Her mahogany eyes pierced through my soul, like she was reading my very essence. "To know who the bearer of this ring is, could set you down the wrong path. You must discover this on your own. It will lead you to a key and return you both home." She slid the ring back to me.

"And how exactly do we use this?" I asked, feeling like I was on the verge of finally finding out something substantial.

"You will know when the time comes," she answered casually.

"What?" I asked, outraged. "What is that? My *time* is up within the next week. Why can't you just tell me?"

"Exactly. Your limited time will be up soon so let's not waste it with silly questions. Your journey is not one that can be tampered with as it is tied in with another's," she scolded.

I felt dumb for throwing a mini fit.

"And who would that be?" I asked, skeptical.

"Unfortunately, you will soon see," she replied as secretively as before. "The powers you have been experiencing, do you want to talk about them?" she lured, the flecks of green in her eyes momentarily shimmering. I stumbled for a moment, my mind reeling with what I wanted to say.

"Well, there are moments where I can control the flame. And there are times where I get this rush of energy pulsing through me and I'm able to use it forcefully. I'm also immune to heat. I've never been burned in my life."

"Is that all?" she asked inquisitively.

"Yes?"

She looked at Fenn, waited a moment, and then continued on. "Let me see both of your hands, side by side, please." Was she talking about him?

Fenn didn't hesitate to lay his left hand down, palm side up. I cringed knowing that we had to stop holding hands. That was my security blanket. I laid my own next to his, palm up, and waited. She traced the lines on Fenn's hand.

"Uh-huh," she muttered. She moved her finger over to my palm and traced a line that wrapped around my thumb.

"You can tell just about anything by studying the lines in someone's hands. For instance," she said, talking to me, "you are very insecure about relationships. Yet your humor and knack for understanding reality is enough to save you from yourself. You also have a very short life line." She never even blinked while airing my dirty laundry.

"A death will come to He that breaks the barrier" is what Mr. Creepy had said that night at the diner. *This can't be coincidence*, I thought as the blood drained from my face. I suddenly felt cold and clammy.

She looked at Fenn and said, "You however are strong and noble." He shifted a little uncomfortably in his chair, but I could see that charming smile taking over his face. "You are experiencing powers as well?" she asked.

He coughed a little as he nodded.

"But your powers differ from hers," she pointed out. He continued to nod, a smile steadily growing. "Your fate is soon coming," she bluntly rushed. "Now, if you could please leave the room so Aurora and I can be alone."

Fenn's undaunted smile vanished.

"No, I'm not leaving her." His eyes blazed as the tone of protectiveness made my butterflies stir. I laid my hand on his forearm and shook my head that it was okay. My skepticism had slowly depleted.

Angst showered his face as he leaned in and grimly kissed my forehead. "I'll be just outside," he mumbled as he turned for the doorway.

"He doesn't like to leave you alone," she stated, her puzzled gaze following his steps as he disappeared behind the curtain.

Well, that was obvious, I thought snidely.

"Your souls are connected to one another. Bound by The Fates," she grandly announced, eyes studying my face.

"What do you mean?" I asked quietly.

"Exactly what I said. When two souls that were meant to be together find each other, they weave together and bind an unbreakable union."

Well, I didn't know what to say or think about that besides, "Why's that?" It was a silly question and I immediately regretted it as soon as it spilled out.

"I don't have all the answers as to why The Fates do the things they do," she replied sharply, her tone questioning my commonsense. "Let me see your palm again." I leaned in and gave her my hand, waiting to hear another negative comment about my character.

A breeze seemed to move in a circle around us, and a feeling of falling asleep crept up on me. *This can't be happening,* I thought in a daze. Her hands stayed locked to mine and her eyes bore deep into my own.

"Seek and thy shall see," she willed majestically as my eyes rolled back uncontrollably. A feeling of being pulled overcame me. Maybe I shouldn't have let Fenn leave.

Chapter 11

~

Hello, Arch Enemy

"HOW ARE YOU IN MY dream? And where are we?" I demanded as I spun in circles inside a crystallized cave. The rushing, quaking sound of the waterfall concealing the entrance, echoed off the walls, crushing out the sound of my voice.

Light shined through the cascading ripples of water and reflected off the giant crystals, casting tiny rainbows through the fine mist.

I thought I was sleeping, but I didn't know why Lady Eve was standing next to me. "Is this going to cost extra?" I asked thinly, realizing that my voice adjusted to the volume of the waterfall. It was my dream, after all, so why not make it convenient?

"No, this won't cost you anything," she said un-entertained. "And you aren't dreaming, Aurora. This is where you must go in order to return home. It is a placed memory that you weren't meant to have until now. In order for us both to see it, you need to let go of what you think is real."

"What—are we in the Matrix? Are you going to ask me now if I want to take the red pill or the blue one?"

She stalked over to me and forcefully grabbed both of my

hands. *I stepped back in defense, but she held me firmly in place.*

"There is a lot you don't know about yourself. A lot that has been kept hidden in order to protect you." Her lips pressed into a thin line.

"Uh...yeah," I remarked under my breath.

"Beginning with the day you were dropped off at your foster mother's house I assume you have questioned why you have no memories before that day." She let the assumption sink in as her brows lifted in expectation.

Okay, now I was convinced. I hadn't told anyone that besides Fenn.

"Well yeah," I stammered awkwardly, "but what does that have to do with us being here?" I felt my muscles tensing, my brain suddenly aching.

"Everything. The choice you have been given cannot be taken lightly. You must know everything before you can make a fair decision. You must be prepared for the future you have been fated." She put her finger to my forehead and tapped it lightly. I felt my body go numb and fall into her arms as the ache in my head disappeared.

"Look inside your mind, Aurora." Her voice was distant, like she was standing on the other side of a door. I could see inside my head. How is this possible? It looked like the hallway back at Mily's.

"Go to the door that you know is right and open it."

"I don't know what you are talking about nor do I know how to open the doors inside my head." This was so ridiculous. I walked over to the nearest door and reached for the handle, but the knob didn't feel right, the handle dissolving in my hand. I huffed and then walked over to the door next to it and tried

the handle. It was locked.

"This is not going to work. The door is locked. This is crazy." I didn't bother trying to shield my frustration as I grimaced. I wanted to be back with Fenn. I wanted to know that I wasn't losing my mind, and quite frankly, the situation I was in wasn't ensuring a positive outcome. They were probably hauling me off to the loony bin while I was stuck inside my head.

"You're not trying hard enough," she called impatiently, annoyance lacing her words. "Forget what you think you know. Believe that the door will open and it will."

I took a deep breath and tried to listen to what she was saying. I tested the doorknob again, imagining the feel of it turning, jumping in excitement when it worked. I stepped through the open door, only to find myself right back in the cave next to Eve.

"Good, see, you've done it. You've unlocked the magical barrier that shielded this memory."

I still didn't understand what she was talking about.

"I'm in the same place I was in before. This is a bunch of bologna."

She spoke without acknowledging my tantrum. "Before The Fates show us what you need to see, you need to understand a couple of things. This may be hard to digest, but there is another realm of time coinciding with your own, under The Fates control." She paused, giving me a moment to consider her words.

"What do you mean coinciding?"

"Imagine two circles next to each other, meeting at a center point. The center point would be this cave-the doorway between both realms. Each circle is its own, different realm, but where they touch is the bridge between both worlds."

"That makes sense, but two realms?" I asked suspiciously. She nodded soberly.

I shook my head. "And The Fates are the Gods who rule both worlds? This is preposterous." I rolled my eyes and sighed. She looked at me with disapproval. "As preposterous," she spat, "as this sounds, you know what I say is true, don't you? You've known all along that you were meant for something else. That you didn't belong in the world you call home." Her eyebrow rose, questioning me.

She was right, exactly right. It made sense, even the situation I was in. No one that I knew of could do what I could with fire. And Fenn's powers only added to the confusing circumstances. We really weren't normal.

My face fell as I caved in. "So what I can do...that's normal where I come from?"

She looked pleased. "For some, yes, but you're special, Aurora. You're one of a kind. Your parents went through great lengths to have you. They-" Before she could finish, a beam of light clapped around her, Houdini-ing her out of my line of sight.

My heart quickened. Now I was alone inside the damp cavern. I felt heat surrounding me and saw the same beam of light appear. I felt myself dissolve inside it and then piece by piece, my body put itself back together.

My first breath as my whole self was a gasp as I clawed at my throat. Eve stood next to me, patting me on the back. I looked up and could have sworn I saw an impish grin before her eyes connected with mine.

"The first time one is summoned by The Fates is harder than the first time one ports. Just try taking deep breaths and think of calming thoughts," she coached as her hand stiffly

rubbed my back.

"Right, calming thoughts. Umm...I'm in a crazy place with an even crazier lady. Fenn has no idea the nightmare I'm living inside my head," I mumbled. I felt a wave of nausea come over me.

"Calming...remember. Get it together or you will miss what is being shown to you."

I scowled at her. God, would it kill her to have a little sympathy?

Then she sighed heavily, pulling me up to stand next to her. Her index fingers touched my temples and instantly the nausea disappeared.

"We are in the Lyceum, the Great Hall of the Pyre Magium," she said. Her tone sounded as if this were the last place she wanted to be.

"What's wrong?" I asked, trying to rub the glaze that seemed to saturate my sight. She moved closer to me and once again ignored my question. Her body seemed almost as if it were shielding me, though from what, I had no clue.

She ignored my question. "This is one of the four Rebell Islands, home to all Mages. Each is ruled by an Arch Mage. The Arch who rules here is Liege Zordon." The disgust rolled off her tongue as her lips quivered. "An Arch Mage is the highest rank of all Mages. And this one in particular will stop at nothing to get what he wants-the Stone of Immortality."

I could feel the shock on my face as my mouth hung open. It took me a moment to gather my thoughts. "Can we back up a sec? I'm a little stuck at Mage. What exactly is a Mage?" I continued to rub at my eyes. Wherever we were, it was very large and extremely bright.

"Part of your heritage, Aurora. I apologize, my patience

is thin. Please try to keep up and accept what is happening. Your time is limited." She took a deep breath. "A Mage is one of the most powerful magic wielding races inside this realm, besides the Draconta."

I gasped which sounded more like I was choking. "Draconta?" I barely stammered out, the word once again hitting home. "You're kidding, right?" I looked up at her, my sight finally clearing.

Her lips were pressed into a hard line, her expression barren and humorless.

"Right, you're not kidding."

"The Draconta is the faction of humans and dragons that live inside the Obsidian Chasm."

"Okay...so dragons and Mages...crazy ladies, oh my." I rolled my eyes. But somewhere deep inside, the pieces were slowly forming into a distorted picture. A picture that resembled me, only I wasn't human...I was something else, something serpent-like with angry-red eyes.

"Look for yourself," she said flatly, stepping aside.

The overwhelming brilliance of the Lyceum subsided as my eyes finally adjusted to the pure-white marble that seemed never-ending, covering the floors all the way up to the ceiling. There was a massive fireplace that took up most of a wall located at the back of the room, its flames burning a greenish-blue. The mantle was made of a gold so bright it could have been carved from the sun itself.

A breath-taking mural of constellations adorned the top of the dome-shaped ceiling. I squinted–the constellations seemed so real, as if the Mages had summoned a clear midnight sky to shine inside their home. The stars twinkled amongst the velvet black background, almost as if moving in a magical flow.

Everything seemed suspended, somehow floating on thin air. Shelves ran up the walls, filled with trinkets and books and globes that floated effortlessly. The tables that were scattered around the room had no legs. There were people, or at least beings, moving around us and through us. We must have been invisible. It seemed busy but silent at the same time. Like magic.

Lady Eve took a step forward, expecting me to follow suit. "Mages of every stature, from the lowest ranking Sage Mage, to a Grand Mage like Myrdinn over there," she said, pointing to a silver-haired man, "dwell here."

My eyes followed her line of sight, lingering on the man she had just mentioned. Didn't I know him from somewhere? Those lavender eyes seemed so familiar. I walked over to where he sat, next to the fire, and leaned in closer, trying to remember.

"And you?" I questioned, still inspecting the man she called Myrdinn, enthralled by his chiseled face and silver hair. "How do you tie into all of this?"

"That is of no importance right now," she quickly shot back, pulling me away from the man called Myrdinn. I was about to yank my arm from her when she suddenly sucked in a hissing breath. I turned to see where she was looking as the room muted and everyone froze, heads pointing to the floor. The air was thick and pungent with fear.

There he was.

My breath caught as my heart slammed against my chest. I couldn't take my eyes off him and felt a weird pulling sensation towards him. I knew him somehow. Zordon.

He looked over to me, eyes flaring with hatred. For a brief second I felt caught and thought that he was going to run towards me. I thought he was going to kill me.

But as the seconds elapsed and nothing happened, I re-

membered we were invisible and turned around to see just where his eyes were piercing. A lady, with long flowing champagne-colored hair that sparkled like a moonlit waterfall, sat alone in the corner. Her pensive face looked familiar.

Eve elbowed my side and whispered, "That is the Arch Mage I spoke of, Liege Zordon, with his two sons, Zane the oldest, and Zhax the youngest."

The room remained silent as Zordon strolled through the Lyceum, his obsidian cloak billowing after his footsteps like a black cloud. The air felt weighted, like a storm was growing stronger with every step he took. His two sons followed on either side of him, their gazes arrogantly sweeping the room, snickering at every head that bowed.

"The lady behind us is his wife," Eve sneered, her lip curling in distaste.

I couldn't take my eyes off the trio; their presence seemed to take up the entire open-aired room. The younger son, Zhax, favored his mother in looks with long wavy flaxen hair and bottomless blue eyes that complimented his gentle face. His soft features didn't fit the brash luster that seeped from his eyes. Zane, on the other hand, aside from his short hair and clean-shaven face, was a carbon copy of Zordon.

Zordon was tall—he had to be over six feet—with dark chocolate brown hair. His eyes matched his hair in darkness, and his face was hidden by a mustache and a thick beard that reached down to the middle of his chest.

I turned to ask Eve if she knew more about him, but she was completely turned around staring at the lady in the back of the room, a doleful expression replacing her once stern face.

"What's wrong?"

She jumped. "Wha-I'm fine," she faltered, tucking away

whatever it was she was thinking. I eyed her dubiously, on the verge of asking again.

Then Zordon spoke, and his abysmal voice trickled up my spine and into my brain–a strange familiarity latching on like flies stuck to a spider web.

"The Seer will be here any minute now so gather around the Table of Thoughts, everyone," he bellowed, grabbing his staff and heading to what looked like a throne of some sort.

He took his seat at the suspended table with his two sons on either side of him.

"How do the tables do that? I mean, suspend like that?" I wondered out loud.

"By magic. This whole place was built by magic," Eve said absently, answering the thought. Seven, tall marble chairs that seemed to have been carved up and out of the floor created the seats that everyone sat in around the table. I now knew who Zordon, Zane, Zhax, and Myrdinn were, but I didn't know who the other three were.

"That is Brohm, a Grand Mage, and the two eldest Mages are Albert and Ghandus. They are ranked Archion which is just below an Arch Mage. They are twins if you couldn't tell. Those three men are the only men worth trusting besides Myrdinn," she pressed.

I was trying as hard as I could to absorb everything she was saying. There were no words forming on my lips as I stood there gawking at what was before me.

She nudged me. "The Fates wanted you to see the prophecy so you must pay attention when the Seer shows up." I nodded.

From out of nowhere a man emerged atop the table. I could see through him as if he was a hologram.

"That is the Seer. He is like me, one who can read the future and tell fortunes," she pointed out. *So this is how she ties into it. She has a lot of explaining to do when we wake up.*

"Welcome, Soothe," Zordon greeted. *My eyes grew wide. Soothe? Is this the same Soothe that set up the security deposit box? It had to be. How many Soothes could there be? Fenn was going to flip.* "Now we can begin," said Zordon, stretching his arm towards the seats, indicating that everyone could sit.

I looked over at Eve. "Is he-" *but she put her finger to her mouth, quieting me. Then she pointed to Zordon who continued to speak.*

"I've been told you've been given the prophecy of the new world. It is rumored that I am a part of this?" When he spoke there was a voracity that tainted his voice. That deep, dark sound of eagerness that I myself have felt before. An eagerness to know who you are and what you are meant to be.

Soothe moved to speak. He was blurry so his features were hard to make out. His eyes were the only distinct thing about him, a pearl color with no pupil. He spoke to the air as if no one was speaking to him.

Eve leaned in and whispered, "The only time a prophecy is given is when major change is about to come. I'm speaking of a revolutionary type of change. That's why Zordon's so eager to know if he is a part of this, since he will affect the New Dawn of our realm."

New Dawn, like my name, *I thought.*

Soothe closed his eyes and exhaled. His arms crossed over his head and came to either side of his body as if in a yoga position.

Everyone in the room sat in deep concentration, but the atmosphere felt almost frantic. All of the men kept their eyes closed while they chanted like Monks, and energy crackled around them, sounding like tiny firecrackers. I turned to Eve to ask her what was going on, but hysteria was written all over her face.

The Seer then threw his head back and spoke. A deep voice, one that seemed to hold all the knowledge of the universe, crept in my ears like tiny spiders.

"Of dragon born a conqueror prevails.
The chosen one fated to protect the dying race.
Third of three deemed protector to the progeny.
The other marked for revenge.
The book of life, pages turn yet unwritten.
The canvas to your mortal soul; the connection to
your immortal enemy.
A death will come to He that breaks the barrier."

The air seemed to freeze as the intensity coming from Soothe spiked. The men looked to one another, a hazy fog emerging from their lips. I shivered, suddenly wishing I was wearing a thick jacket. Those words again. Before I could question Eve, Soothe shifted, something seeming to break his concentration.

He paused, as if listening to something, and then his head descended slowly, eyes glancing sideways in Zordon's direction. The deep inhuman voice re-emerged.

*"**Time now smuggles your other half abroad, where
she awaits the turning of age.
Protected by the divine, the dawn of a new era will
come another day."***

The misty air gave one last punch of cold and then swirled
away leaving Soothe to look up as if waking from a dream.
Zordon glanced uncomfortably around the room, then sat up,
chin defiantly held high in the air.

"I knew it," Eve barked.

"Knew what?" I asked quietly, voice trembling.

"He cut a piece out. He altered the prophecy." I had no
idea what she meant.

"Does this mean I'm going to die?" I asked, my earlier
fear resurfacing from my hand's "short lifeline."

"A prophecy can never be completely solved until it is
lived out. You can only do your best to be wise and cautious
with the information given to you. Think of it as a gift of fore-
sight," she replied callously.

"This isn't real. This can't be happening." I felt everything
around me collapsing as I stumbled forward, on the verge of
fainting.

She yanked on my hand and drew a dagger from out of
nowhere, dragging it ruthlessly across the palm of my hand. I
tried to pull away, but it was too late as my blood surfaced in
crimson bubbles.

"What the hell is your problem?" I charged, glaring at

her.

She glared back. Still holding my hand, she spoke coolly, "Your blood is proof. When this is over, you will see what is real." She dropped my hand.

I pulled it into my chest, the droplets of blood falling below me. My anger stirred.

Zordon spoke, regaining our attention. "You may leave us," he said, wishing Soothe away with the swish of his hand.

"Now let's get down to business. This prophecy must be solved. Myrdinn," he summoned, pointing his corpselike finger in Myrdinn's direction but continuing to look at the other council members, "you will pick this apart."

His sons looked at each other, disappointment seeming to wash over their sunken faces. I almost felt sorry for them.

"Father," interrupted the older brother, Zane. "Don't you think a more worthy Mage should be given this task? A Seer's prophecy is not an easy riddle to decipher." His eyes shot to the ground, ending his sentence much like I did when giving an oral report in school.

"If I thought Myrdinn incapable," Zordon began softly, "do you THINK I WOULD HAVE APPOINTED HIM?" Zordon yelled harshly, anger brewing as he hastily stood, hands slapping flat against the marbled surface of the table.

The marble table shuddered as his voice boomed. "Do you doubt your Liege?" he spat, almost nose to nose with Zane, veins bulging all the way up his arms and neck. His eyes had gone completely black, as dark as the fathomless pit of hell grasping onto innocent souls.

He reached out and grabbed Zane by the throat. Defensively, Zane's hands wrapped around Zordon's in an attempt to ease the grip as the blood quickly drained from his face. Black *crackles of energy popped around Zordon.*

Eve flinched next to me.

"Afflictum!" Zordon shouted, his eyes blazing.

"AGGGHHHHH," came a scream ripping from Zane's throat. His lower body was twisting as if in agony while his face continued to redden from lack of oxygen. No one moved.

Impulsively, I went to move forward to stop what was happening, but Eve held tight onto my arm.

"Careful, little dragon, now is not the time for your temper," she warned. Her head nodded in the direction of a mirror that was close by.

My eyes widened. They were ruby red, and a trail of smoke wafted from my nostrils.

"Little dragon," I repeated, the reality suddenly slapping me in the face. But before I could demand answers, the situation at hand kept unraveling.

"No...sir...I'm...I'm sorry..., my...Liege," Zane squeezed out through his blue-tinged lips as he twisted and writhed. His voice was distressed and cracking.

"My Liege," said Myrdinn, standing to regain focus, his voice as smooth as silk. "I will gladly take this task. Anyone would be honored. That is what Zane meant. He is a youngling who hungers for knowledge the same way we did when we were his age." He laid his hand on Zordon's arm, guiding down the rising temper.

My tensed breath began to ease as Zordon's grip lessened. Zane's breathing became quick as he gasped unmercifully for air.

Myrdinn continued. "I ask that I have leave to find a place of serenity. I need to have a clear mind in order to clarify this riddle. Do you mind picking a place for me? You know this

forest better than anyone, my Liege. " Good, keep his mind oc-
cupied elsewhere, *I thought.*

*Zordon dropped his son. I gasped, thinking that he was
unconscious as he lay unmoving on the cold white floor. Zhax
moved for him, helping him up and walking him towards the
back where their mother sat. Eve's ghastly face was filled with
horror. I reached out and touched her shoulder.*

*"Do you know their mother?" I prodded. Eve nodded in
acknowledgement. I wanted to ask her how, but I didn't feel it
was the best time.*

And then everything began to fade away.

Chapter 12

~

Some Clarity in a Dragon Sort of Way

I WOKE TO FIND FENN and Eve leaning over me. Fenn's face was painted in worry. "Are you okay?" he asked almost painfully as soon as he saw my eyes open.

Of course I am, I thought with heavy sarcasm. *It's not like I just passed out or anything. Or even like a crazy lady invaded my dreams and proceeded to fill my head with even more confusing things.*

I looked over at Eve and then immediately looked at the palm of my hand. There trailed a line of clotted blood, still stinging from the jagged cut.

"You were there," I gasped.

"I was there." She smiled politely, but her eyes were mocking my earlier disbelief.

"It was real, but how?" I asked, muddled. I pushed up off the ground with my good hand and scooted back. I needed fresh air.

"That wasn't a dream, my dear. That was the magic of The Fates. They wanted you to hear the prophecy that was made many years ago before your creation."

And that brought me to the most important question of all. "So…who am I?" I asked, bracing myself for what I already knew.

"Why, you are a Mage...with blood of the dragon running through you," she replied, as if I should have known.

"Wait, what?" Fenn interjected, puzzlement creasing his brow.

"I'm a dragon?" I asked, ignoring Fenn.

"Yes, born of a dragon, fathered by a Mage."

"But how is that even possible?" I asked, mystified. *Of dragon born a conqueror prevails,* replayed through my mind. The beginning of the prophecy. So it really is about me then. I am "of dragon born."

"By a shape-shifting spell," she huffed impatiently. "Do you really think the how of why you are who you are is really important to the matter at hand? You are in danger, child, sought after by the most relentless, bloodthirsty Mage. What is important is that you find the keys that have been hidden," she scolded.

"Who's after me?" I asked cautiously.

"Zordon, of course." She shook her head as if annoyed.

I made a face at the memory of him. "Well, that's just frickin' great. A crazy, delusional man is after me while I have no memories of before or any idea about myself in general," I ranted, standing just to get away from her.

"Do you ever think anything through before you throw your tantrums? Have you not thought that maybe there's a reason that you both have no memories?" she retaliated as she stood to meet my glare.

I paused a moment, letting her insult sink in, and then bit my quivering lip. She was right, I hadn't thought anything through.

"No," I conceded quietly.

"I think that's beside the point," Fenn added, scowling. "How can she think anything through when she doesn't have much to go off of? I mean, besides being here today, we have only had each other." He wrapped his arm tightly around my shoulder, once again coming to my rescue.

Instead of arguing back, Eve sat at the table, her piercing gaze commanding us to sit. She closed her eyes and lowered her face, holding her hands above the table. A faint green glow lit up the underside of her palms.

I jumped back, grabbing Fenn and immediately regretted it as I winced from disturbing the cut. I swallowed the pain and tried to remain brave as Fenn pulled my hand close to his mouth, his cool breath bringing some relief to the wound.

"What are you doing?" I scoffed, thinking that maybe we had pushed her too far.

She ignored me as she chanted, "Appareo." The green glow of her hands grew brighter as something began to materialize underneath them. A book of some sort.

When the book had fully materialized, she slowly opened her eyes as the glow diminished, and looked back at us.

We were huddled together with shock written on our faces, the cut long forgotten. "She's like us," I whispered to Fenn.

"We are from the same realm, Aurora. Come, sit." She beckoned with her hand. "We are running out of time."

Fenn grabbed my arm and dragged me back over to the table. "Can you show us how to do that?" he mused, looking back at me with enthusiastic eyebrows.

A smirk appeared on her solemn face, lighting the flecks of green in her eyes. She was quite beautiful when she smiled, almost intoxicating. She must have felt my probing gaze because her lip quivered and, regretfully, her smile vanished as quickly as it had appeared.

"This Oraculus was created on the day of your birth," she said, resuming her cool demeanor. "You see, in our realm, everyone's fate is written the day they are born. It's written into an Oraculus. All

Oraculus' remain in the Hall of Knowledge-which to you would be considered Heaven. But as I have said before, you are special." She pushed it towards me.

It was a leather-bound book, tethered by a stringy cord. The leather was worn and faded in some spots, like it had been around forever. I ran my fingers over the buttery softness, inhaling the fresh scent.

On the front of it were three symbols that were somehow vaguely familiar. They took up almost the entire front of the book and when I touched them, they lit up as if recognizing my touch.

Fenn was the first to recognize them as he said, "Hey! Those are the same symbols on the ring. Didn't you say they would be on the keys as well? Is this a key?"

Eve smiled again, her eyes gentle as she shrugged.

"What does that mean?" I couldn't help asking, envious of the connection she had with Fenn.

"You will soon see," she foreboded. "I can't just give you all the answers. You have to earn the right to be the Progeny."

I flipped the Oraculus over in my hands, giving up on weaseling information from her about the keys.

"Why is the back burnt?" I asked as I trailed my finger over the burn marks. It seemed like someone had thrown it into a fire or something. Strangely, the deepest burn ran along the edge of the spine.

"Because of who you are tied to," she answered.

I glanced at her quizzically and then opened the book, bracing myself for what it could possibly say. Everything was in a language I didn't understand.

"Well, this is of no use if I can't read it," I said, my words coated with irritation.

"The magic isn't in the words written, Aurora. No one is

supposed to ever see their own Oraculus until they have died and crossed over to the Hall of Knowledge. But in your case, well..." She broke off.

I continued flipping through, noticing that only half of the pages had words. The rest were blank.

"It's not finished," I pointed out.

"Like I said, you're special. Your history is different because it is tied to Zordon's. It's-" A shuffling noise sounded from outside before she could finish. She got up and went out of the room and then came back in a rush.

"Take it and keep it safe, at all costs. You must understand that this is your lifeline," she said, emphasizing the last words.

"Well leaving it with me is not going to keep it safe. I am the worst with keeping track of things." I pushed it back towards her hoping she would understand.

"Oh, really? Well I guess I'll just keep it then," she replied, pulling it back towards her.

I stopped her mid-pull, gripping the edge of the book tightly and preventing her from pulling it any further.

"Wait just a second," I said, a strong sense of possession rising deep within me. "You said lifeline? What does that mean?"

A coy smile crossed her lips. "Oh, but you said you couldn't take care of it," she mimicked, still smiling. "In our realm, a Mage cannot exist without an Oraculus. If your Oraculus falls into the wrong hands, you are dead. To burn an Oraculus is to fatally wound a Mage."

She let go of the book.

A sense of dread and responsibility swelled within me. "So what you're saying is that if this book is ruined, my life is basically over?"

Her eyes filled with recognition as she nodded. "You feel it, don't you?" she asked. "You feel that deep need to protect this…at any cost."

I grimly nodded. "Good," she said as she stood from her chair. "You'll be surprised with just how safe you'll be able to keep this," she finished with a wink, her scold long gone.

"What should she do with it?" Fenn asked.

She didn't acknowledge his question as she said, "You must go now. Our time is up."

"But wait…aren't you going to help me find the keys? This map isn't the most readable," I said as she started directing us towards the door.

"Even if I wanted to help you, I wouldn't be able to. This is not my journey to take, Aurora," she hedged.

"But I can't read it," I admitted in defeat.

"You can. You're just not reading it in the right place. Try saying *Apparatio* the next time you're alone with your Oraculus. It might help you figure some things out. And go to the historian in town. He will unintentionally lead you to the next key. I am not to influence your decision anymore so."

"What's the right decision?" I asked, more confused than ever.

She answered with a smile and patted my arms. "Keep your eye on that," she said, pointing to the Oraculus. "Remember, it is a matter of life and death. It will have the answers. Your choice affects the lives of many so please make the right one. Okay then, buh-bye, stop by sometime." And she practically shoved us out the door.

We both stood on her porch, blank expressions on our faces.

"Aurora?" Fenn asked. "What just happened?"

I looked at him, bewildered. "I was going to ask you that. She didn't even ask for payment." I was thoroughly perturbed by her behavior.

"Should I go in and pay?" And as if she was listening to us, all the lights flicked off and we heard a click of a lock on the door. "I guess not then." Fenn grabbed my hand and tugged me down the stairs back towards our motel room.

"She was in my dream, well, she said it wasn't a dream, but she was there in my head, I guess. Apparently there are two realms, anchored together by a cave on this island. There was an evil crazy man named Zordon—my fated enemy." I paused as something hit me. "I felt tied to him. Like it could really be true. I'm not sure what to think or make of it."

Fenn laughed as if questioning my sanity, putting me in instant defense mode. "I'm not lying or crazy, Fenn Aiden." His eyes flashed over to me and then his lips twitched, as if fighting the urge to smile.

"Besides the fact that I love it when you say my name like that, I wasn't laughing at you," he said sincerely. "And we both know that you are crazy, but that doesn't mean I don't think of you as credible. With everything that's happened lately to the both of us, I'm not going to doubt anything. I've seen and felt the magic myself. She wouldn't know what she knew if it wasn't real." He nudged into me, chuckling as I stumbled to catch my balance.

I frowned. "I just wish I knew what to do with all of this information. I mean, if I pursue my past then I have to deal with all of this, but if I just let the moon phase come and go, well, she said that a lot of lives hang in the balance. I don't want to be the cause of something bad happening," I admitted as we turned into our parking lot.

His face went serious as he quickly looked at me and said, "I believe in you so I can see why you would be prophesized about. And I believe that you will do what's right. If you gained anything from what just happened, gain that you were sent here for a reason, and apparently that reason was to keep you safe and to give you a choice. It is your choice, so don't fret." He rubbed my hair, leaving his hand to rest along the back of my neck.

I shrugged my shoulders. "I guess you're right," I surrendered, giving him a weak smile.

He laughed and said, "I'm always right...I'm a man, remember?"

I punched him in the arm as we headed up the stairs, and I felt a great weight lift as he turned the key in the door.

Chapter 13

~

A Kiss

FENN CAME UP BEHIND ME and rested his chin on top of my head after I took my shoes off by the door. I set my Oraculus down on Fenn's couch. I smiled as a feeling of euphoria consumed me, and I spun around to face him. I don't know what possessed me, but I didn't even hesitate to kiss him with every beautiful emotion in my being.

Butterflies flew crazily in my stomach, making it hard to concentrate, and the lullaby kicked into gear, stealing all rationality. My heart seemed to sync in time with the harmonious song that had unleashed between us like an untamed fire. His lips were so soft and gentle. My knees melted into oblivion.

Time seemed to cease around us, and I wished that it would remain that way forever. Why had I denied myself this for so long?

I grabbed the back of his head and twisted my grip in his thick wavy hair, not wanting to lose this perfect moment. His hands roamed down my sides and up my back, finally resting in my hair and twisting it just as yearningly.

On my tiptoes, I leaned hard into him and found that I wanted to show him the part of me that was real, a part that I had rarely even shown myself.

But then Eve's words replayed in my head, "Your choice will affect many." And I remembered the reflection of my blood-red eyes.

I suddenly shoved Fenn off, taking a few steps back to put distance between us. He had a look of awe written across his face, eyes still shut tight.

"Rory, that was amaz-" I cut him off before he could finish. "That was me not using my head. We can't do this. This can't happen right now." I looked to the floor, desperate for the right words.

"You don't mean that," he said, and in two strides he was face-to-face with me, eyes drowning my resolve. My breath caught. His lips were the only thing I saw. Perfect upper lip that was just a bit bigger than the bottom, soft and loving.

He tucked a piece of my hair behind my ear as he leaned in for another round.

My hand met his chest. "No," I forced out in a whisper, his lips just inches from my own.

"No?" he quizzed softly.

I closed my eyes, wanting so bad to say the hell with it, but I saw Zordon instead.

"No," I answered firmly. "I need to figure this mess out before I can commit to this. I need you as my friend right now. Adding romance is only going to complicate things. And besides, what if it doesn't work? I can't lose you."

He bitterly took a step back and without looking at me said, "As you wish," then turned and headed to the kitchen, pulling out leftover chicken and lettuce to make a salad.

I wanted to make sure he wasn't mad, but I knew that I had hurt his feelings. "Umm, can you look up the number to that historian Eve mentioned? I'd like to go first thing in the morning if you think it's a good idea," I said awkwardly.

I needed to change the subject and that was all that popped into my brain. He looked at me or more like right through me.

"Okay," he said vaguely. This wasn't going to get better soon enough.

"Listen," I leveled, "I'm going to take the car back to Mily. I think we could both use a little space right now." I uneasily edged away and snatched up my Oraculus before I walked out the door.

I took off in a hurry, hoping that the speed would beat the feelings I tried to leave behind. What was I thinking kissing him like that? I smacked my forehead with my palm and was instantly reminded about my bruise, regretting the smack.

Mily's house was only ten minutes away, which was good because the bus wouldn't be too far behind.

Eve popped into my mind as I drove. I remembered her saying that if I opened myself up, then maybe I would understand everything more. I glanced over and looked at the Oraculus on the seat next to me. "Ugh," I moaned.

Thoughts flourished as I raced down the highway. The music I blared wasn't enough to keep everything away so I smacked the power button off and rolled the windows down, letting the night air glide over me.

This was all so crazy, yet I knew it was true. I knew it would lead me to the answers that I had been looking for. The answer to who I am. That was why the decision should be so simple—find the keys. But then there was Fenn.

I was growing doubtful about the worth of finding out the truth anymore. I could simply let the full moon come and go and just live happily with Fenn.

Butterflies stirred again. Maybe that was what I should do. I mean, my parents did give me up so I could make my own choice after all and I could keep the freaky scary side of myself locked away. If what Eve had said was true...I'd really be something other than human. I wasn't quite sure I was okay with that.

I sighed as I turned into Mily's driveway, shutting off the lights so they wouldn't wake anyone. I grabbed my stuff and quietly eased the car door shut. A light was on in the house. I knew it wasn't late enough for Mily to be asleep, but I didn't feel up to chatting. I put the keys under the potted plant and headed over to the bus stop, plopping heavily onto the bench. No one was around, which gave me an idea.

The words written had an ancient scroll look to them, letters curved as if written by a regal hand. I ran my fingers across the rough, stained page and felt a light shock course up my arm. Eve's earlier advice sprang forth.

"Apparatio," I said aloud, letting the word roll on my tongue as if I'd said it before. I felt the energy inside me awaken, as if it recognized the magical language. I paused and looked around to make sure no one was behind me. Only the crickets chirped.

"Apparatio," I repeated, this time pushing my energy into the word. Little blue sparks popped around me and what felt like pure lightning rushed through my veins and coursed through my heart.

I was doing it. I was using magic.

Hunger for more burned in the pit of my stomach, growling and intensifying with each repetition of the word. I felt connected with the other side of myself. I felt alive.

Blue fizzles popped and sizzled around me. I was now unperturbed by the fact that I was out in the open. "Apparatio," I commanded one last time, forcing my power into the word.

My vision became blurry as a blast of blue light shot out from both of my hands, light streaming from the tips of my fingers. It was instant and then gone, but I felt myself fading, being pulled into the other realm like before.

The last thing I saw was the Oraculus glowing in front of me in the same blue-green hue. A void opened around me as more words began to scribe across the page. Then everything went black.

Chapter 14

~

The Fates Speak Through Me

FOR THE SECOND TIME IN twenty-four hours I found myself in another realm of time. Zordon sat in what looked like a bedroom that must have been located in the Lyceum. The walls were made of the same white marble, and everything, including the bed dressed in blood red linens, seemed to suspend in air.

The room was wide open, the ocean air gently breezing through the balcony's sliding glass windows. Zordon's back was resting on the chaise that sat at the foot of the bed. And as if he knew I was there, he tensed and sat straight up.

I wanted to turn and run, but that wouldn't do me any good. I didn't know where to go. I quickly assessed the room for a place to hide, choosing a thick crimson curtain that hung on the wall behind me. As he began to turn in my direction, I darted behind the curtain, praying that he would pass off the disturbance of movement as the ocean breeze.

Moments passed as I tried to calm the frantic pace of my heart, waiting for the inevitability of being caught. The moments seemed to stretch on like a prolonged round of torture.

Instead, his footsteps carried him away from my direction. I peeked around the inside of the curtain. He was facing the mantle of the fireplace reaching for a crystal ball.

"Are you awake in there, Lev?" he spoke to the crystal menacingly.

My hand flew up to my mouth, in an attempt to hold back a gasp. How could he put a person in a prison like that?

"If anyone ever found out that you hadn't deserted us, I don't think they'd be so eager to follow me." He laughed a knowing, chilling laugh and continued, "But if anyone ever tried to desert me, they would only end up like you. So I guess it doesn't matter either way."

His smile made my insides turn. How could I hate someone so much that I barely even knew?

"Gazing into your crystal again?" interrupted the beautiful lady with hair like white gold who had sat in the corner of my earlier dream. Her face was as expressionless as a rock.

"Ah, Gwenevere, you'd think after thirty years of marriage you'd know not to defer my train of thought." He set the crystal down and rolled his head in her direction, lips as thin as paper. "But since you have, what can I help you with?"

Walking over to her, he put his arm around her waist and pulled her towards the open-arched windows. His white-knuckled grip was digging into her hip.

She kept her face expressionless and moved with him, but at the same time I noticed the little bit of distance she tried to maintain by leaning her head slightly away.

"This is my room too, you know. Though I wish you would take up my offer and move me across the Lyceum near our boys." Every note of her voice was flat like the drab hum of a motor. Zordon let out a low growl.

She somehow managed to free herself of his grip and walked over to where I stood. For a second, I thought she was going to no-

tice my form behind the curtain, and I cringed in anticipation, but she never looked my way. I let out a lengthy breath.

She sat at the vanity, next to where I was standing. The misery creased in her face reminded me of Lady Eve. My heart twisted in agony.

Inside the mirror, black smoke twirled and then Zordon's face began to take shape. A Grinch-like smile stretched across his face. His eyes were completely black with only the faintest hint of a raging fire burning in the pit of his irises. No sign of human compassion burned there.

"I've missed you while you were away," he derided, head bobbing in the mirror like a ghost on thin air. His body was still by the window standing motionless, eyes glazed black as his magic pulsed around him. "I feel as if we don't spend as much time together like we used to." The cruel curve of his smile revealed a set of perfect white teeth, somehow adding to his mocking tone.

His dark black eyes held no verification of his words. He moved from the window to stand directly behind her, his face disappearing from the mirror in a puff of smoke. His hands picked up a strand of her fair hair. With care, he bent down and sniffed it, pausing with eyes shut tight to inhale deeply. The knots in my stomach tightened even more. Her face remained unmoved.

She gently took her hair from his hands and began to run her comb through it. How could someone as beautiful and pure as her, marry a man like him?

A crackle of black energy popped around her head, and in an instant her chair spun around, leaning on its back two legs. His nose met hers, her eyes as wide as saucers. His energy was exploding around him.

"What ARE YOU HIDING?" he shouted, the venom in his voice penetrating the air as he crowded her.

My fingers dug into the palms of my hands as I clenched my jaw, biting the inside of my cheek. I should do something. I should help her. The anger flared inside of me.

"I don't know what you are talking about, my Liege." Her voice faltered with betrayal. "You can ask any of the guards and maids. They are with me all the time."

For the first time I saw her look into his eyes. Her own light blue energy sizzled around her, ready to unleash. I had no idea what was going on between the two of them, but it seemed like some kind of ongoing mini-war.

Carelessly, Zordon laughed, grabbing his stomach and throwing his head back. What is wrong with this man? *I thought.*

"I'm not serious, Gwen." He spat her name as he spun her chair back around. "As if you could hide anything from me. You know I have my people watching you." I could see the mist growing in her eyes, but she never let it form into a tear.

"Oh, I hear the dinner bells chiming," he mused, changing the subject like nothing had happened. He placed his hand to his ear, leaning in to hear more. "Be at my side in ten minutes. One of the Mages has insight about the prophecy and we will be discussing it over dinner. I hear the cook has made my favorite again, heart of cow and yams. Oh and wear my favorite gown. The red one—you always look stunning in it."

She winced as he smiled with delight. As soon as he left the room she slammed her brush down on the vanity and stormed towards the window, affectionately holding her lower stomach. Letting all reservations go, I followed her and was taken aback by the view. The room was located a few levels above the main hall overlooking the beach.

She walked to the ledge and looked down. Waves crashing over the jagged rocks matched the rolling skies and promised a quick death should someone fall.

Oddly enough there was no railing to keep someone from tumbling into an untimely death. My heart dropped. She had moved to the very edge, balancing on the heels of her feet.

This was not what I needed to see right now. I didn't want to watch her die. A tear fell from her eyes, and she tilted her head down as if watching it fall into nothingness. Then her head went back and her arms went straight out to her sides. She looked like she was ready to dive.

"NO!" I screamed and ran towards her. Blue energy shot through my hands. As I grabbed her waist I expected my hands to move completely through her like they had before, but the energy that was flowing through them latched onto her. For a moment, our minds connected and I felt something more powerful than me, more powerful than anything, speak through me to her. "There is another way; this doesn't have to be the answer." And then the moment was gone.

She was limp, and it took everything in me not to fall with her as I tightened every muscle in my body and jerked backwards. I couldn't let her do this, my future depended on it. At least that was the thought that echoed in my mind the moment she went to jump.

A split second later I fell back onto my butt with her in my hands. She was unconscious, maybe from the scare of choosing to die or maybe from the mind meld that had occurred between us.

I looked down to my hands, still blue and humming. There was an incandescent yearning to use it some more, to practice. It was natural, what I was meant to do.

Now what? *I thought to myself. I sure as hell didn't want Zordon to come back and find me here. I wasn't sure if they could see me or not now that I had physically touched her. I looked at my hands again, amazed at what I had done. Was that magic? It felt good, whatever it was. It felt right.*

Gwenevere stirred and then sat up, scooting quickly away from me.

"Who are you?" she asked, tucking her hair behind her ear. What did I say to that? Umm, I'm a person from another realm? "I'm the one who just saved your life."

I stood up, looking to the sky. A little help, Aurora? Now would be the time to wake up.

"Why?" she asked accusingly, staring vacantly out into the ocean. I tilted my head in puzzlement. "I hate this place, I hate my husband, and most of all I hate how he has tainted my sons." She pulled her knees up to her chin and looked up at me with golden eyes of a doe. I swear I had seen her before, before all of this began.

"Do I know you?" I asked guardedly.

"I don't think so. How did you manage to get by the guards?" She seemed so young, like my age young, but Zordon had said they had been married for over thirty years. She couldn't be my age.

I shook off the unimportant question. "It's a long story. Look, you really shouldn't take your own life over this guy. Why don't you just leave here?" I didn't know how long this dream was going to last, and I didn't want to leave not knowing if she was going to live or not.

"It's not that easy to leave him. He is more powerful than any-one I know, well, besides the Dragon King, I guess." She moved to stand up, a faint light replacing the despair in her eyes. But then it disappeared, as if she had ruled out hope. "He's after revenge and he won't stop until he has it. I'm stuck here. I can't go on like this anymore. I'm not living and haven't been for a long while now." She turned back to the oceanic grave. "I won't let him ruin another one of our children."

Then her image began to fade. "Wait," I said, hoping that I could hang on for a moment more, but she disappeared.

I felt myself returning to my realm, but grabbed onto the memory of Zordon. I had to know Gwenevere would be okay. I had to stay a while longer. "Apparatio," I commanded, allowing the energy to encompass my body.

After standing in nothing but swirling darkness for a moment, I was once again in the main hall of the Lyceum. This time it was different. Everything seemed chaotic. The suspended objects pulsed wildly in their places.

Zordon paced in rage. He yelled for someone named Gabe and began moving objects angrily with a swish of his hand. He picked them off the shelf and slammed them into the fireplace where they burst into flames. His eyes were even darker than before. I ducked out of habit to avoid the flying objects.

I tried to seem inconspicuous as I quickly receded to a shadowed corner. The few Mages that remained to witness Zordon's rage were too busy ducking to notice me.

"FIND MY WIFE!" he screamed, the Lyceum air turning a dull gray. A well-seasoned storm churned outside the archways. His robe billowed behind him as he stalked through the room, shoving monk-like men out of his path. Trails of paper flew everywhere from the scattered wind.

A biting breeze, hissing like a rattler's tail, entered through the open windows.

Wait, did he say find her? Find the sweet Gwenevere? Oh no, what did she do?

"My Liege," said Gabe, taking his plated helmet off and bowing to Zordon. That face, I knew that man's face. All I could think of when I saw his face was a gentle smile on a full-mooned night. My head began to throb.

"What?" asked Zordon, ruining the slow appearance of a

memory. "If it's not the answer I'm looking for then you better leave me at once." He was scowling at Gabe. Gabe's weight shifted.

"We think we may know what has happened. I'm very sorry. Your wife is dead." His voice broke off in sorrow on that last word, carrying the realization on the hissing wind. He backed up a step, perhaps in fear of Zordon's outrage, but Zordon stood silent for what seemed like an eternity. The skies rolled furiously.

Sorrow replaced my anger. I let this happen. I didn't try hard enough to save her.

Lightning struck just outside the Lyceum, splitting a tree in half. The sound of the cracking wood and the smell of the burnt sap infested the hall, singeing my nose.

After a long enduring moment Zordon spoke. "What do you mean she's dead?" he dissented on a growl. He grew an inch, looming over the armored man. "She cannot be dead. Do you know why she can't be dead?" Spit flew from his mouth as Gabe squinted from the vile debris. Everyone else had left the hall.

"No, my Liege, I don't," he answered squarely. He kept his eyes leveled with Zordon's. The hissing of the wind hollowed out. Claps of thunder ripped at the quiet while the lightning flashed savagely, illuminating Zordon's sunken, shadowy face. Then his teeth gleamed in a twisted smile.

"She can't be dead because I trusted her with your men, Gabe. You wouldn't train your men to fail me, now would you?" His words were laced with anger, heavily pronounced, emphasizing his disapproval.

"My Liege," Gabe implored, wincing as another lightning bolt hit outside the opened hall. "I am sorry to have failed you. We aren't sure what happened. We think something may have been slipped into the guards' drinks because all three of them fell asleep. I unfortunately wasn't with them on this trip..."

He was cut off by Zordon shouting, *"Why weren't you with her? It was your task to escort her!"*

Gabe shifted again and moved his helmet to the other hand. *"Sir, I was also on task to check in on Myrdinn and ensure he was working on deciphering the prophecy. I was only gone for a few hours. When I returned, I found the guards unconscious and the Lady Gwenevere gone."* Zordon didn't respond, but he continued to glare daggers at Gabe.

"We've ridden all day, trying to find her. We had a Seer scan the area to see if they could pick up where her trace is, but there is nothing. There is no trace of where she may have gone or of her life force. She just disappeared. I will report this to the Counsel. I'm truly sorry to have failed her, my Liege." He bowed his head.

A deep-bellied laugh grew from the pit of Zordon's dark soul, spilling over into madness. The tumbling sky went charcoal. He pointed his finger at Gabe's chest. *""You should be sorry to have failed me, not her. You are my commanding officer and you have lost my most prized possession."*

Gabe winced at that remark.

All of a sudden Zordon's tone changed and the skies returned to a normal sunny day. With resolve he added, *"You will find her, Gabe, and she won't be dead when you find her. Understand? You will spend every waking moment personally looking for her, and you are not to return here until you have found her. If I see your face before then, I will kill you. It will not be a pleasant death either. You will beg for me to finish with you."* He turned his back to Gabe and stared out of the windows into the skies. *"No one takes what is mine."*

Then all of a sudden, I felt myself being pulled, forced back out of the realm.

I was back on the bench. My cell was flashing through the thin material of my purse, and the bus driver was getting ready to shut the creaking doors.

"Wait!" I called out, shoving the book into my purse and bolting to the door, almost slipping on the graveled sidewalk. Of course he was still closing it when my fist landed on the outside of it. He smiled an evil smile, and I imagined lighting his head on fire. If only.

He slowly opened it back up, still grinning from ear to ear. "Thank you," I said snidely, giving him a sarcastic grin. *Why can't he find a different passenger to torture?* He sneered and I shot him a nasty glance as I made my way to the back of the bus.

My heart skipped a beat as I locked eyes with Mr. Creepy. He was staring at me, as expected, so I boldly sat on the opposite side of him, knowing this was my one chance to ask about what the prophecy means. "Of dragon born a conqueror prevails," echoed in my head.

The barren bus took off slowly, engine sputtering. I glanced over at Mr. Creepy, who was still staring at me, and then looked up to the rusty bolted roof. *It's now or never*, I told myself as I turned to face him.

"I'm ready to learn," I said, hoping that he would have a little sympathy and shed some light on my situation.

"Where's your protector? He should never leave you unattended," he chastised, ignoring my question.

"I don't need a babysitter, you know. I am the chosen one." I felt my face flush from his disapproval of leaving Fenn. "And it's not like I need a guy anyway. Besides, he wouldn't have let me go. I was in a hurry and left him. Believe me, I'm sure he's freaking out right now," I rambled on. "The important thing is that I'm here now, and you're here, and I want to know about the prophecy. I want to know about me."

"I told you I was done," he dismissed, now facing forward.

"Please," I begged, "I need to know."

"Do you even know *who* you are? Have you at least figured that much out?" he asked, annoyed.

"I'm a dragon," I replied, the words feeling foreign on my tongue.

"I see you've met Eve then."

I paused a moment, taken aback that he would know that, and then asked, "Are you following me?"

He smiled, ignoring my question with one of his own, "And you saw the prophecy given?"

I nodded.

"Then that is all you need to know," he said with a sharp nod of his head as if ending his side of the conversation.

"What do you mean? Before you said that you would help me, that I needed to know things, and that you were going to show me. I have until the full moon to find these keys, which obviously doesn't give me much time." I leaned over and pointed to the almost full moon hiding inside a cloudy sky.

"I told you, girl, you're on your own," he recalled, eyes pointed in irritation.

Anger rolled through me. "Oh, I don't think so," I replied, feeling my energy awaken inside of me. Searing heat began as a ball in my chest, suddenly rushing through and bursting out the tips of my fingers.

My unstable tone made Mr. Creepy look up in acknowledgement and twitch as if he was startled. "Careful, young dragon, you're revealing yourself," he commented, pointing in my general direction.

"Yeah. I keep hearing that yet somehow I don't care." I glanced to where he pointed and saw in my reflection wisps of smoke trailing out from my flared nostrils. But it didn't seem to matter anymore.

"See, what you don't understand...is that you don't get to pick what you do or do not help me with. I need to read this map, and you can help me understand it, yet now you won't? Now that I've asked for your help? Don't you see the contradiction in that?" A growl slipped past my lips and I stood up. "I *need* to find the keys," I finished. "People's lives depend on it." I thought of Gwenevere.

He stood to face me and said, "You have no idea, do you? You still haven't realized the importance of you being in this realm. You're so eager to jump into something you've barely begun to understand. Things don't just get handed to you. You have to fight. Prove that you are worthy and then maybe the answers will be found. The Fates help all those who look to your return as their saving grace." Sarcasm laced his judgmental words.

I felt everything begin to vibrate from the angry energy I was unleashing. A small part of me knew that this had been a long time coming. All of my past frustrations were surfacing. I saw red.

"Sit down back there," the bus driver yelled, bracing the wheel as the bus shuddered from the stress of the energy streaming through my hands.

The few passengers on the bus hung on for dear life as the bus shook, the anger continually building within me. Eyes watched as Mr. Creepy and I stared each other down.

He smirked as if this were simply a mere annoyance to him. The bus driver shouted once again for us to find our seats.

"Yes, young one, do sit down. And how do you young people say it...chill? Yes, I believe that's right." He turned away to regain his seat as the bus tires found a pothole, jarring the passengers around. At that moment in time, the worry and concern that was strewn across their faces didn't matter. I was too focused on the smug twinkle in Mr. Creepy's eyes.

"I will ask you one more time. Are you going to help me?"

"Miss," the bus driver called out again, this time sounding more like a plea than an order.

I continued to ignore him, waiting for an answer from Mr. Creepy. Time dragged on as he ignored me. He had to have felt my anger rising as the energy began to gather in the palms of my hands.

The bus was now vibrating so hard you could hear the bolts in the roof jingling out of socket.

"That's it! I'm pulling this bus over and you are getting off!" shouted the bus driver.

"You shut up!" I shouted, pointing towards him. The balls of blue energy that had been forming flew towards his head. But another jarring pothole caused the stream to miss him and hit the dashboard instead, flames roaring to life on contact.

Uh-oh, I thought as I glanced back at Mr. Creepy, wide-eyed and looking for help. He just continued smiling.

"No brakes, NO BRAKES!" the bus driver shouted as he tried pumping them repeatedly. Headlights lit up the inside of the bus as we headed straight towards a semi with no power to stop. He swerved. But it was too late. Everything went flying from the impact, including me, as we spun out of control. The windows on the opposite side of me shattered and showered the passengers with broken glass.

I was thrown ahead into a seat and my head smacked the window. Then I flew up and into the next seat only to be shoved onto the ground and somehow rolled into the aisle. That's when I felt a snap in my arm.

A scream ripped out of me as the fiery burn raced throughout my body.

My arm had caught on the seat and bent the absolute wrong way. When the bus finally stopped, I opened my eyes and gently pulled myself out of the awkward position. My purse was behind me and so was Mr. Creepy. He seemed to be knocked out. I poked his forehead and watched as his head lolled back and forth for a moment. Yep, he was out.

My arm was definitely broken. The bone was protruding underneath my skin. A wave of nausea rolled through me. I bit the inside of my cheek and promised myself not to look at it again. With my good arm I grabbed my purse while registering moans from the other passengers.

What have I done? I slid the purse over my neck and noticed a glittering object next to Mr. Creepy.

It was that necklace. *My necklace*, I thought strangely. Instinctively, I snatched it up. *This is mine and he shouldn't have it.*

"Miss," a man called from behind me. I shook my head out of the trance and quickly pulled the large necklace carefully around my neck as I turned to face the voice. "Miss, I work up at the hospital. Let me help you up."

He was nice and I was suddenly very tired. As soon as my feet touched the floor everything began to spin. My horse knick throbbed from the collision with the window.

"I don't, I...don't...feel..." The floor rushed up to meet me.

Chapter 15

~

History, Fun...

"RORY, WAKE UP," FENN WHISPERED while rubbing the side of my head. I pried my eyes open and there was his beautiful face, fatigue written all over it. "I called Mily. She was about to wake up the triplets to come, but I told her you were okay, just some bruising. She said to tell you she loves you and is here in thought. Oh and she let me borrow her car. I had one of the guys from the restaurant drop me off at her place. She said we could use it tomorrow to get around until they get the bus thing figured out." I smiled and nodded in acknowledgement.

The hospital bed felt lumpy. I looked down and noticed my arm resting on top of a crisp white sheet. The overhead fluorescent lighting blinked rapidly a few times then straightened itself out. *Hospitals*, I thought with a grimace.

Then I shot straight up. "What have I done?" I asked as panic rose inside me. How was I not in handcuffs right now?

"What do you mean?" Fenn asked, confused.

"The bus, the accident, it was entirely my fault," I whispered to him.

"You must have hit your head pretty hard." He laughed. "There was engine failure which burned the brake lines. How could you have caused that?"

"No, Fenn." I grabbed his arm and pulled him close. "Mr. Creepy was there, on the bus, and I kind of got mad, and well you know what happens when I get mad, and long story short, magic shot out of me and into the dash which caused the engine failure. All those people—hurt because of me." I broke off, suddenly overwhelmed with guilt.

"Relax," he said as he rubbed my back, "no one was seriously injured."

"Mr. Creepy must've erased everyone's memories," I stated.

"Well, at least he's done something right," Fenn reassured.

I cringed at the memory of bone poking underneath my skin, but it wasn't anymore. Now there was large bruising covering the skin. "But this wasn't..." I started as the doctor pulled the curtain open.

"Ah, I see you're awake now, Miss Megalos. I'm Dr. Portel. How are you feeling?" he asked while extending his hand towards my good arm. His hand felt cold and clammy, and I instantly wanted to rub my own against the bedding. With a splash of hand sanitizer. I really hated people touching me.

I smiled awkwardly, noticing the smile lines that creased his hazel green eyes. Silvery white hair offset by his olive toned skin matched his sweet and wise grandfatherly voice. For a moment I felt myself slip into his comforting gaze, but the long white jacket adorned with probing trinkets brought back the reality of where I was. I hated anything doctor related.

I sat up, my hand moving to the side of my head where I had smacked it. I tested the sensation with the tips of my fingers. Although it was a little tender, there was nothing there—no bandage, no lump, no sign of any damage taking place. A strange feeling sank

in. "I'm feeling good actually. What kind of medication did you in-
ject me with?" I felt no dizziness, no sudden need to spew my empty
stomach.

Dr. Portel started to laugh. "We haven't given you anything,
Miss Megalos. We haven't needed to. We took X-rays and CT scans
while you were unconscious and they all came back normal. The
funny thing is, the man who was first on the scene swore up and
down that your arm was broken and that you most likely had a concussion."

I shrugged my shoulders dismissively, not knowing how to answer. The truth was, my arm was broken. I felt the bone snap, but
how could I tell him that when now, my arm was clearly not broken.

"I don't remember," I stuttered, "it all just happened so fast,
you know?" A classic, well-used, yet believable sort of lie. I looked
over to Fenn who was rubbing the back of my hand. His eyes were
so sympathetic. "How long was I out for?"

"A few hours. That in turn alarmed us and led us to doing the
CT scan, but we've seen patients react like you before. Usually a
lot of trauma to the head can cause a person to respond to a minor
concussion the way you have."

"I don't remember anything," I said, barely audible, watching
my pulse on the monitor. Could it show a lie?

"Well, we can keep you overnight if you feel you need the ob-
servation, but if you are feeling fine, you can be discharged. There's
no real concern for you to stay." He looked at my medical records,
shaking his head. "That guy swore…" he muttered under his breath
while walking away.

"I want to get out of here, I hate this place," I admitted to Fenn.
He started helping me up. I instantly frowned as I felt the uncomfortable breeze from the back of my hospital gown. *Let's add humili-
ation to the recovery process*, I thought, rolling my eyes.

Luckily a nurse brushed the curtain aside and handed me a large bag that held my belongings. The pendant sparkled under the fluorescent lighting. "Here are your things, Sweetie. We took them right before we decided to send you for a CT. That necklace sure is pretty." She paused to look at it. "Make sure you sign these papers before you leave," she finished with a smile. She set a clipboard down on the edge of my bed.

"Thanks," I mumbled, pulling my pants from out of the bag. She smiled softly and then slid the curtain shut.

"So did he give you this necklace?" Fenn asked, handing it to me. I smiled and slid it back around my neck. He turned his head away so I could slide my jeans on underneath my gown. I inched them up slowly, still bracing against the expectation of pain. Nothing came, no shooting pains through my arm, no dizzying headaches. It was a miracle.

"Am I completely, horribly rotten if I say no?" I asked, pausing mid-pants to glance at the necklace. My hand reached up instinctively, and when I clutched it, my hand warmed to the core. "It was on the ground in the aisle, next to him. Is he even here?" I asked nervously.

I definitely did not want to give it back.

"He's not here. Somehow he managed to sneak by everyone before the ambulance showed up."

"Well, I guess the necklace is mine for now. Let's get out of here." Fenn nodded and took my hand. No jittery feelings surfaced, only comfort, thank God.

I woke late the next morning to the sound of Fenn's shower and the sun peeking through the dark curtains. I felt unnaturally good curled into my cozy blankets. Actually, I'd never felt better in my life. My whole body was roaring with life.

I pinched myself...nope, not a dream. The bruises on my arm were gone, and touching my forehead proved the tenderness had disappeared as well. Not normal.

What a strange night.

I slowly sat up, in case there was some pain that I hadn't noted, but there was nothing. The weight of the necklace bumped my chest from the movement.

Oh yeah, about that. I wondered if it had something to do with my rapid healing. Of course Mr. Creepy would be the only one with the answer, and I wasn't sure I was quite ready to deal with him again.

I replayed yesterday's events over and over again, reminding myself that I needed to tell Fenn about Gwenevere and then stumbled over another issue I had yet to address—the Fenn kiss.

Lost in the memory, my fingers climbed up my chin and ran over my blushing cheeks. They trailed back down to my lips where I let them linger, thinking of his lips pressed to mine.

Thankfully my thoughts were interrupted by him coming out of the bathroom, in a towel of all things. Steam billowed behind him in curling mists, carrying the scent of bar soap. In that moment, he was unaware of me, and I found myself staring at his perfect body. I still didn't know how he managed to have perfectly chiseled but slim muscles when he did nothing physical besides play his guitar.

"Oh, you're awake. Feeling okay?" he asked, disconnecting my eyes from his body. I nodded and he gave me a small smile while still clutching his towel and reaching for his stuff right outside the door. "I thought you'd still be sleeping...forgot my clothes."

"I'm feeling great now," I said, amazed.

He was blushing, either from the steamy shower or from my presence. Either way it didn't help my feelings any. I jumped out of bed and quickly walked over to his clothes, handing them to him with a little too much eagerness in my step. Our fingers brushed against each other, sending a jolt through my body. It took a great deal not to gasp.

"Sorry," we both said. I plastered a dopey smile on my face while he ducked his head back around the door and closed it. Can we say awkward? I knew this wasn't going to be easy. I walked over to the bed and fell onto my back. Maybe this wasn't such a good position to be in when he comes back—all splayed out. I sat up but wasn't satisfied with that position either. A bed was simply not good.

I got up, defeated by my mixed emotions and walked over to the window, opening the slightly dusty curtain. My eyes squinted at the burst of midmorning sun.

Turning away and waiting for my eyes to adjust, I got my outfit ready.

"So, no bruises, huh?" he asked dressed in khaki shorts and a graphic tee adorned with skulls.

"Yeah, it's really weird, like nothing even happened. I think it may have something to do with this necklace." I ran my fingers around the edges of the vines that encased the ruby.

"Hmm…well, now you have my super healing powers, just like you asked for," he added with a smirk. "Even your horse knick is gone."

"It has to be the necklace then," I repeated.

"I'm glad you're okay though. Lord knows I would've hated having to cart you around everywhere all broken and battered. Spoon feeding is not in the cards of our friendship," he teased playfully. For a brief moment the awkwardness disappeared, the ease of our friendship returning.

"Mm-hmm, sure. You know you would've spoon fed me. And liked it." I stuck my hip out, flicking my hair over my shoulder in confidence. When he joked like this, everything felt right again.

"Yeah, maybe. It's all yours," he said with torment clouding his eyes that shot to the floor. My hope sunk. It was painfully obvious, the effect we had on each other. I headed to the bathroom so I could wash the weird night away. He moved and made sure not to look at me or touch me.

"Thanks," I said almost too eagerly. I quickly went through my morning routine—brush hair, wash face, teeth, dress, smell good, and then a quick once-over in the mirror. I don't know why I was in such a hurry. When I was finished we still wouldn't know what to say to one another. That stupid kiss. Well, I shouldn't say stupid because I thought it was great. Either way, it had certainly strung up some kind of roadblock between us.

I stepped out of the bathroom, tucking the necklace inside my shirt and taking in a breath for confidence as I found his beautiful blue eyes. He was fiddling with the remote, flipping endlessly for something on TV. When he saw me he tossed the remote to the edge of the couch and stood, moving toward the kitchen.

"So about that historian," I quickly babbled.

"Yeah, about that. I called him before you woke up this morning and asked him if he had anything on dragon lore and map reading. He said that was his specialty and to come in whenever we're ready, that he'd be there all day. Maybe he'll see something we missed," he informed as he looked up at me.

"Cool," I replied casually.

"Mily doesn't need the car back until later, so after we're done, I'll take it back since you can't handle that on your own." He stood at the sink, turning to throw that last remark with an impish grin before turning back to the dishes.

I squinted in sarcasm, lips turned up with a fake smile. "Ha ha ha, good one." I was grateful for the attempt at humor.

He was chuckling to himself as he pulled out the mug I'd bought him from the cupboard. He must have made coffee while I was in the bathroom. My nose jolted to life, picking up on the sweet smell wafting through the air. I loved that the room smelled like a coffee shop. Maybe I could revel in my urge to pick up a good book and just relax for the rest of the day.

"Would you like some?" he offered.

I smiled and said, "No thanks," then sat next to him at the table. I cleared my throat. "I umm-I crossed over to our realm last night while I was waiting for the bus."

He stopped mid-sip to shoot me a questioning look, so I kept on.

"Strangest thing happened…this lady named Gwenevere, who was married to Zordon, I think committed suicide. Remember in the prophecy it says 'the other marked for revenge?' That must be what it means…if she died, then he must want revenge for that. Maybe he blames me? Maybe he found out that I was with her or something?"

I stopped mid-thought, tapping my chin. Something was missing. Some detail that I overlooked. I scrunched my nose, trying to remember what it was that was dangling on the tip of my tongue.

My finger shot up into the air. "What a minute, she told me that he would stop at nothing because he was after revenge. That was before she died." My shoulders slumped in defeat. "That means he couldn't be after revenge because of me or because of her death. Now I don't know what to think."

"Wait, she talked to you?"

"Yeah, weird, right? I think it may have something to do with using my Oraculus, but I'm not sure. That was something I was hoping to ask Mr. Creepy about, but you know how well that turned out." I sighed. "A part of me doesn't want anything to do with this, you know? It's almost too much to take," I admitted quietly. "Do you think that makes me a bad person?" I looked at him, seeking his approval.

His face softened. "I think the opposite, Rory. That letter and Eve said you have a choice to make, and it's your choice alone." He paused, seeming to struggle with his thoughts. Then he sighed as well, as if caving in to whatever was bothering him. "To be honest, I'm not real sure I even want you to continue with all this. I mean, with what's happened so far…who knows how much worse it can get." He trailed off, worry replacing his confidence.

I sat there for a moment, considering what he had just said. It was starting to sound like a good idea. Especially after seeing what I would be returning to.

"I think I'll base my decision off of what we find out when we go to the historian. Eve said he would 'unintentionally' lead us to a key. And if he can't help us, then I'll give up," I reasoned.

"I think that's a reasonable idea," he replied with a forced wink. I ignored the instant spark that shot through me, causing goose bumps to rise up on my skin. "That's why I called him. I also called the diner and let them know that we'd be out for the next few days due to personal issues. They were very understanding, considering the bus accident."

I felt the creases of my mouth turning upward as I nodded. Then my eyes moved a little south, betraying my mind that was yelling for them to stop. When I looked up again, his eyes were on my lips. I saw myself kissing him, letting myself go, but turned my head instead.

"That's why you rock," I pushed out, hoping my uneven voice didn't give away my thoughts. "I guess we can go when you're done with that mug. No use wasting a perfect morning," I hurriedly added, getting up from the table and walking over to the TV. I fumbled with the remote.

"You okay?" he asked, picking up on my inner struggle. The disappointment was apparent in his voice. This was just one problem I wasn't ready to sort through.

"Yeah," I replied, and then I forced myself to turn and look at him. "Just nervous about what we're going to find out." I was lying. I hated lying to him. I hated lying period. He watched me, examining my face skeptically. He saw right through my lie, but thankfully let it go as he carried his mug to the sink.

His scent distracted me from where I sat. The delicious, homely smell, caused me to again picture myself grabbing him and kissing the hell out of him. I added, "It should be interesting," as I moved to the door where my shoes and purse sat.

He stalked over to me and turned my shoes around so I could slide them on. How did he manage to think of half the stuff that went through his brain? Then he stood and was once again face to face with me, in the very spot where "it" had happened. His demeanor was so easy for me to read. I knew he was still thinking about it too. How could he not? We were a constant reminder to each other about what had happened. And the feelings still remained.

I coughed nervously, clearing my throat, then turned to open the door. I ran down the stairs and jumped into the car. My eyes rested straight ahead and noticed someone staring directly at me through their motel window. A small portion of the curtain was peeled open, enough for me to see one eye and half of a nose. The person stared at me for what felt like forever so I made a contorted face and childishly stuck out my tongue. The curtain angrily closed shut.

We both buckled up, and then Fenn pealed out in reverse. "What a weirdo," I said, miffed. The person's questioning eye stood out in my mind. It had a glaze to it that was almost unnatural. Where had I seen that before?

"Yeah, he did that when I first came here to look at the motel room. The manager said that he rarely ever leaves this place." He adjusted the rearview mirror, looking back to our room and then pulled out onto the highway.

"So it's a he? I couldn't tell."

Chapter 16

Fenn's Awakening

WE PULLED INTO THE DRIVEWAY of the historian's, the orbed sun making its way to the middle of the cloudless sky. The grass was sated and lush from the recent storm, and butterflies fed from bloom to bloom. The breeze was steady but low, sweeping my hair off my shoulders as we shut our car doors.

A rugged, old, two-story building built out of coarsely weathered wood sat painted in coral colors. The windows were trimmed in a darker rose color, and the light blue door seemed to fit oddly. The overhang, made of the same battle-scarred wood, had all sorts of wind chimes twisting and singing in the quiet morning breeze. A sign on the front door read "Open" so we walked right in.

An old man standing on a polished ladder in the far left corner of the room was busy putting books on a bookshelf. He peered over at us as we entered. Sunrays peeked in through the many windows surrounding the building, emphasizing the dust that glittered off the books as he put them away.

The entire first floor was an open room, filled with bookshelves that looked pretty ancient. They were made of some type of dark wood carved with spirals and vines that whispered stories of fairytales. The scent of aged paper mixed with Pine Sol permeated the air. Classical music played softly, the old man humming along. I was home.

"Welcome to the Public Library," the old man said. He was wearing khaki pants and a plaid yellow shirt laden with a sweater vest.

"My name is Bob. I'm assuming you're Fenn and Aurora?" He pointed to each of us as he said our names. "We don't get many visitors here; these days the younger crowd thinks reading is overrated." He was smiling to himself like he had told a good joke. How cute and old man-like.

"Yes, sir. I'm Fenn and this is Aurora, and we don't think reading is overrated," Fenn replied, shaking his hand a little too enthusiastically. He was a sucker for old people. "In fact, Rory here reads as often as the sun rises."

Bob climbed down the ladder and handed a couple of books to Fenn with a thump. "Well, I understand that you two want to learn the mythological history of dragons." He kept talking as he walked to the back of the room, leaving us to sum up that he wanted us to follow him. Fenn walked quickly ahead, reaching his arm back so I could grab hold of his hand.

"He seems nice," I whispered to Fenn.

"Yeah, I think he is. I really liked him over the phone." He pulled me to walk in front of him and put his hand on the small of my back. The smarter part of me knew that I should keep him from doing that because it only made things more complicated. But my heart wasn't quite strong enough to make him stop.

We walked through a door that was in the very back of the main room and entered what I guessed was a parlor of sorts, striped in green and white. A few different couches and chairs created a pleasant atmosphere to kick back and read in. I could see myself coming here and relaxing quite often.

"Well," said Bob pausing for the first time and tipping his glasses down on his nose to get a better view of us, "take a seat. I've pulled a couple books for reference, in case I find myself missing a piece. This isn't a popular subject around here, but it's one that I myself have put a lot of research into. I've always held a keen fascination for all things fantasy."

Come on Fve, please be right, I thought with a glint of hope.

Fenn laid the books Bob had handed him on the table where we sat. Bob sat down in a loveseat in front of us, crossed his legs, and then took a deep breath.

"Where to begin," he said, tapping his finger to his chin. He looked up. "The beginning would be best, I suppose. I tried to stay local with the lore-keep things interesting. Did you know that we actually have lore on this island concerning dragons?"

We shook our heads as he changed his glasses, pulling a reading pair out of the pocket on his sweater vest. He had a Star Trek communicator pin fastened to the pocket. I tried to refrain from giggling. Bob grabbed one of the books off the coffee table that sat in between us.

He cleared his throat. "Now, are you two aware of the ruins on the Eastern side of the island?"

"Somewhat," Fenn answered for both of us.

"Those ruins were actually once a place of worship, back before the settlers came. The Shaman who led the founding tribe passed down stories about another realm of time." He smiled blissfully.

I leaned forward, biting my lip to hide my smile. If he only knew.

"The Shaman held awakenings in a cave not too far from the ruins. It was a religious practice performed the night before the tribes would harvest their crops. Legend has it that one night, while the Shaman held an awakening inside the cave, he witnessed a phenomenon." He shifted in his seat, excitement gushing from his words. "An unusual man appeared from out of thin air, right inside the cave."

I blinked. "A man?"

"The Shaman wrote that this man spoke of a realm full of magic and hope."

"What happened?" Fenn asked Bob.

Bob smiled. "The Shaman took this man into his tribe and offered him shelter. In return, the man shared his insight. He claimed to be a god from the other realm."

"A god?" I blurted out.

Bob chuckled. "You see, the man claimed that in his realm he had four other brothers. They were known as The Fates. This man-the fifth brother-broke a law. He created a new race, dragons, without the consent of his brothers."

Fenn stiffened, slowly sliding his hand in mine. Eve had talked about The Fates. I squeezed Fenn's hand.

"And the Shaman believed all of this?" I asked, dazed.

"It is written here, in this journal," he informed, tilting the journal in my direction. "It was deciphered by our college as a part of our island's history. The Shaman wrote that this man was someone he could trust"

"If he was trustworthy, then why would he leave his realm after breaking a law?" Fenn asked, confused.

"Because the other four Fates didn't approve of the creation of the dragon. They looked at it as an abomination. And since they had no punishments set for this unimaginable crime, they attempted to terminate the entire race."

I gasped, covering my mouth.

"But the fifth brother knew something the others didn't," Bob continued, deep into his story. "He saw something coming-a grim future. He told the Shaman that he believed one day, a spawn from his creation would save our two realms from the destruction he foresaw in a vision. A savior."

Bob's words drifted away as I stared absently out of the window, my mind spinning. I felt shaky and a little nauseous as my thoughts touched on Mr. Creepy's prophecy. Of dragon born a conqueror prevails. Am I the savior-the conqueror?

Fenn coughed, nudging me.

"...this was why the man, as you inquired Fenn, fled his realm," Bob kept on. "He told the Shaman it was to ensure that the savior would be created. If he stayed, his brothers would've eliminated the race of the dragon. To prevent this, as penance for his crime, he put his immortality into a special stone and laid it deep inside a volcano. He left it there, in the other realm, and asked the Dragon King to protect it. He then crossed over here and lived out his days as a mortal."

My heart accelerated. I understood why I needed to visit this historian now. He might not know *who* he was talking to, but he certainly knew a lot.

"What did the brothers do after that? Did they destroy the dragons?" Fenn asked, taking the words from my mouth.

Bob's brows lifted as he shrugged in uncertainty. "No one knows. Alas, the journal is incomplete. It ends shortly after the man died and the Shaman disappeared." He looked up from the book with a sad smile and then closed it, placing his palm lovingly on the cover.

"What did the Natives do after that? After the Shaman left?" I asked, thirsting for more.

"They created an altar inside the ruins, worshipping the Fate who sacrificed his immortality for the fate of our two realms."

Zordon's face came to mind then. I briefly remembered Lady Eve mentioning something about a stone that Zordon was after. My mind buzzed with information. Was the stone the Fate poured his soul into the same stone Zordon was after?

"I was told that you have an ancient map that you'd like me to look at?" Bob asked. I stared at him for a moment, trying to make out what he had just said.

"Show him the map, Rory," Fenn muttered under his breath.

"Oh! The map, here," I rushed as I pulled it out of my bag and unfolded it, laying it down on the table for Bob to see.

"Ahh, this is quite old," he commented, tilting his glasses down and leaning in. He compared it to the pages of the leather book, brows furrowing as he tried to make out the picture. "It's a hand-drawn layout of our island, similar to this one," he explained, pointing to a map in the journal.

He leaned down until he was almost nose to nose with the map, then said, "Actually, your map looks like a treasure map. There are focal points on here, but the hand that drew it was unsteady, it's hard to tell. There is however, a heavy emphasis on the ruins. You see how it takes up more space than needed on the map? Maybe something is there. Who gave this to you?"

I wasn't sure how to answer. I wasn't sure how much I should give away. I shrugged.

"Hmm," he pondered. "Well, I can't really help you in this department. My knowledge only goes as far as what I've shared. If this were mine though, I would definitely investigate the ruins. There is an island tour, the group travels to the altar and the cave. You never know what you may find." His gaze filled with yearning as he looked down at the map.

I snatched up the map and put it back in my bag. "So other than recognizing the ruins, it's unreadable?" I pointed out, trying to deter him from wanting the map.

"Precisely," Bob replied, disheartened. I leaned in again to glance at his map that was drawn up by the Shaman and was caught off guard by his excitement. "Is that a Lapis?" he asked, grabbing my hand and holding up my middle finger. The ring had obviously sparked his curiosity.

"Lapis? I don't know what you're talking about." I tried to gently pull my hand back, but he brought it closer to him. From his pocket, he pulled out a small magnifying glass, similar to one that a jeweler would use. Who carried those things around?

"It's a type of stone. That ring you have on," he gestured with his eyes, "it is set with a Lapis. In jewelry form, it was said to hold great power. The odd thing is, the altar I told you about, the one they built to worship the Fates sacrifice, is made entirely of this stone. It was the only thing left undamaged after the settlers came. Hang on a second." He practically jumped out of his chair and headed back into the main room.

As the soft pad of his loafers drifted away, Fenn poked me in the side with his elbow. "I bet this ring has something to do with the temple. This has to be the clue that Eve wanted us to hear. Must be where a key is."

I was thinking the same thing. I slid the ring off and laid it on the table in front of us.

"That's great...if I decide to continue," I reminded. "This whole map thing is bumming me out." He shrugged his shoulders and looked up to Bob who had jogged back into the room. He had yet another book in his hands—so resourceful.

"See here," he said, flipping the book open to a creased page and guiding our eyes with his finger. "This is a modern-day picture of the altar." He pointed and gave us a moment to take it in. It looked like a really big block of dark blue stone that the native people carved intricate pictures into.

Like the pyramids in Egypt, it was perfectly cut. And like the pyramids of Egypt, I couldn't begin to imagine how it was built without technology.

Pictures were chiseled all around the four-sided stone. On the right side was what looked like a large dragon standing before humans bent over in worship. It seemed to be harmonious.

"What do the pictures represent?" I whispered, curious to know more and even more curious as to why I was whispering.

"There are a few different interpretations, but for dragon lovers like us, I'll tell you what I believe." I could feel his excitement building once again as both his hands came out to sway to the sound of his voice. He liked to use his hands while telling stories, a trait I found intriguing.

"I believe this carving represents the savior. I believe the Natives carved this image as a reminder of the vision the man spoke of to the Shaman-a reminder to pray for the realms salvation."

Now this was something I could work with. Maybe there's a key inside this altar. My blood began to rush.

He flipped the page over. More carvings appeared. A human stood in the center with what looked like a stone in his hand. "I believe this is the stone the Fate poured his soul into. Many will covet, but one will attain this stone. An evil that will threaten the safety of our realms. The Shaman wrote that the savior would be the only one to prevent this from happening."

I knew it. It was all coming together.

"Hmm…something I haven't noticed before. Look here," he said, pointing to the left of the human with stone. "A piece of the altar is missing." It wasn't a large enough gap to be distinct, but he was right. It looked like someone had chipped it out.

"Maybe it is just coincidence that the altar was chipped. I

mean, it is after all, a ruin. Damage does occur," Bob noted, "but you know what would be intriguing?" he asked as he scooted forward. A strange looked crossed his face, like he wasn't sure if he should continue or not.

"What?" I coaxed.

"Well, I was just thinking, it'd be marvelous if the stone in your ring was created from the piece of stone that was chipped. I doubt it though, you can buy Lapis anywhere," he finished, brushing aside the thought.

But it was just what I needed to hear.

"Anyway," he said shaking the thought, "that's that as far as the history goes." He shut the book and sat back in his chair, staring off into the distance. I glanced back down at the ring on the table, respecting it more than I had before.

This was a good idea, I thought as I gave Fenn a reassuring smile. I knew where I needed to go to find at least one of the keys. *Thank you, Eve, wherever you are.*

"I just received this yesterday, if you can believe it. To make things even more interesting, I have no real inkling as to who gave it to me," I admitted.

"That is interesting indeed. Are you going to look into it?" he asked, distracted.

"You know, that's part of why we're here today, to help me decide. What would you do?"

"That's a silly question. I'm a historian, Aurora. What do you think I would do?" My cheeks went red as his smile grew.

But of course, I thought with a laugh.

Fenn slid forward and stretched his arm out, swiping the ring from off the table and sliding it onto his middle finger. It fit him perfectly. He sat there for a moment as stiff as wood before he moved again. Something was off. I don't know how I knew, but something in me stirred at his stillness.

"Do you think this ring really came from that altar?" he asked with an odd look on his face. His hand was still outstretched, eyes darting between the ring and Bob.

"It was just a theory. It's hard to say though. I'd like to think that the Natives would have left something for the savior to find. Something that would help them in their journey," Bob answered, completely unaware of Fenn's strange reaction.

Maybe something like a key to return home. Maybe this ring is one of the keys. I instinctually reached out to Fenn, placing my hand on his arm in hopes that I would magically know what was going on. He flinched at my touch, moving just enough to knock my hand off.

"Is it supposed to give a tingling, buzzing feeling?" He looked over at me with a glaze to his eyes. "Rory, when you put this on, did you feel funny, like your head was dizzy?" I shook my head no, alerted by the alarm in his tone.

"What do you mean? It's only a ring," Bob said curiously.

"Yeah, you're right, I…I'm just being silly. Where are your restrooms?" he asked as he jumped up. He paused long enough for Bob's quick directions before hurrying away. I wanted to follow him, to make sure he was okay, but Bob turned back to me, interrupting my departure by asking if I wanted to see his personal gem collection.

"Sure," I managed politely, trying to hide my nervousness. I kept glancing to the doorway, waiting for Fenn to come back, but he didn't. That worried me.

Chapter 17

~

The Fight

FIFTEEN MINUTES HAD PASSED WITH no sign of Fenn. I politely excused myself from Bob and his extensive collection of stones and went looking for him.

It was eerily quiet inside the main room as I walked through the maze of dimly lit bookshelves. I wasn't too sure where he had gone so I checked each aisle of books, just to be sure. I found dust mites and pages of history, but no Fenn. I headed to the back where the restrooms were and called out his name.

"Fenn?" I asked as quietly as possible. No need to stir up Bob. Nothing.

"Hello?" And then I heard a moan. I grabbed the antique handle to the men's bathroom and turned it as quickly as possible, hoping that it wasn't locked. It creaked open but then stopped midway, as if something was blocking it. I pushed a little harder, opening it enough to peek my head in. There he was, in a heap on the black and white tiled floor.

"Oh my gosh. Fenn, are you okay?" I asked, easing him out of the way so I could fully open the door. Concern burned through my belly. I had never seen him like this before. He looked completely dazed and disoriented.

"Aurora?" he muttered, trying to move to a sitting position. I stepped forward into a puddle of water rippling beneath my foot.

"Yeah, Fenn, it's me. Should I get help?" I crouched down, helping him up and grabbed his face so I could see his eyes. He groggily blinked a few times, trying to focus on my face. After a brief moment of swaying, he steadied, his gaze intently boring into mine. I let him grab onto me to help him stand. I had never realized how heavy he was before. Or maybe I was just weak.

"I'm okay. Just got dizzy is all." He smiled weakly and splashed cold water on his face. I hadn't even noticed the running water that was overflowing onto the floor like a waterfall. I placed my hand on his back, running my fingers soothingly along his spine.

"What happened to you, really?" He wiped his face with a paper towel and shrugged his shoulders, shutting off the water.

"Don't know. But if I remember, I'll tell you all about it." A frail smile came from him and he stepped for the door slightly off balance. "Let's go home, okay?" I nodded and helped him walk to the front door.

Luckily Bob was already there so we could make for an easy exit. "Hey there, oh, you look sick."

Fenn stood on his own, seeming to regain most of his strength and balance. A strange look of recognition crossed his face as he stared straight ahead. I nudged him in his side, hoping to bring him back to reality. He looked at me, his eyes full of sorrow. He was somewhere else, seeing something else. I reached out and took his hand, squeezing it. Then he shook his head, replacing the sorrow with a forced smile.

"Wha-oh, yea. We better be going now," he said bleakly, shaking Bob's hand again. He grabbed mine and I waved at Bob, not sure why he was tugging so hard on my arm. And what about the mess?

The frail Fenn that I had just found on the bathroom floor was gone. Here's to a rapid healing ability.

He rushed us toward the car and got into the driver's side, slamming the door. I hurried, not sure what his issue was. One second he's lying on the floor, passed out, and the next he's a raging maniac. He must've hit his head pretty hard.

"What's wrong, Fenn?" I asked, grabbing his arm off the stick shift gently. I didn't feel comfortable with him driving like this. I wanted him to talk to me first.

"Nothing, okay, just drop it," he barked, his tone harsh and barren. He threw my hand off his and then put the car into first, peeling out onto the road.

That caught me way off guard. Fenn had never yelled at me before, and I couldn't help the feeling of dejection that came with it. I had no idea what to do for him, but my defenses went up immediately. I felt my temper brewing, the power in me heating up.

"No, I won't just drop it. What happened to you when you put that ring on?" I asked and then waited expectantly. Something had to have happened with the ring. People didn't pass out in a bathroom for no reason.

He glanced over at me, his eyes hard and cold and then back at the road, the speedometer still rising. The muscles in his jaw flexed in agitation.

I crossed my arms and huffed loudly, hoping that it would be enough to get him to spill.

He looked over at me again and I raised my eyebrows impatiently, holding my own against his glare. His shoulders slumped as his cold eyes melted.

"Aurora, there's nothing wrong okay. I-I'm tired and dizzy. I think I just need to lie down. And I haven't eaten anything. It's probably just the caffeine from the coffee that's upset me." He glanced over in my direction, his eyes now empty.

He was lying, but why? My stomach clenched in knots as I foresaw what was coming but pushed the thought to the back of my mind, knowing that things would work themselves out. He loved me in one way or another.

But I knew deep down—his time had come as well.

My shoulders slumped as well as the sick feeling rose to the top of my throat. "Okay then. As long as you feel better. That's what's really important. Eat and get some rest. And when you're ready to tell me the truth, I'll be here." I was trying not to sound as pitiful as I felt.

"I'm sorry Rory. I…I just need some time alone okay. I need to figure some things out." He looked straight ahead, his tone as dry as a desert but somehow edged with sorrow. I hated that I noticed all these little things in his behavior. Why couldn't I be more naïve?

"I guess everyone's warranted their alone time. I'm as good as gone when we get back," I replied blankly, trying to hide the hurt.

When we arrived at the motel I let him head up the stairs to be alone. The roof needed to be tested out anyway. I liked to stargaze and watch the sunset, and now seemed like the perfect time to do just that. Since the building was only two stories there was an easily accessible ladder around back beside the dumpster. The air was tinged with dirty garbage. I hoped the roof had a fresh breeze.

I climbed the rusted ladder, wiping on my pants the yellowish-orange tinge it left on my hands. Gross. Where was my hand sanitizer when I needed it?

Taking in a deep breath and trying to exhale away all the problems in my life, I looked around the desolate rooftop. There was an air conditioning vent and some aluminum pipes, but that was about it. I scuffed the gravel with the toe of my shoe and walked over to where some plastic chairs had been placed.

Just when I thought I had Fenn all figured out, he confused me again. I hated feeling like this, not knowing what was going on inside his head. And worst of all, I didn't want him to be in the same strange boat that I was in.

The steamy sun was past mid-day when my thoughts began falling into place. I must have sat there for hours trying to rummage through the events of the past few days. I was determined to leave the rooftop with an answer.

If I was going to try for this, I would need to somehow make it to the ruins. Assuming I would find one of the keys there, I would still need to find the other two keys. With a map that was unreadable, my odds weren't looking too good. And time was moving quickly.

I stretched my legs out and looked up to the faint stars twinkling above me like a field of diamonds. I breathed and let everything go. Two stars shined brighter than most, the two stars that Fenn and I had claimed as our own one night on a break behind Paradise Diner. In those moments I felt the most alive and complete.

I sat straight up. Suddenly I knew what I wanted to do. I just needed to make sure Fenn was on board.

My legs ached from not moving for so long and seemed to cry out as I raced over to the ladder. My nerves were in knots, but I had to face him sometime. So we had a fight. Maybe I was just overreacting. People were allowed to be upset every now and then, and he was definitely due for it.

I unlocked the door but couldn't find Fenn anywhere. "Hello?" I called out. I waited for a response but nothing came. I turned back around and looked out the door. The car was gone. He must have taken it back. I hadn't even heard him leave when I was up on the roof.

I sighed and shut the front door, uncertain about what to do with myself. I thought I had given him enough time, but apparently he really wanted to be away from me. I stood there for a few moments as my stomach dropped to the floor in disappointment.

"Aurora," he said, startling me. I was lost in my thoughts and didn't hear him ease open the door. "Please don't be mad at me. I was an idiot today." Tears rushed to my eyes. In that split second, the thought he was gone hit home, stinging worse than any wasp could.

I smiled and leaned into the hand cupping my face. Fighting was so unnecessary, especially with him.

"I'm sorry too, for everything lately. I've come to a decision, Fenn." I wanted to tell him everything, excitement pulsing through my veins.

"And?" he paused, anxious to hear what I was about to say.

"And I'm going to give up. I want a normal life." It got so quiet you could hear the TV next door playing through the wall. *What if he didn't want that?* I started to doubt.

"You sure?" he half whispered, tilting his head forward and searching my eyes.

"One hundred percent," I answered.

He walked around me and went to the closet, reaching for something.

"Go sit on the stairs and close your eyes," he instructed.

"Why?" I countered.

"Rory Jay, just do it, okay?"

I gave up and stepped back out into the cool night air. I took a deep breath and sat on the edge of the top step, looking again to the stars.

A moment later, he said, "Okay, open them." I spun around and looked up to his looming figure. "I, umm, I wrote you a song."

"Fenn," I started, cut off by the strum of his fingers on the guitar. I loved when he played. Many a night he would play for me after a nightmare, or if I had a really bad day, but lately we had been so busy... It had been forever since he played for me.

He closed his eyes and let his fingers work their magic as a silken breeze wove around us. Beautiful notes played softly in my ears while his velvet voice hummed along. I knew this song. I had heard it before. I leaned in, trying to remember where I knew it from, when suddenly it dawned on me. It was the same song I heard playing whenever an intimate moment occurred between us. Eve had said our souls were bound by The Fates...

He opened his eyes. They burned with an intensity that touched my soul as his voice continued humming, pulling me to a place I had never been before.

I was so completely enthralled by him and by the delicate notes he strummed. I closed my eyes and for a moment was lost in our future. Hand in hand, having children and turning grey together, laughter lines etched around our mouths. My heart slowed as it recognized the truth.

I was wholeheartedly in love with him.

The music stopped and he laid his guitar down and took a seat next to me, nudging my side with his elbow. I was still mesmerized, gazing at him dreamily. A smile lit up his face and then he said, "Look Rory, a shooting star!"

I followed his gaze and caught sight of the tail of the star falling. "Make a wish," he whispered into my hair. I squeezed my eyes as tight as they would go, wishing that Fenn and I would get through this together in one piece.

Suddenly, I felt heavy. The dream began to fade as blood red eyes replaced the laughter lines and silver hair. The pressure to fulfill my destiny and the responsibility to figure everything out before I ran out of time was too much to handle. It will always be there no matter how much I want to be normal. I can't escape it.

I stood to excuse myself, caught up in the moment and needing some space. But Fenn grabbed my arm.

"Rory, look, I'm in love with you," he confessed, his eyes full of passion.

No, don't do this to me, not right now. This isn't how I imagined easing into things.

"I just don't know what to feel. That kiss, it was, it just, it happened, and now I don't know how to come back from that, how to move on pretending that I didn't kiss your beautiful, perfect mouth."

He grabbed my face and stared at my lips, making my knees feel like jelly.

"Fenn, I can't." I pulled my face from his hands and went back inside. He followed me in. I stopped and faced him. "I don't want to ruin what we have. What if a relationship doesn't work between us? I mean, you haven't even told me what happened back at the library."

Tears fell as I put my head in my hands. Why was this so confusing? It should have been easy. I love him, he loves me… But I had never worn my heart on my sleeve so it wasn't that easy.

Fenn took two steps and stood in front of me, holding onto my arms. "Tell me you don't feel anything. Tell me you didn't enjoy that kiss and that you don't want more," he begged through pained words. "Tell me that you haven't felt this way for a long time. Put all the other crap aside…you've decided to give it all up, Rory, for what?" He let the question hang. "That tells me something, Rory. Whatever it was that brought you to that decision, hang on to it. For once, be honest and fair to yourself. I know you've heard the lullaby before tonight. It drives me insane every time it plays in my head. I can't seem to shake it." He was frantic, making it harder for me to reject my feelings. I didn't want to let him down or even let my own heart down, but how could I go along with this? One of us had to salvage our friendship.

"All I want is to love you, Rory. I want so much more than our friendship." He looked up to the ceiling with the most angelic smile I'd ever seen on him and then continued with laughter tingeing his voice. "I can finally say this after all this time of denying."

His eyes were desperate as he waited for a response. I couldn't lie, but I hoped that I could hide the shock from him. I had heard the lullaby, and I had felt this way…for a really long time. I may not have paid attention, but my heart had always pounded for only him.

"Fenn, I…" I hesitated, contemplating my answer to make sure I was being fair to myself. I should just go for it, I should. But a knock came at the door. Once again, a stupid sign.

Fenn looked over and headed to answer it. A second knock sounded, reminding me to exhale. At least I had another moment to think.

"Who is it?" Fenn asked, his voice going an octave lower. I had to admit that I found it sexy when he got territorial. He looked out the peephole and waited for the person to respond. I fidgeted, straightening out my shirt and checking my breath.

"I've got a message for you," came the voice from the other side of the door. It was close to midnight. Was it someone from the other realm?

I was going to mention that before he opened the door, but he beat me to it as parking lot lights flooded our dimly lit room.

"One sec," he said as he cracked the door. Whoever was on the other side must have handed him a letter because a moment later he was standing in front of me, a note in his hand.

"What is it?"

Fenn stood there for a second examining the delivery.

"Well, it's a letter to…" He flipped over the envelope and read, "Fenn?"

"It's for you?" I asked as my earlier dread resurfaced.

He ripped open the seal and unfolded the crinkled paper. His eyes danced wildly over the words as he read silently to himself. No emotion showed on his face. It seemed like a millennium of waiting. I bit my fingernails in nervous anticipation.

"Well?" I asked impatiently.

He paused and looked up at me with a strange look in his eyes. Where had my Fenn gone?

"It's from my mom," he answered in disbelief. He rushed over to his suitcase and started throwing anything and everything he could into it. It startled me so I followed him, trying to stop him with my hands on his chest.

"Fenn, stop, listen to me. What's going on?" I asked. "Where are you going?" I paused, waiting for his answer that didn't come. "What are you doing?" The questions kept rolling but he kept ignoring me. My worry had built to boiling point. I felt him slipping away. I could no longer maintain my cool.

"Stop it, Fenn!" I shouted, shoving the clothes out of his hands with force. My voice had changed slightly, my dragon side trying to take over from the swell of emotion.

He stopped, looking up at me through new eyes. "I remember," he said, his tone strangely detached. His face held such pain, it twisted a knife into my heart. The something that I had known was coming just made its sparkling appearance. I had known all along that one day he would eventually leave me, but why did it have to be today?

"What do you mean, you remember?" I shoved him away from his suitcase and got into his face. "Fenn, what's going on? What are you hiding from me? Why are you doing this? I thought I meant more to you," I kept on, pushing him back with my hands, letting all of my frustration surface. His eyes filled with anger, his pupils shrinking, and I felt my own rage flourish from the betrayal. "I knew you would do this to me," I shouted. "I knew you would leave me, everyone always does!"

Fenn looked up with a dark gaze, one I had never seen before. In a flash he had me pinned to the wall I had backed him into. "YOU DON'T KNOW ANYTHING!" His fist landed beside my head, leaving a hole as a trace of the moment.

Both of our chests panted heavily as we realized that the level of anger had gone too far. "You're scaring me," was the only thing I managed to say as my face fell, the adrenaline subsiding. Fear and pain pushed tears to my eyes. His whole demeanor had changed, like there was a stranger standing in front of me. He closed his eyes for a brief moment, drawing his forehead down to rest on mine.

I felt him soften. "I remember everything from before, Rory. And now you're in danger because of it. I should never have put on that ring. It's mine, and it was my way to return home, but I shouldn't have put it on until after we found all the keys. I've screwed it all up, Rory," he said, breaking off on the verge of tears, "and now I have to leave because if I stay, they will find you. My memories are traceable and weaken the spell that is protecting you. Being around me is…not safe anymore," he broke off, barely able to finish. "I'm so sorry, Rory." His voice was strained, his teeth clenched tight.

"Who are *they*, Fenn?" I asked, my voice guarded.

"Zordon…he will find you. I have to go, like right now. The letter enforced what unlocked inside me this afternoon. Remember the prophecy? Well, I'm the third of three, deemed protector to the progeny," he finished, repeating that line of the prophecy. "I don't know how I am third of something, but I do know that you're the progeny and I am your protector, and right now leaving is the best way I can protect you." He resumed packing. I was as still as a statue, trying to absorb everything at lightning speed.

He stopped and walked back over to me, grabbing hold of my arms. "Are you listening?"

I nodded.

"I need you to keep going. Giving up would have been a mistake. Everything makes sense now, and it will for you soon. We will be together again, I promise. You just have to stay safe and get to the altar. Here," he said, taking the ring off and handing it to me. "It will unlock the altar which holds a key. Bob was right about that. Find the keys, and you will find your way back to me. They're waiting for me. I have to go now okay? I love you, Rory," he finished hoarsely, firmly kissing my forehead, holding my neck with both hands, and then pushing away from me.

They?

I slid the ring back on and watched in disbelief as he impatiently finished his packing and zipped up his bag. Then he headed towards the door.

"Stay with me," I heard myself saying, or did I say it? I must have been in shock because I couldn't think or see anymore. Tears clouded my vision. I heard Fenn pause at the door, and then, just like that, he was gone. My heart shattered.

Just when I thought I had made my decision and found my life, it was cruelly stolen from me. This couldn't be happening. Not to me, not to us. In between all of the craziness of the past few days, I'd somehow managed to believe that we were going to make it through all of this…together. But it was too late now, too late for me to prepare myself and too late for me to change the situation.

Chapter 18

～

Wake Up Already!

TIME HAD NO SIGNIFICANCE. I sat in our room that night, barely moving from my place on the floor where I had collapsed in a fit of tears after he left. I found myself thinking Emo thoughts, like if my heart stopped, then maybe this ripping pain would go away.

It was the worst and most un-like me moment of my life. Being a zombie was not something I enjoyed, but it was all I could muster.

The next morning I numbly stood in the shower for hours, lost in despair. The sting of ice-cold water shocked me into turning it off. Where had the comforting, numbing burn of hot water gone? I grimaced. I must have emptied the hot water heater.

I was shivering as I tried to uncurl myself from the bunched up position I sat in. It took me a good minute since a few of my muscles had fallen asleep.

I wrapped a towel around me and then another around my hair, finally looking at myself for the first time. My eyes looked permanently red and swollen. I reached up and gently ran my fingers around them. My skin felt raw. "I'm a mess," I said out loud.

Being like this was not going to cut it. I needed to pull myself together. Worse things had happened to me, right? That thought almost had me sliding further into the pit of despair I was trying to pull myself out of.

I left the bathroom and found tissues scattered aimlessly around the room, making me feel totally pathetic. Nothing had ever affected me this much, but then again, I'd never been left completely alone before. If I could take my parents leaving me, then why couldn't I handle this? I huffed to myself as the answer hit me. I knew and loved Fenn, as opposed to my parents who I didn't even remember.

Anger began to rise up from the depths of my belly. How could he do this to me? I had picked him, had decided to give up on my destiny so we could have a life together. And all for what? For this? For him to selfishly leave me? What if he's in trouble? And he expects me to do all of this alone?

Boy, did I make a wrong choice. It was then that I noticed the stars on the ceiling, the constellation he had carefully mapped out for me after we had first moved in. Stupid shooting star. I cursed myself for jinxing us last night.

In a hazy blur I tore each and every star from that ceiling, vehemently throwing them into a garbage bag. Cursing each one. Cursing Fenn. But most of all, cursing myself for listening to what my heart wanted.

It felt good to wipe him away, to try and burn the evidence of the hole he'd left in me. It felt like I was getting back at him.

"Screw you, Fenn," I screamed, tears welling up again. What was I thinking, falling for him? I knew it would never have worked. If my parents deserted me so easily, why would I expect Fenn to stick around? I mean, come on, do I have some sort of "Abandon me" expiration date stamped across my forehead? He didn't have to leave. We could have made it through the danger together. I know we could have.

I put the engorged garbage bag full of my heartbreak by the

door, thinking that I would take it to the dumpster later. I dusted off my hands. The room was barren. No more stars on the ceiling, no more posters on the wall, no more of Fenn's clothes that he'd forgotten to grab lying on the floor. It was as if he was never here.

And suddenly I felt like the most selfish person in the world. Erasing him didn't erase the hurt I felt, and it didn't justify giving up on him. He told me to find him. It's not about my destiny anymore, or finding the keys. It's about finding Fenn. He had to go back to our past...without me...and I needed to get to that place so I could tell him that I loved him. So I could make things right.

I looked around with a sudden burst of hope. I had to find those keys if I was going to find Fenn. Nothing was going to stop me.

First, I needed to find Mr. Creepy.

I locked up and headed down the stairs towards the infamous bus stop. I needed to eat, and I needed to bump into Mr. Creepy. That always seemed to happen when I was out.

As I walked past the rooms on the bottom level of the motel, I popped a piece of chewing gum in my mouth to curb my hunger. One of the dingy moth-eaten curtains moved, and a set of pale, bloodshot eyes met mine, instantly freezing me on spot. Oh...my...god. Those are Mr. Creepy's eyes. My blood began to boil at the sight of him, energy instantly rushing towards the palms of my hands.

I walked right up to his window and pointed against the glass where his nose was, squinting at him. His face went even paler than it already was.

"You've lived under me this whole time and haven't bothered to tell me or to help?" I scolded, ready to blow his head off in frustration.

He shut the curtains as quickly as he had opened them. I could hear things crashing over, and I imagined him stumbling about, knowing he had been caught. I couldn't believe this crap.

I waited, giving him a moment to open the door, but there was only silence. *Oh, I don't think so.*

"Excuse me," I said loudly through the glass, "I know you're in there and you better come out or else I'll," I broke off, looking down at my hands and smiling in reassurance, "or else I'll blow your door in." I mentally debated if I really wanted to go through with that threat or not.

Thankfully though, I heard movement and then a click of a lock, and then another, and another, and, ugh, another. *Geez, how many locks did one person need?*

The door cracked open. "I've already told you. You're on your own." He spoke quietly, keeping half of his face covered up by the door.

"That's rubbish, and you know it." I grabbed the door handle, ready to push it in should he try to close it on me. "I need your help...how many times do I have to ask? Haven't I proven myself to you?"

He waited a moment and then slid through the small crack of the door, shutting it quickly behind him.

"All right, since you are so desperately needy and persistently annoying, I'll tell you where to find the first key. But that's it," he said. "Nothing more after that."

"Okay," I agreed, crossing my fingers that this would pay off.

"Go home," he said flatly.

"What!?" I asked in amazed irritation. "Are kidding me? You just said you would hel-"

He put his hand up to shush me. Then he closed his eyes and pinched the bridge of his nose. "I did say I would help. I am helping. Go home," he repeated, his voice indignant.

"You know what..." I said, putting my hands up in retreat, "I give up. You are a big waste of time, thanks for the help," I criticized. "I'll 'go home' now." I turned to head back up to my room.

"You must have a hearing problem, girl."

I stopped and unwillingly turned toward him.

"Must I spell it out for you? I said to go home. Where is home? Home is where you were raised," he stressed.

"Mily's?" I questioned.

"Yes, girl," he replied with a sigh, rolling his eyes.

I threw my arms around him, ignoring the strong scent of cleaners as I hugged him tightly and said, "I knew you had it in you. Thank you, thank you!" I called, racing towards the bus stop.

Chapter 19

~

Revisiting the Past

THE BUS ROLLED UP ABOUT ten minutes later, following a dreaded conversation with my now ex-boss. Susan called wanting to know when I would be returning to work, and honestly, I didn't know what to tell her with everything that was going on. Even with the vague answer I gave, she said she understood and told me to take all the time I needed, promising that I would have a job should I decide to return.

As I hung up the phone, I boarded the bus and was greeted by a new driver with a pleasant smile. "Aloha," she said.

"Aloha," I replied as I moved to take my seat near the front of the bus. I cranked up the volume on my I-Pod and easily got lost in my thoughts. I found it somewhat amusing that I'd spent my entire childhood questioning who I was when apparently there was a key to my past right under my nose.

It had been days since I had last spoken with Mily. Of course we talked after the bus accident but not much since then. She always loved when I showed up for a surprise visit.

As the bus drove off, I stood for a moment in the sea-shelled driveway, listening to the sounds of my childhood. The triplets were out back, playing a game of make believe, their soft cries of joy inviting and taunting my inner child. Un-admittedly, it felt warming to come back here.

I walked up to the strangely distant but familiar door and put my sunglasses and I-Pod away. For some reason my hands were trembling, and I was dreading going inside. To return home without Fenn was almost embarrassing. What was I going to say when she asked me where he was? Hopefully I wouldn't have to say anything. I just needed to focus on finding this key. It was the only thing that would bring me closer to finding him.

I leaned over to turn the waterspout off. It was a habit of Mily's to forget that she had turned it on. She kept it running sometimes to water the lawn and annual flowers that ran alongside the house. Purples and pinks that I once believed could bring out the fairies in the world. The plastic sprinkler had been on for a while. The puddle of muddied water was becoming obvious as the freshly mowed grass went for a swim.

It was probably stupid of me, but I rang the doorbell while wiping my dirt-soaked shoes on the "Come in Silly" mat. I noticed the blue-stained planks of porch wood needed to be replaced.

Mily pulled the curtain aside on the door window, and a smile appeared instantly, promising a glass of sweet tea or a piece of homemade pie. I could hear her mouthing my name as she opened the door and pulled me in for the tightest hug I had ever received from her. My breath staggered and caught. When she stepped back to look at me, my face fell as her eyes scanned to my left and then my right. My heart dropped to my feet. She was looking for Fenn.

With a weak tremble to my voice, I answered her unspoken suspicion. "He's not with me." I kept my eyes on the spiky floor mat as she sighed.

"Well, come on inside, dear," she beckoned encouragingly. I

appreciated that she did not probe into why Fenn was not with me. I was also glad that she did not bombard me with questions about why I didn't answer her more recent calls.

Once inside, her famous baked macaroni cooking in the oven welcomed my nose and stomach, and the scattered toys along the way to the living room made me surprisingly homesick.

"It's so good to see you," she said softly, reaching out to pat my knee. She was sitting in her favorite chair. The same chair that had rocked me to sleep many a night. The heat was building in my throat and behind my misting eyes. I swallowed hard.

"It's good to see you too." It was impossible to hide the sadness I felt about losing my best friend.

"How's work?" I could hear the nervousness in her voice. Small talk was never really her thing, but I was grateful for her efforts. She never could keep her curiosities at bay, and this time I couldn't blame her.

"I actually quit today. I didn't tell you before, but I received a letter from my family and have been caught up in trying to figure all of that out," I admitted sheepishly. "That's actually why I stopped by today. I think I left something behind that I need," I started, not quite sure how to explain what I needed since I had no idea of what it looked like.

"Oh…well, do you know what it is? I can help you look, but I think you got everything when you moved out."

"Oh no, it will only take me a minute…I don't want to bother you, umm, but I am thirsty," I said, adding in a cough for good measure.

"Would you like something to drink?"

I silently cheered myself on as the diversion worked.

"Sure, do you have any sweet tea?" I asked, hoping that she didn't so she'd have to make it, giving me time to search.

"I don't, but I'll make you some," she offered. I smiled as she stood and headed towards the kitchen.

I jumped up and walked down the hall, pausing just outside his old door. It was cracked open. I could see his bed sitting in the far corner, freshly made. Mily always made sure to have a bed ready in case of emergencies.

Why was I being so dramatic? It's not like he died. But something inside of me had when he betrayed my trust by walking out on me. The pang of remembrance hit hard, but I took in a deep breath, trying my best to push it away, ironing my heart as stiff as a freshly pressed uniform.

I pushed the door open and waited for the creaking to stop as rays of sunshine bathed the cherry wood floors. It seemed bare and desolate without his posters and scattered books. But it also seemed the same. Like time was frozen in place. Could the key be in here?

I rushed over to the desk and went through all the empty drawers. Then I knelt down to look under the bed. Nothing. *How would I even know if I found something?* I thought glumly. *Would it look like a key or something else?*

I crept back out and ran up the stairs to my room, pausing for a brief moment to remember what it felt like growing up here. My walls were still an aqua blue, my bed still covered in zebra print. Everything used to be so simple.

I quickly rummaged through my dresser and then behind it, dropping to the floor and glancing under my bed as well. I came up with the same results. A big fat nothing.

I headed for the backyard. There was nothing I could think of that could even possibly be a magical key. I started thinking it was just a bunch of crap.

I walked through the kitchen and told Mily that I was going out to get some fresh air. She nodded in her motherly way and then stopped me as I reached the door. "The triplets went next door with Amy, just so you know. I don't want you to worry when you don't see them." I smiled at her and then shut the door behind me. Plopping down on the steps, I pulled my pant legs up, crossing my arms on my knees. Where would a good hiding spot be for a key?

A soft humming vibration rattled in my ears. I rubbed them with the palm of my hands, trying to soothe the ringing, but it didn't help. I'd forgotten about that ringing. It always happened when Fenn and I played out here. Fenn always said he never heard it. Just like he didn't hear Lady Eve that night.

I sat straight up. Wait a minute…could the ringing have something to do with the key?

I jumped up as I tried to remember the first time I'd actually heard the ringing. I stood still for a moment, looking around, listening closely, trying to let the vibration coax awake my memories.

It was so long ago, it could have been anything. I stepped onto the grass and walked towards the fence, noting that the humming grew fainter the farther out I went.

I paused and squinted my eyes, the answer right there on the tip of my tongue.

"It's out here," I said to myself. I stepped backwards, smiling as the ringing picked up. My steps continued until it was as loud as I could take, which had me standing back on the porch. *So it's here,* I thought as I kneeled down to begin my search.

There wasn't much on the porch besides a rocking chair and a potted plant. The Koi fish pond sat next to the porch. When we were kids, Fenn and I had decorated the pond with rocks that we had found at the beach…Wait a minute.

I crawled over to the pond and leaned in, searching slowly with my eyes. Then I saw it. It had to be the key. A quarter-mooned chunk of stone that was no bigger than my hand with an infinity symbol carved into it. That's why the symbols on the Oraculus looked so familiar. Three keys, three symbols. My heart jolted.

I glanced around me, making sure no one was watching, and then reached in, careful not to harm the fish. The stone flashed on the bottom of the shallow pond, sunlight highlighting the symbol. When my fingertips touched the stone, the water began to bubble. The symbol lit up in a white flash of light, illuminating the inside of the pond. The light shot towards the sky, reaching as far as the eye could see.

I quickly pulled my hand out as the stone rattled inside my palm. It took everything to keep from dropping it. I tried tucking it inside my shirt to hide its brightness, but the material of my shirt wasn't thick enough.

"Dang it," I said aloud. How was I going to hide this?

"Anela?" I heard Mily's voice call through the kitchen window. "What was that light…is everything okay?" Anela. It meant angel, something she called me since I was little. If she only knew.

"I'm fine…I, uh…I don't know what that light was. Weird, right?" I called back as I fumbled with the stone. "Please stop, please stop," I whispered to it, hoping that the light would go away. It didn't.

"Did you find whatever it is you needed?" she asked, her voice trailing towards the doorway. I took a deep breath and focused on the energy that I knew was inside me. If there ever was a time to try and get a grip on the powers I harnessed, now would be it.

I felt the palms of my hands heat up and let the energy seep from my hands into the stone, connecting with it and merging. And just like that, the vibration stopped.

I opened one eye, praying that the light would be gone and let out a huge sigh of relief when I realized it was. Actually, there was no stone either. What the…

"The tea is ready," said Mily from behind me.

I jumped, the energy disappearing as I turned to face her. "Great," I replied with an innocent smile. I followed her with a backward glance to make sure I hadn't dropped the stone.

Nope, it had simply disappeared. That was just wonderful. I had the key in my hand and somehow I lost it.

Mily and I talked for a few hours about nothing in particular before we finally hugged and said our goodbyes. Of course she made me promise that I would make visiting her a regular thing. I really did want to. I just needed to figure out all of the other things happening to me before I could fully commit.

On my way home, I hit up the grocery store to grab a few things to get me through the full moon and then walked from the bus stop back to the motel. I set the bags down outside Mr. Creepy's window, waiting for him to open the curtain. He had to have known I was there. He seemed to have radar for my activity. I didn't even bother with trying to look unsuspicious. It was time for the stalker to become the stalked.

He peeked through the window and glanced at me, then shut the curtains. Right on cue. I reached for my necklace safely hidden beneath my shirt. I wondered if he missed it. The locks clicked one by one until finally a portion of the door opened.

"I assume you found it," he said plainly.

"Well, then you assumed right," I replied, my tone acerbic.

What I thought was a smile appeared at the corner of his mouth, but it might have been a twitch.

"Congratulations. Now if you'll excuse me."

I put my hand on the doorknob to prevent him from shutting me out. "Wait," I said, my eyes to the floor. "I have a slight problem. The key is gone." I looked back up at him as my words spilled out in explanation. "One second it was in my hand and the next it disappeared. Was that supposed to happen?"

"The answer lies within your Oraculus," he answered, yanking the door from my grip and slamming it in my face.

"How rude!" I shouted as I stood back and picked my bags back up. At least I got something out of him.

Back home, I opened my curtain to let the setting orange sun illuminate my room. Blood red shadows cast an eerie glow to the walls, and I shivered, running my hands up and down my arms. I hated being alone, so quiet and empty.

Zordon's eerie face popped into my head. His hollow black eyes called to the being within me. He looked powerful, scary and determined, but determined for what? I wondered what had happened to Gwenevere.

The sky had turned a charcoal gray as the sun tucked itself away, revealing the mystic stars and almost full moon. I sighed as I locked the door and shut the curtains. Then I smiled inquisitively.

I plopped onto the bed and pulled the covers over my legs for encouraging comfort. Reaching inside my nightstand, I found the Oraculus. I ran my fingers over the inscribed symbols on the leather cover. The symbols of The Fates.

The infinity symbol suddenly lit up, burning like fire. I untied the tether and flipped open the cover, running my fingertips along the inside of it.

The other two symbols remained unlit. Did this show that I still have the key?

I shut the book, tied the tether back, and tucked it neatly back into my dresser. *One down and two to go*, I thought, hoping that tomorrow I would be able to pry another clue out of Mr. Creepy. Who needed a treasure map when I had him? The map was still in my bag where it would remain until I figured out how to use it.

For now I would rest and pray that the moon wouldn't complete its cycle before I had a chance to return home.

Chapter 20

~

You've Got to be Kidding Me

MY EYES SNAPPED OPEN AS I sat straight up in my lonesome room. I glanced over at the clock. 10 a.m. The clock ticked annoyingly, rubbing in the fact that time was running out for me.

I turned the TV on and watched a commercial for a local beach. *Very appealing*, I thought as I continued flipping the channels until I reached the news.

The meteorologist was giving the seven-day forecast. "Clear skies for the weekend," he said in his cheesy voice, "and for all you astrology lovers out there, stay tuned for an update on this Saturday's super full perigee moon."

My mouth dropped. Today was Thursday. That meant I had only two days to find the other two keys.

I went over to the table and opened my laptop. Google popped up. I typed in "perigee moon" and waited, tapping my fingers against the table.

Most of the sites were speculation about a super full moon that had occurred—wait a minute, had occurred eight years ago in December. The same month and year that I had appeared on Mily's doorstep.

"...The moon will be almost fifteen percent bigger than a normal full moon, something that hasn't happened in eight years and shouldn't be happening for another ten at least," called the weatherman on the TV.

This can't be coincidence, I thought. "And I know just who to ask," I said to no one as I jumped up from the chair and headed to the bathroom for a quick shower.

While in the shower, I had formed a back-up plan. If Mr. Creepy couldn't pull through in giving me answers, then I would brave up and go see Eve. She may be able to help since she had known so much.

My flip-flops slapped the underside of my feet, echoing off the walls as I rushed down the stairs two at a time. As I stepped up to his door, a little note fell through the mail slot and landed at my feet. Okay?

I bent over to grab it and flipped it open, peering around the corner to see if his nose was sticking out of the curtain watching me. Nope. I glanced around, checking to see if someone other than him was watching and was delighted to find no one. I read the paper:

You're not supposed to know I'm watching you. Therefore I cannot help you. Do us both a favor and pretend I'm not here. And no, I cannot help you find your keys. They are your mission.

I quickly grabbed a pen from my purse and scribbled back:

Why are you "watching" me? You know it's against the law, right? I could report you! You'd better help me or else!

I slid the note back through the slot and waited. The seconds that ticked by felt like eons, but soon enough, the letter reappeared. I caught it this time, anticipating its fall.

I don't follow the law in this realm. Enjoy the amulet.

Zordon's face made another appearance in my mind, and his voice pierced my memory like a sharpened blade. *"I don't follow the law."* Exactly how was Mr. Creepy tied into all this?

I quickly jotted:

What's your name? Do you know a man named Zordon?

I waited, hoping for an answer, but nothing came. My hand rose up in a fist, tempted to knock on the door and demand an answer, but something stopped me. Was I really ready to know exactly who he was?

What if it was like Fenn had said? What if he was on Zordon's side? I had no way of knowing. Dread filled my stomach as my mind swarmed with conspiracies. What if he was setting me up to fail? Then I would never find Fenn. I kicked at the gravel and turned back one last time hoping to catch him peeking out into the world. The curtains remained unmoved.

I was more than a little perturbed by my neighbor. Because he never answered, it left me feeling like maybe he was tied in with Zordon. Why else would he have ignored my question? Guilty conscience? I shook my head at my internal fight.

Plan B was now my only available option. I headed to the bus stop and boarded a few minutes later when it peacefully pulled up. Maybe Eve would be willing to tell me more about Zordon and even Mr. Creepy. She'd told me to come back and I needed her assistance now more than ever.

My stomach began to stir as I got closer to her place. What if she proved to be as difficult as Mr. Creepy? But my stomach dropped as the bus pulled up to where her house was. The signs were gone and the lights were off. A real estate sign sat staked in the front yard. Why would she have packed up and left so suddenly? She told me to come back anytime.

I got off the bus and walked up to the front door, hoping to find some evidence. It didn't make sense. Everyone in my life was disappearing.

Peeking in through the window brought even more confusion.

The previously painted walls were a bare white, and where a curtain once hung as a door, a real wooden door now sat. All of the furniture was gone. It was as if Lady Eve had never even existed.

I looked at the sign and pulled out my phone. Maybe the real estate agent would have an answer on where I could find her. I should have gotten her phone number before.

It rang twice before a lady picked up. "Hello?" she asked hastily.

"Umm, yes, hi. My name is Aurora. I was calling in regards to the property located on Intuition Avenue." I paused to wait for her answer.

"Ah, yes, are you looking to buy?"

I contemplated lying but went with honesty instead. "No, ma'am. I was just wondering if you knew where the owner moved her business. Her name was Eve."

"I'm not sure you have the right place in mind. This is my personal property. It's been on the market for years now." She sounded annoyed.

I felt my stomach drop even lower. Nausea kicked in. I stepped back onto the gravel and took another look at my surroundings. This was the place we had been to before, I knew it.

"Okay, thank you for your time," I finished and hung up. "What is going on?" I asked out loud.

I walked around to the back of the house, hoping to find something that would give me some kind of assurance about my sanity. The place was fenced in and luckily unlocked. I tried to look inconspicuous as I walked around the backyard. I found nothing. No trace of what transpired the other night. I peeked through every window hoping for something. Still nothing.

The wind picked up again, caressing and almost pulling me around to the back of the yard again. I instantly noticed footprints caked into the sand. These weren't just any footprints—they were a woman's footprints. They trailed all the way to the back, stopping in front of the fence.

"What the hell?" A small shred of cloth that looked as if it had been ripped from an outfit was snagged on the chain link fence. I leaned in closer and pulled it off. It was the same material that Lady Eve wore when we had visited her. I looked over the fence. There weren't any footprints on the other side or leading away from this spot in the backyard. She had walked all the way back here and stopped, but where did she go?

I contemplated calling the police, but what would I say. "Umm, hello, this lady that I only know by first name who broke into someone's house and claimed it as her own den of psychic wisdom may be missing." Yeah, that would fly real well. In the back of my mind, fear struck. What if something had happened to her? She had been scared of Zordon, and she was definitely scared when she pushed us out the door, ending our time together. My emotions were overwhelming.

Suddenly, the blinding sun felt suffocating, and I couldn't breathe. My chest heaved up and down in an unbalanced cadence that I couldn't steady. I laid my hand over my heart, trying to will it to calm down, but it continued to race wildly as if it were going to beat out of my chest. In the pit of my stomach I felt a strange being stir. Such heavy emotions seemed to be a trigger for my dragon side.

Think calming thoughts, I told myself. *Breathe, breathe, breathe…* But I felt something creeping up my arm like tiny crabs. I looked down to brush them off and instantly panicked.

Red mirrored scales began to run up my arm, scales like you would find on a…a dragon. I tilted my head away from them as they rushed towards my shoulder in a wave. *This was not happening*, I thought as I went to scream, but my scream was interrupted.

"Hello, Aurora," said the quirky voice of a girl.

For a moment I stopped breathing. Everything stopped actually. And then like the crazy wave in which they had rolled up my arm, the scales rolled back down, disappearing, as if they had never been there at all.

"What the hell is going on?" I questioned as I tried to shield the rays of sun that surrounded her.

"Good timing on my part," she answered with a laugh. "Looks like the dragon's out of the bag," she finished with a knee slap.

"I'm glad you find this funny," I retorted. "Scales, shiny red reptilian scales, just took over my skin. Wait," I said, peering at her. "Why am I telling you this?"

"Aurora, this may sound odd, but you and I are about to become very well acquainted. I'm from the other realm, and like you've been warned, time is of the essence."

My heart found its rhythm and a sense of calm set in. The girl was about my height with short, chunky brown hair and was wearing leather pants and a weird looking long sleeve shirt. It was well over 98 degrees out.

Was she a customer I'd waited on? Wait, she said realm. I should have been weirded out, but her voice sounded so sweet and intoxicating. It was as soft as rose petals and I felt pulled to her, like everything she was saying could only be the truth. I shook my head, trying to shake the connection I felt to her. It was as if she was inside my head, coaxing me to believe her.

"I can see that I didn't approach this right," she said unsteadily. "I'm not very good at this sort of thing…umm…" She looked back and forth and then back to me again. "Why don't we go somewhere private so I can explain everything a little better?" She grabbed my hand, starting to pull me away from the house.

I yanked my hand from hers and stepped back, faltering on the sidewalk and falling straight onto my butt. She leaned over to offer me a hand, but I gave her my best scowl and stood up on my own.

"No, thank you," I said evenly. "Now if you don't mind, I will be on my way." I turned to walk away, but she was right on my heels. "Alone."

She opened her mouth as if to say something, but I cut her off by saying, "No, no, that won't be necessary. Keep your comments to yourself." Her mouth went shut. I gave a fake smile and turned, walking as quickly as I could back to the bus stop. I wasn't going off with some random girl who could have been peeking over my shoulder. I didn't care if she seemed nice and helpful and could possibly have the answers I was looking for.

I am doomed for all eternity, I thought as I looked to the skies. Why? I reached the bench and laid my stuff down, anxious to get back to the safety of my motel room, when I felt someone breathing on my neck.

"What?" I said as I turned around and collided noses with the pixie girl. She was so close I could see each and every tiny freckle on her face.

"I'm sorry. I guess I forgot to mention that you don't have a choice in this," she said, and the last thing I saw was a glowing green light exuding from both her hands.

"Insomnus," she chanted as I felt myself slip into a slumber.

Chapter 21

~

Who Are You and How Did You Find Me?

I CAME TO BEHIND THE wheel of a car, driving I might add. "What the hell," I said as I slammed on the brakes, nearly causing the car behind me to run into us. My hands were shaking as I tried to register how I was driving with no memory of getting in the car.

A glowing green light brought my attention to the passenger seat where that crazy pixie girl sat. She was magic. Her green energy shot towards the car behind us.

"Why the hell am I driving a car?" I asked on the edge of hysteria. "I'm pulling over. I want out of here." I jerked the car off the road and came to a hasty halt, then closed my eyes, breathing deeply and exhaling slowly.

"This is my life, this is normal for me. I have nothing to worry about," I chanted to myself.

"Aurora, don't be difficult. I'm here to help you. You brought me here after all," she said with a laugh. "Sure, I'm a little late." She broke off, glancing out the side of the window at the traffic whizzing by. Then she turned back to me. "I can't very well just walk away and leave you here alone. You need me, now more than ever." Cars were honking as they zoomed by us.

"I brought you here? Why would I do that? How could I do that? That doesn't even make sense," I rambled. "I don't even know you." I turned to her, perturbed by the fact that she was picking at her nails, undisturbed.

She looked up a moment later and pointed to my necklace with a silly smile, a smile I wanted to smack off her face. "You weren't supposed to have that just yet," she replied easily. "Actually, the only reasons you would have that necklace are if you were dead or crossing back over." She laid her two fingers on the artery in my neck. "And you're not dead."

I frowned.

"Wait, what? This necklace brought you here?" I shook my head dizzily and braced my fingers to my temples. They suddenly began to throb as panic rose up and seized my train of thought. Something was breaking open inside me. Doors were flying open in the hall of memories. I could feel an anxiety attack on the brink.

"Aurora, just breathe. You're working yourself up for nothing," she said lightly, rolling her eyes.

I puffed up, irritated by her indifference. "You talk as if you know me, but I've never seen you before. You don't think I have a reason to work myself up? My world is falling apart piece by piece." The sorrow in my voice was poorly disguised.

She sighed. "Look, I sympathize with you, really, I do, but we don't have time for you to break down right now, and I don't know how to operate this thing." She glanced around the inside of the car, lip curled, then added, "especially not when danger is right around the corner and your shift is in progress."

"Shift?" I asked groggily.

"The scales running up your arm thing…" she said, registering my look of shock. "It will all be explained soon enough," she said as she grabbed my forearm. I felt a calming sensation wash over me. "Just get us to where you live and I will explain as best I can along the way. At this point I would only be giving you the answers you're looking for so what have you got to lose? You have questioned everything, I'm sure."

I paused a moment to let myself breathe as she suggested. *She definitely had a point*, I thought as I glanced at her goofy smile and feather light hair.

"Whose car is this?" I asked, leery to the fact that it could be stolen.

"Relax, Aurora, no one will miss it and it will be returned when we're done using it," she reassured.

I huffed. I was going to tell her that I would be perfectly fine walking back to my motel, alone, but instead it came out as, "Explain everything, or I will walk back to my motel, alone." I emphasized the last word. "You have until I get to my place to convince me."

She smiled, content with my proposition.

I eased the car back onto the road, keeping my hands at ten and two. It was the closest I could get to feeling like I had some control over my stability.

"That's plenty of time," she said confidently. "First off, my name is Alexis, but you can call me Lexi for short." I braked at the stoplight waiting for it to turn green. "So you already know about the magic—you've experienced it by now—and it's all real, including the power you harness over fire, although that comes from your other half.

"Our two realms are connected by a doorway, a cave on this island. The doorway cannot be opened without the keys of

The Fates, which I'm sure you know by now."

I nodded as I kept my eyes forward, absorbing what she was saying, what Eve had basically already explained.

"Wait, so there really are gods?" I questioned.

"Yes. Four to be exact."

"But I've heard there were five. What really happened?"

"Oh yeah, the fifth brother," she sighed heavily. "He created the barrier between our realms by crossing over."

"Because he was trying to protect the dragons?"

She smiled like a proud mother. "Yes. The other brothers were furious, blaming him for upsetting the balance after he created the race of dragons behind their backs. They ordered all dragons to be executed. The fifth brother couldn't handle the despair that weighed on his soul and pleaded to the other brothers. His life for the dragons, thus creating the infamous Stone of Immortality. Many in our realm have sought after this stone, yearning for the power of a Fate, but it is protected by the Draconta and nearly impossible to attain."

"So, Zordon won't stand a chance in taking the stone, right?" I asked, a spark of hope igniting within me.

"I am a Draconta," she said matter-of-factly. "I live with the dragons inside the Obsidian Chasm. We heavily guard the entrance to the volcano to protect it from evil. There's no way he could get past our defenses. At least, I don't think…"

Wow, I thought, staring ahead.

"So why am I in this realm?" I asked, glancing in the rearview mirror out of habit. Lady Eve only said that it was so I could choose. But why the need to choose? What would have prevented me from choosing?

"That's an easy one—because of your importance, it was necessary to keep you hidden and protected from those who would harm you for their own purposes." She leaned into me, whispering, "Rumor has it, two of The Fates are corrupt. They tried to end your life the night Astral sent you here. If it wasn't for him, you'd probably be dead right now."

The Fates wanting me dead would surely be a reason to remain in hiding.

"Why don't they just find me and end it already," I wondered out loud.

She looked taken aback. "Because Aurora, you are very special. The powers you harness, they're one-of-a-kind rare."

"How so?" I asked.

"You have the ability to shift, Aurora. You have the power of a dragon and the magic of a Mage in you. And that's not all. You harness the power over fire. No one in our realm has that power, not even the dragons."

I swallowed hard, for once, happy to be me.

"This obviously puts you in danger. And since the doorway between here and there was sealed with your departure, it was impossible to detect you here. I stress the was," she finished quickly, glancing out the window again.

"What do you mean was?" I asked warily.

"I mean, you were undetectable before you put that necklace on. Now, not so much. It links you to the other realm. It's a part of you," she answered. "The Fates…Zordon…anyone who is looking can easily trace it."

I went to take it off as if it were a poisonous snake. "Well, here…take it then," I said, but her hand stopped me.

"No! The damage has been done, and you need to keep that on. It protects you," she stressed. "I've just been sent as an added bonus since Fenn had to leave," she blurted out.

"Fenn? You know him? How is he? Is he okay?" I rushed

out, but she stopped me again.

"He's fine, Aurora, calm down. Sheesh. He had to return because his presence put you in danger…without training, he could no longer protect you from what will be coming."

"But he said it was because he put the ring on," I replied, confused.

"No, the ring simply unlocked his memories that were taken from him when he was sent through the portal with you. In a sense it would have put you in danger had you not put the amulet on first, but you did, so you beat him to it. *You* put yourself in danger, and in turn he had to go because he would have been useless against who has been sent after you," she explained.

"And exactly, *who* is after me?" I asked hesitantly.

"Not fully sure, but I've been told it's one of Zordon's men. I don't think we have to worry about The Fates. They don't step in unless they absolutely have to," she replied easily. "But don't fret, I am fully skilled," she added with a smile.

So I had been the reason Fenn left. All this time I had been blaming him…

"Look, before we go any further, there is something you should know." She grabbed onto my forearm again.

Maybe I felt comfortable because she seemed so familiar to me, even down to the gestures she made and the smile she wore on her face. And the way she braced me so comfortingly when trying to tell me something I may not like. It reminded me of somebody…

"What's that?" I asked, moving my arm quickly so she wasn't touching me.

"When you crossed over, your memories were erased and most of your powers were stripped. When you were reunited with this necklace, you were supposed to have gained everything back, like Fenn." She paused, then asked, "Did you?"

"No," I stated.

"I figured," she replied.

"Why is it so important that I remember everything? Can't you just tell me? Or can't you just do a spell to undo it?" There had to be a way.

"It's not as simple as that. Crossing through the barrier to this realm was a part of the spell that sealed the doors of your memory shut and bound your dragon form to the amulet. So crossing back over must be what brings everything back. We need three keys to do that."

"I've already found one."

"You did?" She jumped in excitement.

"Yeah…I found it yesterday. That's how you found me actually. I was hoping to find Eve, this psychic lady who knows about me. Do you know her?"

She nodded.

"Wait, how did you both get here if the door is supposed to be sealed?" I asked.

"From our realm, we don't need keys to cross the barrier," she explained. "We just need very powerful magic. The only downfall is, every time we cross, it weakens the barrier between our realms so it's highly discouraged," she leaned in, winking as if I would understand what that meant.

"Why do I need keys and you need powerful magic?" My curiosity was slowly turning into frustration.

She shifted in her seat as if moving would help me better understand what she was saying. "My realm is a magical realm whereas yours is not. You need those keys, with their magical energy, to cross the barrier to my realm," she said very slowly. She paused, waiting for a sign of recognition to appear on my face.

I grasped the necklace in the palm of my hands, blaming it for all of my recent problems. "I get it," I said simply, staring straight ahead. Nothing could ever come easy for me.

I glanced over at her as I turned into the parking lot of the motel. She was fidgeting with the button that rolled the window down, watching it rise and fall and rise and fall. "I crossed over the night Fenn left, that way the barrier would only be breeched once. Otherwise, he wouldn't have been able to do it without the keys. We Mages sure can multi-task," she giggled to herself. "By the way, this is so cool." She was still messing with the electronic window.

"Totally," I responded with heavy sarcasm.

She must've heard it in my tone. She stopped what she was doing and looked up. Her eyes filled with understanding. "You know," she said hesitantly, "you've never been alone on this side. My mother's a Seer and she's watched over you. Over both of you actually."

"Why?"

"There are higher powers interested in your well-being," she admitted reluctantly.

My hands began to tremble as a sense of dread crept in. I tried to clear my throat quietly. "So your mom must be pretty powerful then…to be able to watch over me from the other realm," I fished. I started to see why she looked so familiar now that I took the time to look at her. "What's her name?" I asked, trying to hide my suspicions.

"Eve."

My stomach dropped. I went completely still, trying to quickly decide if I should run or knock her out and then run. *I knew this was a set-up*, I thought with disappointment. I slowly reached to turn the car off, hands unsteady with fear. "Aurora, what's wrong? Why are you so pale?" she asked with concern, eyebrows furrowed and head tilted like a puppy dog. It was a trick, a psychological trick. Either she was a great actress or... she was sincere.

"Eve. What is this? Some kind of sick joke?" I asked, trying to sound angry though my voice faltered. She looked perplexed.

My internal struggle was driving me mad because deep down, I was willing to wait and find out. She was the closest thing to my past that I had at the moment. But the being inside of me let the feeling of betrayal take over my sensibility. I could only see the worst.

"I don't think anything is funny, do you?" she countered, tipping her brows in wait.

I stiffened my jaw as I spoke through tight lips. "Eve's your mother? Are you two some kind of scam artists? Have you been spying on me or using some kind of witchcraft to get into my head? Because I specifically went to see her today, and she just up and vanished. So how do I know if you two are the ones 'after' me or not?" My throat tightened with the possibility of tears.

With puzzlement, Lexi replied, "No, it is as I have said. She's been watching you since you were little by the Draconta's orders. The night I was told that Fenn was returning, I was instructed to help you find the keys so you can return home. I would never betray you. I'm only here for your best interest, Aurora."

She leaned into me, staring deep into my eyes. I felt another pull from her and then a sort of calmness easing its way into my mind.

"Stop it," I said. I knew she was doing something to me. I could feel the power. My own energy surged inside of me.

"Stop what?" she asked, never moving from my eyes as a faint green glow emerged from her hands. "Sedatum," she whispered softly. I thought about pulling my own gaze from her, but I couldn't. Panic rushed through my blood. *This is it, this is it. I'm done for.*

"Get out of my head!" I yelled. A surge of energy burst out of me. I felt my hair standing up like static electricity. When I re-opened my eyes, I saw a blue glow fading from my hands.

I looked back at her, almost scared to see the damage I may have caused, but saw only amazement written all over her face. Both her hands were bracing her temples as she steadied herself in her seat.

"You're extremely powerful, Aurora," she noted, mystified. "That was a really hard spell to counter, and you literally threw me from your mind. Without chanting, I might add. I'm really sorry if I invaded your space. I just want you to be comfortable with me, not afraid." She was smiling like I had done something right and not just knocked the shit out of her mentally. Her smile was contagious as I felt my own twist up.

"I'm sorry. This is just a lot to digest. I mean, I saw your mother and then she disappeared. I wasn't expecting her daughter to show up."

"About that, she had to leave. She's not supposed to interfere with your fate under His orders, but the Dragon King felt differently. And she agreed with him. So she came and stayed as long as she could, before He found out."

"Who's 'He'?"

"His name is Astral. The one I was telling you about who sent you over here. He's the one who wants you to have a choice. If I'm being honest," she leaned in to me, her voice dropping to a whisper, "I think he wants you to stay. He doesn't want you to get hurt. Sweet right?" Her voice picked back up as she practically bounced with giddiness.

"Astral?" I said, testing the name. It sounded so familiar, but I couldn't place a face with it. "So she's not hurt then? Zordon didn't get to her?"

"No, she's fine. I saw her before I ported here," she reassured.

I sighed. "What exactly is a port?"

"A portal is a way of transportation. It's like moving through time, and it's how we get around where we're from. It's actually..." her words trailed off as she stared in the other direction, worry taking over her pixie-like features.

"What are you staring... Oh," I said as I looked in the same direction, "that's just Mr. Creepy. He actually had this amulet...wait a dang minute. You know who he is, don't you?" I asked. She nodded and got out of the car. I responded quickly and shut the engine off, following closely behind. This couldn't be good. "Is he the one who's after me?"

I don't think she was even paying attention to me as she sniffed at the air and said, "He must have followed my mother's my portal." She noticed my confused face and quickly explained. "When you open a portal, even though it closes up, its trace can be followed minutes or even hours after, depending on how strong your magic is."

A sudden blast of light along with a rumbling earth shudder came from the room in front of us. I stumbled back a couple of steps. Whatever that was, it was so powerful it had blown the door open with a loud crack.

"Oh fizzle, he just ported," said Lexi rushing up to the

open door, hinges creaking from years of use. There was a weird electrical smell coming from the faint breeze that seeped through the gap of the doorway. Lexi walked up to the edge of it and flattened herself against the wall, peering in from the side. It was weird seeing his door open for anyone to glance into. So unlike him.

"Aurora, go back to the car." She was already in a fighting stance. Curiosity overruled and I followed behind as she ventured into his room. I couldn't help but feel a little triumphant after he ended our conversation today. Now I was inside his home, spying on him.

But I was instantly freaked out. Pictures of me covered every visible surface. "He's been here a lot longer than just a few days, Lexi. These pictures go back to when Fenn and I first got here." I started backing out of his motel room, trying not to lose my lunch. I guess I got what I deserved for being curious.

Just as I reached the door she called, "He must've felt my arrival and ported, that Rotten Harpy. I can still smell the trace of his port." Her nose lifted in the air, taking in that awful electrical wire smell. I was uncontrollably shaking my head no. I guess subconsciously I thought that by doing that it would make this go away somehow. But it didn't. This was real, and it was too much to accept.

"I can't…" I said, interrupting her. "Look, Lexi, I'm going to go take a shower. I can't…" I gave the room another once over, all the private moments of my life pinned up for prying eyes. "I can't deal with all of this right now." Realms, creepy men, portals, it was just too much. My brain was fried. I felt so helpless, so out of control. Dizziness crept in. I braced the rail of the stairs on my way up hoping I wouldn't fall.

"Okay, Rory." I stopped in my tracks at this term of endearment. Not just anyone called me Rory. I hadn't told her to call me Rory. She must've picked it up from my missing best friend while she and her mother "watched" me. Everyone seemed to have "watched" me. And that did it for me. Anger flared up. I was tired of everyone prodding into my life, a life that everyone knew about but me.

"Fenn called me that, as I'm sure you already know. Don't…over," I said through a low growl. I paused, suddenly unsure if I really wanted to unload on her or not. Instead, I continued up the stairs. Nothing good would come from what I had to say and she was not a verbal punching bag.

Of course she followed me up the stairs and into the room asking, "You really love him, don't you?" She was like a bug, a bug that I wanted to smack.

I turned to face her and said, "I'm going to take a shower now. Help yourself to whatever you see in here. Please do not bother me unless it is an extreme emergency. I will be done in a while. And yes, I do love him. He was there with me throughout my entire life. He helped me become the person that I am and then he had to leave. Because of me, I might add, which doesn't make it any easier to swallow." Again she looked confused.

I grabbed some clothes from my dresser and headed to the bathroom. I wouldn't be coming out for at least an hour. Turning the water to scalding hot, I stepped in, anxious to feel the comforting burn. I let it all go for the moment. There was no point in trying to decipher anything so I closed my eyes as the mist filled my pores.

Chapter 22

~

Holy Cow!

I KEPT TO MY WORD and stayed in the bathroom for at least an hour. After the water ran cold, I put comfy clothes on and opened the door to face Lexi.

For a brief moment I thought I saw Fenn's face, my heart jumping with hope, but then I realized it was Lexi's face I was seeing. She was sitting on the edge of my bed with my Oraculus resting on her lap.

"What are you doing with that?" I felt immediately shaky and walked over to her with nervous hands, energy firing up inside me. My eyes never left hers as I leaned in and gently pulled it off her lap, prepared for anything that might come. I didn't want anyone touching my Oraculus—even if her mother had given it to me.

"We should talk about this, Aurora. Do you even know what that really is?" I shook my head no and braced my book to my chest like it was the last good burger on Earth. Eve had never gone into detail about it, but I knew it was as connected to me as Zordon. "You know how everyone has their own Oraculus, written on the day of their birth," she eased, "well, your case is different. Your Oraculus is only half of a whole. The other half is in the Hall of Knowledge, and it has an owner," she said gravely. She didn't have to say it out loud. I knew whose it was.

"Zordon," I stated, sitting down next to her.

"Yes. I wasn't supposed to say anything, but I felt it's something you should know, something you should prepare for. Have you ever seen him before?"

"I have, yes, but not lately."

"That's odd. But it's not like anyone knows exactly what an Oraculus can do for someone who has it in their possession. Especially in your case since your Oraculus was split in half-the other half being Zordon's. Our law says that no one can see their own Oraculus until they die and cross over into the Hall of Knowledge. So how did you manage to see him?"

"I saw him once with Eve. She told me to say Apparatio while holding my Oraculus, so I did, and somehow, I saw him again. That was the last time."

"That word, Apparatio, is a spell Seers use in our realm to see what The Fates want to show them. What happened?"

I filled her in, delighted that she was interested. Maybe she would be able to help me figure it out. I told her about Zordon and Gwenevere and Gabe and all that had happened. When I finished she took a deep breath.

"I've heard of Gwenevere before. They say her disappearance was plotted," said Lexi.

"Plotted? To get away from him?" I asked, hopeful.

"Well yeah. My mother swears that she's dead, but she said Lady Gwenevere hated Zordon. She was promised to him and had no choice but to marry him." She leaned in and said in a whisper, "I've also heard she was pregnant."

I looked up, remembering her clutching her lower stomach before she went to jump.

"I think she was," I admitted. "She was holding her stomach when I saw her."

"Well, like I said…my mother says she's dead. It's one of those things we'll never know because if Liege Zordon ever found out… he'd kill her himself."

That's reassuring, I thought as I shook my head. What kind of world was I heading back to?

"Open the Oraculus, Aurora," she instructed.

I did as she said. "This is the language of The Fates. There is no interpreter besides the person who the book belongs to and The Fates themselves. It is your entire life mapped out. Well, not yours because obviously it's not completed, but everyone else's is."

"The book of life pages turn yet unwritten. The canvas to your mortal soul, the connection to your immortal enemy," I repeated out loud. "That's what the prophecy means. That's why I'm connected to Zordon," I said, excited that I was figuring it out.

"So then you can understand it and connect to Zordon?"

"No. I've read it, but I don't understand a word it says. But I think it does have a way of bringing me to Zordon." I was flipping through all the pages that did have writing, trying my best to translate it.

"About that," she coughed, "the owner kind of has to be dead in order to understand it. It's a condition of The Fates in case something like this happens. *This* meaning when the owner is alive and has the book. You're not meant to know your fate."

"Well, that may very well happen." I broke off thinking about Zordon. "So was Mr. Creepy after me then?"

"Who, Soothe? No, he was the Seer who gave your prophecy," she answered. "I just wanted to talk to him. He didn't have to port like that."

"Wait, his name is Soothe?" I asked, "The same Soothe who set up my bank account?" At least I didn't have to continue searching for the mysterious Soothe any longer.

"Yes and yes. And he kind of is the reason you are in danger," she edged.

"Like how much danger are we talking here?" I hedged.

"Like a lot of danger. But don't worry, Gabe is our insider, and he told my mother before I left that Zordon was onto the fact that you were over here. Gabe is doing everything he can to divert action from being taken."

"What about Soothe? Why is he here?"

"That's part of why you're in danger. You see, he altered the prophecy by keeping a piece to himself. And no one knows what that missing part says. So that left Zordon questioning. In the meantime, Astral sent Soothe over here to hide that pendant, which he apparently failed to do, and to watch over you. Gabe said that Zordon has a Seer working for him called Sayer trying to uncover the missing piece and that he may be able to locate Soothe. This brings us back to the problem. You're in danger."

"And what if they find me?" I turned to her, dread growing like a prickly vine.

"That's why I'm here, Aurora—to protect you should that happen."

"And what of my parents? Do you know them? Are they safe?"

"Yes, they are safe. Just give it some time for everything to sink in. You can't expect to understand it all in one night. Remember that I'm here to help. We will get through this, together. I think what you need right now is sleep. It will be easier to talk about this tomorrow with fresh minds." I agreed. I was beat. I lay in my spot and pulled the covers up to my chin. It didn't take long for sleepiness to kick in and for my eyes to grow heavy and close.

"Goodnight, Aurora," was the last thing that I heard.

"Aurora." I awoke to someone shaking my shoulder in jerky motions. "Aurora, wake up. We need to talk," said Lexi with worried eyes.

Oh great, what now? I thought to myself. "Okay, just give me a second." I sat up in bed, knees pulled up to my chin.

"It's about Soothe." She sat down next to me on the bed.

"What about him?" I asked, instantly interested.

"He said he's willing to talk to you about the prophecy." Her words rushed out in excitement.

"Back up a sec...you talked to him?" I was jealous.

"That's exactly what I did. After you fell asleep, I went back downstairs and into his room. I had to know what he's been up to. It's my duty to protect you and I had to make sure he hadn't snapped or gone Rogue." She was so sure of herself.

"Why'd he leave so quickly?" I asked, getting up to get something to drink.

"I used the Repetio spell to trace his port trail. Your realm doesn't take to our magic very well. He left because he didn't want me to confront him about his screw up. His port trail lingered long enough for me to follow it. I found him hiding out in the woods near the cave."

I sat down at the table and poured cereal into a bowl. After adding milk, I stirred my chocolaty mass of goodness and watched the milk change color. Drinking it was the best part. The whole time, Lexi sat there watching me in wonder. I tipped my brow towards her, asking if she wanted some, but she shook her head no absentmindedly.

"So Soothe wants to meet and *finally* help me out. Convenient. You know, this whole time I've been trying to get him to help me and he's been dodging me like the plague," I said in between mouthfuls. "I guess beggars can't be choosers."

She gave me a look of confusion at the crunching noise my cereal made. "Are you sure?" I asked tauntingly, swirling my bowl under her nose. She ignored me.

"So ho said to meet him around noon," she explained.

I sipped the best part of my balanced morning breakfast and quickly rinsed out the bowl, tossing it into the dish drainer.

"Where are we meeting him?" I asked, suddenly remembering all the pictures. I really didn't want to talk to him in an atmosphere filled with stolen moments of my life.

"Near the cave where I found him last night. He says he feels the most relaxed there ever since the voices stopped."

"The voices?" I asked.

"Yeah, the voices of The Fates. When Soothe broke the law of prophecies, his power was stripped and the voices stopped."

"Okay then," I replied, deciding to let that one go.

A little before noon, I locked the door and we ran down the stairs in a flurry, heading to the "borrowed" car in record time.

"Why don't we just port there?" I asked, not sure why we had to drive.

"Because, Rory, I told you, using magic in this realm is different. Things could go wrong, like you getting lost in the chasm or something, and I don't want to take that risk. Besides, we don't really have a good inconspicuous spot to do magic at the moment.

You want your motel door left open?"

"No, sorry, I was just curious," I replied, getting into the driver's side of the car. She got in and buckled up, following my lead of safety first while I turned the car on. I was just about to put the car into reverse when she braced my arm.

"Rory, wait," she said as she pulled my arm from off the gear shifter. "Someone's here." She was looking around the car for whomever she thought was present.

"Yeah, there are a lot of people around." I tried to pretend like I didn't notice the alarm written all over her face and in her voice, but it was undeniable.

Her nose tipped up as she sniffed the air before saying, "We need to go, NOW!" She quickly unbuckled herself and me and bolted out of the car, yanking me from the driver's seat. She was a moment too late as a fiery ball of energy whizzed past us, barely missing our heads.

"Go back to your room!" she yelled. Out of nowhere, another energy ball flew at us, smashing into the brick building. Debris instantly showered us, the bits of rock shattering windows. We had both dropped to the ground, blood trickling from our hands and faces. I was shaking from limb to limb, the gravel biting into the palms of my hand as my breath came in rapid torrents. Zordon had found me.

Lexi grabbed my hand and yanked me towards the stairs, not stopping for a moment. Her hands lit up and she chanted, "Protectio."

A bubble surrounded us as another energy bolt flew towards us. It hit the outside of it and I tensed in horror, waiting for the bubble to break, but the spell was absorbed instead.

"Pulsecto!" Lexi shouted as she threw her energy in the general direction of the attacker.

"Ahh!" I heard a man's voice cry out.

I scanned the area, trying to find the culprit, but she pulled me inside my room, slamming the door behind us.

"Talk to me, Lexi, what's going on?" I said between breaths.

She paced back and forth. "He must have followed through my port trail. Damn it! I told my mother to get someone better to do it." She stopped and looked at me. "Okay, listen carefully. The guy who is here, he is from the other side. He wants to kill you, Rory. He works for Zordon."

Zordon? I thought. *No way, this is not happening.*

"Listen to me," she said as she snapped me from my thoughts. "We don't have much time. He is here and this is happening. I'm going to have to port us after all, and you aren't going to feel very well when it happens. You have to hang on to me no matter what, okay?"

I nodded in acknowledgement, but I really felt like everything was happening around me and not to me. "Okay, come over here." I stepped over to her in a daze as she grabbed my arm and wrapped it around her waist. I winced from the sting of the fresh wounds.

"What do I do?" I asked, not sure where my part came in. She looked at me with sympathetic eyes and said, "For now, just trust me," and I watched as her eyes went from a honey-kissed brown to a deep mahogany. A light green glow emerged from the palms of her hands, the energy pouring out of her and into thin air.

In front of us, a void began to open as the energy swirled and began to form a picture of the other end. I could feel the pull of gravity. Her green energy was shooting from her hands towards the void, powering it as a crazed look overcame her face.

Outside I heard heavy footsteps and a man shouting, "Come out, come out, little dragon." A second later the doorknob rattled.

"Lexi," I said, fear swelling up.

"I'm going to count to three," she whispered. "When I say

three, we're going to jump into the port. Hold your breath. It will only take a few seconds to get through, but when we get to the other side I want you to count backwards from ten. It will help with the nausea."

I shook my head in agreement and waited. "One...two...three."

I didn't pay any mind to what was around me as I was being sucked through space. I did however feel every molecule of my body being moved and rearranged. Our feet landed with a thud on earthy forest ground. *I guess we made it to our destination after all,* I thought sarcastically.

"This was where we were heading, right?" I asked, hoping that Soothe was nearby. Then I toppled slightly as the first wave of nausea hit. "Ooh man, ten, nine, eight..." I began to count like she had said while she sat me down on the ground.

"I figured this would be the best place to deal with who's about to follow us. Soothe should be somewhere around here," she said as her eyes scanned the forest. "This guy will be following my port trail. We don't have much time and you need to hide."

"Wait a minute. Exactly who is it that we are running from?" I asked through blurred vision, my head spinning.

"His name is Zane, he is Zordon's son." The look on her face wasn't a very hopeful one. I knew exactly who she was talking about—the same guy that Zordon had choked in my dream. It was a shame that he had to send his own son to do his dirty work.

Dread suddenly filled my pores. I'd left my Oraculus in my nightstand. What if he found it? I could almost feel the life draining out of me as sweat beaded my forehead. Lexi told me that she had cloaked it in a protection spell, but it didn't feel like enough. I held onto my necklace for support. It warmed my palm, easing the panic just enough to let me breathe.

"And what are we going to do when he shows up?" I wasn't

prepared for this. I wasn't ready to fight someone or deal with magic from another realm when I didn't even have answers to the million questions that constantly pounded through my head.

"We won't be doing anything," she said firmly, stressing the plural. "You have no control over your powers which puts you in more danger rather than helping us out. I need you to hide behind that tree while I figure this out."

She was pacing again, rubbing her temples, panic radiating off her. "You don't need to worry though. I have formal training, with the Dragon King, I might add," she reassured shakily.

Somehow I wasn't relieved. I didn't know what Zane was truly capable of. What Mages were truly capable of. My visions were the closest thing I had to knowing what was happening and they only showed me snippets of what might happen.

Like lightning, a crackling sound resounded off the trees as Zane popped out of the air and landed on the ground in a fighting stance. He was instantly recognizable. He looked almost exactly like his father.

I shuddered.

"Zane," spat Lexi as she crouched ready to fight. I looked down at my hands, hoping that this whole heart-racing, mind-pacing thing would be enough to ignite my powers, but I felt nothing.

"Alexis," he toyed, "I see you've grown into quite a beauty." He walked casually towards us. "It's amazing that a girl from the market, working for those serpents," he said disgustedly, "can look as good as you. Though, you'd look better as a wife."

His smile made me cringe.

"At least some of us know how to make an honest living," she threw back at him. Then she clasped her hands together, and a green ball of crackling energy began to emerge between them.

A smile ran across Zane's face as he stalked towards us. There was nothing I could do. The nausea I now felt had nothing to do with porting.

A snarl came from the pit of her as Lexi threw the green tinted energy again. Instantly, an invisible shield sprung up around Zane, causing the spell to deflect and hurl towards me. I wasn't quick enough. The energy caught the ball of my heel, a scream ripped from my throat. I was on fire. I had never been burned in my life, yet whatever had just hit me, had ignited my skin, the pain so white-hot I felt on the verge of fainting. My chest heaved rapidly as I tried to see through the pain. But I couldn't think of anything but the never-ending burn. It wouldn't stop.

Lexi looked pissed when she looked back at me. She said something I couldn't comprehend as her energy connected with my heel, the pain instantly relieved. I scurried backwards like a crab, not really knowing what to do. "I'm okay," I said quickly, pointing to the approaching Zane.

"I see this will have to be done the old-fashioned way." She sprinted towards him faster than I'd ever seen anyone run before. He began to run as well, and they came together with a colorful thud.

After that, it was hard to make out everything that was happening. I heard shouts of pain and fighting as various trees fell from the dodged energy. My hair stood on end as tree limbs cracked and sizzled.

She shouted, "Occidium!" which caused Zane to lose balance and then followed up with a move that made him slam into a tree. When his back hit, he slid down, the breath knocked out of him.

He didn't look too pleased as he stood up and quickly shouted, "Afflictum," hurling a red ball of energy back at her.

She tried to dodge with her own invisible shield, but her magic wasn't strong enough, and after only a second of the magic pushing against her barrier, it broke through and caught her leg. Her gut-wrenching scream echoed my earlier agony.

I jumped up from the ground at the sound of her scream, panic rising. It seemed Zane had forgotten about me up until that point. I cursed myself for interfering.

"The fight is not with her, you coward. Finish what you started!" Lexi barely stammered out from behind him, stopping him in his tracks as he headed towards me. She was lying on the forest ground in a heap, blood pooling around her leg against the rotted leaves. Fear of what was happening clouded my judgment.

"All right then," he said in a menacing tone that I didn't trust one bit. As fast as I could blink he was at her throat, holding her up against a tree. "Slither back to your cold-blooded reptiles, you traitor," he seethed. Her eyes went wide with shock.

She was scrambling helplessly, trying to get out of his grip like an animal in a trap. "Such a shame though. You truly are a beauty. Too bad things couldn't be different."

Then I felt it. I felt the power building up inside of me like a volcano ready to erupt. It was scary at first, but then that crazed delicious feeling returned. Something stirred deep within me. The dragon wanted to break free.

I glanced down and sure enough the blue energy was pulsing around my hands, red scales prickling up my arms. An evil smile crossed my lips.

I didn't know any spells, but I certainly had my instincts. I noticed a small log lying at my feet. I knew this would be my only real chance to rectify this situation. I focused on the log and saw the energy pouring from me and around the log. I focused on levitating it and watched as it floated higher and higher, my hands rising as it rose, and still I didn't feel weak. It was like picking up a feather.

"Not this time, shithead," I declared, catching Zane's attention. For a millisecond his eyes went wide before I sent the log flying towards his head. I thought I would have cringed on impact, but it felt good to watch him slink unconsciously to the ground. Whatever was inside of me liked it as well. I felt the stir of energy coursing through and wrapping me in a warm hug of approval.

Lexi slowly sunk down against the tree, trying to catch her breath as she grabbed at her throat. There were red welts where Zane's hands had squeezed.

I knelt down with her, whispering that she was okay, trying to help her focus. Although the energy surge had subsided, I couldn't help but be satisfied that I had finally done something to help. I had finally taken control of my power.

"Thanks," she muttered with a halfhearted smile. "Pretty amazing stuff you pulled back there." She coughed, her voice hoarse. "You really shouldn't even be able to," she coughed again, "be able to do that. But cool nonetheless. You saved me." Her eyes met mine and I could see the thankfulness.

She took another breath and then glanced down at her leg. "We've got to fix this fast," she said, the blood continually oozing from the injury. "I need you to combine your energy with mine for a moment. I'm too weak to heal this on my own."

"Okay…" I replied, not sure exactly how to do that.

"Just focus on healing my leg and say 'Mendaro.' I'll do the rest," she explained.

I nodded and focused on the open wound, letting the energy flow through me once again. I imagined it sealing from the inside out, healing and returning to normal as I chanted "Mendaro" over and over. I felt her energy flow into mine as the leg began to heal in front of us.

"It's working," I declared excitedly.

Then she stood up, testing its sturdiness. "All healed," she said with a smile.

She walked over to Zane. He lay there limp and lifeless though we both knew he was still very much alive.

"Stand back. I don't want you to get pulled in," she said as she began to weave another portal. I was still smiling distractedly inside, feeling like I had finally done something to control at least a small aspect of my life. No one but myself made me get up and do what I did.

When the portal opened, I helped Lexi pick Zane up and throw him into it. "I'll be right back," she said, jumping in after him. I paced the forest, avoiding the puddles of blood that had formed from either Lexi's leg or the blunt trauma to Zane's head.

What the hell was happening? I couldn't do anything but think of how proud Fenn would have been in that moment. To see me finally take a stand for myself.

I practically caught Lexi as she fell back through the port.

"Thanks," she said. "He won't be back for a while. We might have enough time to find all the keys before he makes it back. The problem is, now he knows what you look like. And that you're the one," she finished, pointing to my necklace. She didn't look too pleased. "Next time we may not be so lucky, and he may not come alone." A smile slowly formed on her face. "We make a good team," she said. I couldn't help but smile as well, letting myself bask in my moment of glory.

"Now let's get moving. We have a date to catch."

Chapter 23

~

Our Cozy Little Meeting

WE FOUND SOOTHE ALMOST AN hour after the time we were supposed to meet him. He was farther into the forest, resting on a rock near a waterfall.

"Hey!" Lexi shouted over the sound of the crashing water. "Come over this way so we can hear each other a little better."

Soothe leisurely rolled his eyes as he hopped off the rock and strode casually towards us. "I can hear just fine," he replied when he was in front of us. "You're late."

"Well, I'm not shouting," she retorted. "And of course we're late. Zane spotted her."

For a brief second his eyes lit up, like he was concerned and ready to take action, but then his face resumed that cold, blank expression.

"Indeed," he replied. "That's truly unfortunate. And before she had a chance to find all the keys. My-my savior, you truly are proving your worth, aren't you?" he sneered.

I frowned. "Are you going to help me find the rest of the keys or not?" I bit back, hoping that having Lexi with me would help.

"Do you still have the map?" he asked in return.

"Yeah, it's right here." I reached into my bag and pulled it out. Lexi gasped. "You didn't tell me you had that," she chided as she took it from my hands. She unfolded the worn hide, her face lighting up in awe.

I shrugged. "I figured you knew. I mean, weren't you told everything before you came?"

"Well, yes, but no one said anything about this. I mean technically you shouldn't even have this. If we were back in our realm, you'd have to face The Fates and explain why this is in your possession. Do you know what this is?" she asked, her voice heightened.

"Judging by your face I'd say it's something pretty important," I guessed, glancing over at Soothe.

"It's a portal map," he answered dryly. "They're very rare and impossible to find. There are a total of four, one for each of The Fates. It shows the way to any object you seek to find. In your case, the keys. This is the most coveted map you could ever find. When I left, there was only one missing. This one."

Lexi cleared her throat. "Scouts were sent out with another map to try and find this one shortly after it was taken," she said quietly.

"Well they won't ever find it, now will they? The maps only work in the realm you're in," Soothe reassured smugly.

A bleak expression replaced Lexi's confidence. "Before I left, the scouts went missing."

Soothe's face paled. "Let's pray it hasn't fallen into Zordon's hands," Soothe concluded.

"I can't even begin to piece together how any could be stolen right from under The Fates' noses," Lexi wondered.

"What if the other map is with Zordon?" I asked, a part of me not wanting to hear the answer.

"If that happens," he said gravely, "then finding the keys and returning home will be the least of your worries." His face fell. "And every sought after object in our realm is now in danger."

There was a long moment of silence as we all digested the reality of what Soothe had said. I haven't even made it back and already my future was looking hopeless. I thought about Fenn and how he was over there, possibly dealing with the danger that seemed to be my destiny. I needed to get the keys, fast.

"Look here," said Lexi, pointing to an X that hadn't been there before. It looked like it was around Mily's house.

"That must be where I found the first key," I said, suddenly excited. "Only it's missing too," I added.

"It's not missing, Aurora. It is where it should be. That is a part of The Fates' magic...to protect what is theirs. Trust me," said Soothe.

"Well, why don't I see where the other keys are?" I asked. "There isn't an X anywhere else."

"Have you used the second sun's light?" asked Soothe.

"Second sun?"

"Yes, that's where the Hall of Knowledge is. I'll show you," Lexi reassured. "So we don't need your help after all," she said to Soothe. "This map will get us the rest of the way."

"I do have a question though," I interrupted. "It's about what you said that night at the diner, about the last line of the prophecy," I said, fidgeting uncomfortably.

"Yes?"

"A death will come to He that breaks the barrier...what does that mean? It's the last piece that I can't figure out," I admitted.

"What do you think it means?" he asked in return.

"Well, at first I thought it had to do with the portal I came through and that maybe Fenn or I would die if we tried to go back, but now I'm not so sure. I mean, if I'm supposed to protect the dying race, then why would I die so early on? And, it says *He*; I am a she.

So basically, I have no idea," I finished.

"But you see, Aurora, I cannot tell you what it means. That is not a part of my job," he said artlessly.

"What about the missing piece? You weren't supposed to withhold a piece of the prophecy so it appears that rules mean nothing to you," I retaliated.

I saw a quiver of a smile at the corner of his mouth.

"You're wiser than I assumed," he said quietly. "Rules do apply to me," he said slowly, "as does your purpose. As you already know, I gave up my ability to protect you. In return, I simply ask that you trust me when I say I cannot tell you. Now is not the appropriate time for that," he finished solemnly.

I paused a moment, then sighed. "Fair enough."

"Well then, now that that's settled," said Lexi, stepping in between us and facing Soothe. "Are you coming or staying because we have keys to find and one night to find them."

He turned back to the cave and stared at it for a moment before facing us. "Staying," he said. "I have a feeling we will run into each other again," he finished with a wink in my direction.

"Then if you'll excuse us, we will be going now," she said, tugging my arm in the direction away from him.

"What now?" I asked.

"Now we find the next key."

Chapter 24

~

Aloha Hotel

"WHERE EXACTLY ARE WE GOING?" I asked, trying to keep up with her pace as we trudged through the forest.

"To find the next key," Lexi replied as she opened the map. "But we can't do that until we make it out of this forest. We have to be directly under the sun."

"In all my life, I have never noticed a second sun," I said under my breath as I shambled along behind her. The far off sound off the waterfall was calling my name due to the afternoon heat that was steadily rising.

"You usually can't see it," she verified. "You just know it's there. I mean, it's the Hall of Knowledge," she said as if it was common knowledge, "the place where all Mages hope to cross over after death. And technically, it's not a 'second sun'. It just appears that way if you are lucky enough to catch a glimpse of it. I've read that it was created from the purest light."

"Sounds complicated," I grunted. I quit focusing on swatting at the shrubbery and looked up. The edge of the forest was just in sight. "Finally," I mumbled, wiping the sweat from my brow. We exited the forest and came out into a lush valley. The grass was slippery from an afternoon shower.

"Show us the keys" said Lexi, holding the map up to the sun. The rays banned around her and the map, shining through the ink on the hide. Suddenly all of the scribble made sense. Somehow, the light made the lines of the ink impress upon the grass, becoming a sort of holographic image. And where the X was, a small sliver of light shone through. It was much like the beam of light that came from the key when I found it.

So the map was real.

"See," she pointed, "it's showing the other keys." Her finger was in between the ruins and the cave. They were surrounded by a pulsing glow.

"The altar and the cave," I stated. I mindlessly twirled the loose-fitting ring on my finger and thought back to what Bob had suggested. "Was Fenn's ring created from that altar?"

She nodded.

"Why?"

"That's easy enough. He's your protector. Why do you think the Natives worshipped the fifth brother? Because he sacrificed himself for something more, he *protected* the Draconta. Astral felt it was worthy of holding and restoring Fenn's memories."

I slowly nodded as it all took shape in my mind. Fenn, the fifth brother, both looking out for someone (or something) other than themselves.

My lips puckered in sadness. "Why couldn't Astral have instructed Fenn to hold-off on putting the ring on in the letter he gave us?"

"Astral has a reason for everything he does," she consoled, "maybe I was wrong about him wanting you to stay here. Maybe he intended for it to happen this way so you would have no choice but to return."

"It sure is a cruel way to make me choose," I said, my voice almost inaudible.

She patted me on the back sympathetically.

"So what are we waiting for?" I asked, suppressing a sigh.

"Not a thing." She smiled softly and started in the direction of the ruins. "They should be just over this hill."

She was wrong.

It wasn't "just" over the hill. We walked for what seemed like forever. When we finally reached the other side of the hill, the excitement to get to the ruins had all but left me.

To add to it, Lexi's shoulders slouched over in disappointment. "Great," she muttered darkly.

"What?" I asked as I came up behind her. "Oh." The ruins were full of tourists.

"There's no way we can get in and out without anyone noticing," she brooded.

"Can't you just perform a spell? Soothe did something like that before," I offered.

"Magic doesn't always take well in this realm, Aurora. And look at the numbers. The ruins is crammed full of people. I would deplete my energy if I attempted that."

I huffed, shaking my head sadly.

After a long moment of not knowing what to say, I asked, "What now?" It was inadequate for the situation, but the best thing I could think to say.

She frowned. "I need to think. Come on, we'll grab our things and find somewhere other than your motel room to sleep since it's known." She folded the map and handed it back to me.

This time I was the one patting her on the back.

Back in the room, I started packing a spare change of clothes and my Oraculus. The sun was already starting to set as Lexi slumped over, staring blankly out my motel window. Defeat seemed to have poisoned her. I had to do something.

I quickly jumped on my computer and searched for a place to stay, just to get us moving. There was a hotel right off the ruins that would be perfect. I selected it and waited for my authorization code, when an ad popped up.

My face immediately lit up.

"You know," I said craftily, "Bob had mentioned checking out the tour that is offered for the ruins." I peeked sideways at her with a hopeful expression.

She looked at me, her expression still blank.

"And I was thinking, maybe it would be a good idea." I gave her a meaningful look, hoping it would sink in.

She stared at me for a moment, puzzled. And then slowly, as the thoughts turned in her head, awareness seemed to overtake her bummed mood. "We would always be near people," she began to formulate, "so we would have the protection of safety in numbers." Then she frowned. "But what about the people?" she reminded.

"We could separate from the group and get the key when they head for the cave. We just have to get it before the next tour group gets there," I explained. She was beaming now.

"We can meet back up with them near the cave since it showed up on the map for the third key and is where we need to be when the full moon hits. Your powers and memories will be restored and we'll be able to make it home," she concluded happily.

Back to Fenn.

With our plan underway, we drove the stolen car back to the beach, to where Lexi had taken it from, and then boarded the bus that would take us to the hotel. We talked about our plan in depth, ensuring that there would be no hiccups. I felt confident that we would make it.

But I still had a lingering question that I had been meaning to ask. "What exactly is Zordon after?"

"Oh," she said, seeming surprised by my subject change. "Well, rumor has it that Zordon is planning an attack against the Draconta, hoping to gain control of the Stone of Immortality. I fear it will have a devastating effect on our people and dragons," she said sadly as she paused and stared out the window. Softly she finished, "and Zordon's rumored army gathering will leave us all with no choice but to run."

"The chosen one fated to protect the dying race," I repeated out loud as it dawned on me.

"Huh?" Lexi face scrunched in question.

"A part of the prophecy says that. That has to be what it means. That has to be my purpose, to protect the Draconta. Maybe I can prevent all that from happening," I reassured.

"It's not that simple, Rory. The army he is supposedly going to gather is one that many fear." She leaned into me and whispered, "The Dark Saar."

"Who are they?"

"They're Mages who never crossed over to the Hall of Knowledge because they never found their balance of light to escape the darkness that follows us. The worst part is, they can only be killed by humans so the Draconta don't stand a chance against them. That's if Zordon's lucky enough to recruit them." Despair weighed on her face.

"There has to be a way to keep that from happening, and I swear to you, I'll find it," I said, squeezing her arm. The bus slowed as it turned into the hotel parking lot.

"I know that, Rory. You are the Progeny. It is your destiny to save us from him," she said encouragingly as she stood up, motioning for me to follow. I grabbed my bookbag off the seat and threw it over my shoulders. When I stepped off, the air smelled of native Jasmine, dazzling my senses.

"This is it," I muttered, sliding on my backpack and following the greeter who placed Leis around our necks. To add to the atmosphere, the path we walked along had little rocks with speakers built in that serenaded us with tropical themed music.

"I wish that my home was as luxurious as this," Lexi remarked, amazement filling her eyes. Her look reminded me of Fenn's eyes filling with joy the day we stepped foot in our new space. I hoped to see that look again, sooner than later.

After quickly checking in, I pointed Lexi towards the elevator. Like a kid in a candy shop, she bolted towards it. *This ought to be interesting*, I thought, wickedly amused.

"Push that square thing called a button," I said, pressing my lips together to keep from laughing. She pushed it, excitement bursting out of her pores as it lit up.

"Ding, third floor please," I said cheerfully as we boarded the elevator.

"This feels kind of like porting. It's so quiet in here. What's this called again?" she asked as we ascended.

"An elevator." I scoffed, still laughing at her wonder.

The elevator chimed as the doors opened, revealing an oasis with banana leaf inspired carpets and sheer white fabric draped across the ceilings and lights. Tropical music played softly, reinforcing the mood.

We found our room and I handed Lexi the key. She looked at me, clearly baffled. "You slide it in there," I said, pointing to the slot. She shrugged and then did as I said. The green light blinked and she pushed the door open to our paradise.

She gasped, her hands clasping over her mouth. "This sure beats cobblestone and jewels," she said taking it all in.

"It better, I booked us a suite," I muttered.

"Suite?" she questioned.

I shook my head, deciding not to go there. Instead I asked, "So is that true? I mean, about dragons liking shiny things? It isn't just lore?"

"Well, yeah, they love rich shiny things," she replied as we set our bags down, "but who doesn't?"

"True," I agreed, poking around the room. It had a full-size kitchen, two double beds, a couch, a TV, a bathroom with a sunken-in Jacuzzi tub, and a desk. A lovely home away from home.

"I can't believe that I'm one of them, you know?" I admitted.

"What do you mean?" she asked as she plopped onto a bed.

I sat across from her on the other bed and replied, "I mean, I've always known that I was different, that there was more to me than just me, but when I step back and think about it all, I mean really think about it, it begins to feel unreal, like I fell and hit my head or something."

She started giggling. "I can tell you now, you haven't hit your head. This is exactly where you're meant to be," she insisted, turning to her side and propping up on an elbow.

"I can feel that it's right, like you say, but I can't help but think what if… What if Astral hadn't sent me over here, or if Soothe hadn't decided to cut a piece of the prophecy out, or if Fenn never had to go…" I rambled on. She put her hand up to stop me.

"Rory, if I could give you any advice on the current situation, it would be this—you can't become who you're supposed to be if you keep looking back on what might have been."

I pondered that thought for a moment, impressed by her depth of thinking. "You're right...onward and upward," I declared with a smile. "Now if you'll excuse me," I said, pushing up from the bed, "I'm going to take a long soak in our tub to prepare my muscles for this so-called hike tomorrow."

"Okay, I guess I will take a walk then and 'soak up' as much as I can of this place," she said, heading for the door with a laugh.

About an hour in, a loud pounding on the bathroom door took me from my blissful quiet time. "Rory!" Lexi shouted from the other side.

I pulled the plug in the tub and ran to the closet, pulling on a robe. "Hang on a sec," I called out. She seemed rushed. That alerted me. *Zane*, I thought.

She practically busted through the door, almost knocking me over before I could reach the handle. "I thought you may have drowned when you didn't answer."

"Geez, you scared the crap out of me," I huffed as I rolled my eyes at her dramatic antics. She followed me over to the tub, chattering in my ear. "I walked myself down to the pool and took a dip thinking that you would be out before I got back."

"Sorry, I was nodding off. Tends to happen when you're relaxing in a bathtub," I explained under my breath, shaking my head.

She was in a hotel robe as well but was wearing it completely wrong. I burst out laughing, tears gathering in the corners of my eyes. She placed her hands on her hips and tilted her head to the side, eyes curious. I pointed to the mirror so she could see what was tickling me.

"What's so funny, prune girl?" she countered as my laughter began to pick up again. I couldn't help it, she was so oblivious.

"Well, nothing really, except your robe, it's all wrong…" I broke off into more laughter. I had never seen anything like it before. I ran and grabbed my purse, taking a quick picture before she noticed what I was doing. Blackmail for later.

"What?" She looked at me, pausing with a raised eyebrow before looking into the mirror. "Oh fizzle." She had somehow fit each leg into the arms of the robe, pulling the end of the robe up halter style and tying it closed. I would have died laughing if I had been an onlooker at the pool. It was a mystery how she didn't flash anybody.

"How could you let me go out in public like this?" she blurted, wrapping her arms around herself defensively. I held in another giggle and said, "You're the one who took it upon yourself to go for a dip alone." She huffed and stalked off.

I walked over to my bag by the bathroom door and scavenged for some jammies, finding the same sweats that I wore the night I kissed Fenn.

Sliding the pants under my robe, I turned my back to Lexi and slid on a tank top. I walked past her and plopped onto the bed, switching on the TV. I decided MTV was a suitable channel to wear me down.

Lexi changed into some sweats and a baggie shirt that I packed for her and then walked back over to her bed, stifling a yawn. She slid into her bed, shifting the covers around her. She was (as with everything else) amazed at the TV.

"To be able to see people from all over the world inside a tiny box is truly wondrous. I will be sad to leave this behind." She adjusted her weight and began twirling her short hair through her fingers, huffing quietly as if pondering something.

She shifted again to face me, staring at the side of my face. She was probably waiting for me to look over so she could say whatever it was she was thinking. I waited a moment just to mess with her, and then turned my head.

"We need to discuss a backup plan in case Zane returns before we find the last two keys. We need to ensure you get there safely, and most importantly, that your Oraculus is kept safe."

I had already packed it into my backpack that rested at arm's reach on the floor. I didn't want to take any chances on someone finding it.

"Zane may come back with back-up this time. He knows who you are now and that puts you in serious danger. Not to mention your amulet is basically a tracking device right now. They don't want you to make it to the cave." This was the conversation I had been dreading.

"Why not?" I asked, unsure as to what cave we were even going to. I knew they wanted me dead so I wouldn't stand in the way of Zordon. I just wasn't sure why exactly they needed to stop me before the cave. What was in the cave?

"Because that's where the doorway you came from is located. And when you are in the cave with the keys and amulet under the full moon, you will be reunited with your powers."

"Do you think he has the other map?"

"I sure hope not," she fretted.

I frowned. "Me too," I replied, trying to modulate my voice.

"In the meantime," she said, changing her tune, "if he does so happen to make another appearance, I will be better prepared. I want to teach you a simple immobilizing spell."

A spell? I was at attention.

"You need to understand that he knows you have powers now so he may expect it and deflect. And the spell may not work because of the realm we're in."

I nodded earnestly.

She almost smiled. "Okay, repeat after me. Immoblatio." Her hands lit up with green energy as she shot a ball at her pillow.

I held my hands up and closed my eyes, searching for the source of power within me. I'd used it enough now that I could feel it even when I wasn't angry. Touching my amulet seemed to help. I opened my eyes and held my hand out, saying the word.

I guess I should have paid attention to where I was pointing because Lexi's eyes got real wide as she toppled over like a stiff board on the bed.

My stomach twisted as my heart raced. "Oh crap, sorry, Lexi. Oh no," I said, sitting her back up and patting her incessantly.

Her eyes were frozen in place as she sat there, unmoving and rigid. "Please do something," I begged, "I don't know how to undo this." Nothing happened.

I huffed.

Then her paralyzed body relaxed as she let out a pent-up breath. "Thank the gods you're not into your full power yet or that would've stuck," she said with a grateful sigh.

I hid my horror.

"At least we know you can do it now," she said smiling. I still felt panicked. "Don't worry. I'm fine," she encouraged through a giggle. "So just use that, and don't worry about me next time. You making it is the only thing you should be concerned about, otherwise this was all for nothing."

I waited for the pace of my heart to return to normal, then said, "Okay, Lexi, I've got this. I actually feel…empowered, if you can believe it." She looked content with that and also a little sleepy. It was the first time I saw her eyes droop. I wondered if my spell had drained her.

"Tired?" I guessed.

She replied blankly, "Just a little. On a more serious note though, I uh…wanted to ask you something," she said quietly, moving to my bed and sitting next to me.

The trust that was growing between us felt so normal. I didn't usually like someone being this close to me, but she was becoming a fast friend. I wanted a friendship, scratch that, needed a friendship. I'd never had one with a girl before. Fenn was it for me. Maybe this was all a good thing. It seemed almost healthy that I break away from the old me.

Then I thought about what she had just said. Me? She wanted to ask me something? It was slightly strange flipping the tables. I was usually the one with the questions.

"Okay, so ask. What's up?" I said, rolling over to prop up onto my elbow. Her hair smelled of chlorine.

"I've been wondering how you knew you were in love with Fenn. Only because there's someone back home that I've been promised to. I've only talked to him a few times and he's really nice, but I'm not sure that he's the one for me. I don't want to be promised to someone that I don't love so I figured if you could tell me how you knew, then maybe I could learn how to fall in love with him."

She exhaled the thought like it had been pent up inside her for days.

I wasn't expecting that. Promised to someone? What am I, in an eighteenth century romance? I didn't exactly know what to say to her. How did you make yourself fall in love with someone? It was kind of like—because you couldn't pick, you would automatically rebel against it. Well, at least I would.

I shifted uncomfortably. "Umm, well, I guess I feel that you just know when you are in love. This is not my area of expertise," I added gruffly. "Ask me how to screw love up instead.

"That's not true, I've seen you with Fenn," she blurted out. "What I mean to say is," she spoke quickly, trying to recover, "even though you may not have looked at it as a relationship, it really did seem like it was one." She was staring intently at me.

"First off, Lexi, it's a little creepy that you watched Fenn and me. As creepy as Soothe and his photos. And now you are asking me to give you advice, well honestly, look what happened. I screwed everything up. I even made him leave. It seems we've been doomed from the get-go. I really don't think my 'relationship' is a good example."

She looked tongue-tied and though a part of me felt bad for being so harsh, I felt better for being honest. "I'm sorry, Aurora," she spoke softly as her words died off. "I didn't mean to impose." Then she rolled and faced the ceiling.

Now I felt bad. She was, after all, just looking for advice. This is why I stayed away from making friends. Too many complications and hurt feelings. But it was time I made a change, in myself.

I backpedaled. "Listen, that special person would live in your every thought, consuming your day-to-day life. He would be as much your rock as you are his, helping support each other through it all. The words 'I love you' would never be enough to profess how much he genuinely means to you." I paused, feeling awfully exposed, and then added, "And I'm not speaking from experience. This was something I picked up out of one of those 'Chicken Soup for the Soul' books. And no, I don't own the book, just read it in a store while waiting for Fenn one day." I hoped she would buy that lame lie.

She looked at me questioningly, mouthing, "Chicken Soup?" and then shaking her head.

"Never mind."

"No...that does help. I definitely don't feel that. I've just never had the chance to talk to anyone about it. Frankly, I don't know how chicken soup ties in with love here in this realm, but hey, who am I to judge?" She smiled and then rolled onto her back. "My mom doesn't believe in love anymore so I never bother her with it. I think my father may have hurt her when he left us, killing her chance of ever loving again."

"I'm sorry," I said softly. "I didn't know he had left you." I could understand what her mother felt, to an extent. I blamed my parents leaving me for much of the reason I had screwed things up so much with Fenn. It was hard for me to open up and trust someone with my true emotions.

She looked back to the ceiling and said, "It's okay. I never knew him. It can't hurt as much when you don't have those emotional ties with someone. Never knowing him saved me from the same despair my mother carries." I wish I had that much resolve when it came to my parents.

"You definitely clarified things for me. I could never feel that for Brohm. I have to figure out how to get out of my promised marriage." She went back to her bed and situated herself under the covers. She didn't sound confident.

"So his name is Brohm? That's a very...um...sturdy name." It sounded so otherworldly. "Maybe you should just try talking to him. You never know, he may surprise you with an amazing personality." She started to laugh, and I joined her. "Okay..." I said, "so maybe not. But I'm sure we'll figure something out. Especially if we can find the keys in time."

She yawned, nodding in agreement as I situated myself, feeling the same drowsiness overcome me. I gave up on trying to think and let sleep take me, anxious for our exciting morning to begin.

Chapter 25

~

The Tour From Hell

THE NEXT MORNING WE STOOD in the hotel lobby in the midst of a small crowd of eight. Lexi was still laughing about almost falling down the stairs after we decided racing each other would be a good idea. She cheated by tripping on the stairs and somehow managing a twisted back flip, landing at the bottom in a cat-like position. If it wasn't for her clumsiness, she would never have beat me.

"Don't be such a sore loser," she said, smirking.

"Don't be such a sore loser," I mimicked snidely.

I glanced around, noticing a couple in our group that clearly believed in PDA. They were practically wrapped around each other, sucking faces as if they were octopuses mating. Maybe this was their honeymoon?

An older man stood a few feet away from them, next to the tour guide and his helper. Over to the left, leaning against a large pillar by an inside waterfall, rested an Oriental guy with a beanie and an Mp3 player. He looked up at me, smiled, and then looked back at his music player.

I leaned into Lexi and asked, "So are you ready?"

"Huh?"

She was distracted by the tour guide's helper who was sneaking glances at her while speaking to the man beside him. Lexi batted her eyelashes in return and did a little finger wave.

"What are you doing?" I asked, elbowing her off balance.

"Eyeing the hot guy, what does it look like? Don't try to steal my thunder." I rolled my eyes. "There is nothing wrong with enjoying the fine youth of this realm."

"Enjoy it while you can, my dear, for we won't be here much longer," I said, laughing.

"Okay everyone, gather around, we have a few things to discuss before we depart," called the tour guide. He was tall, around six feet, with blonde hair and easy blue eyes and was dressed in full hiking gear. His skin was leather brown—you could tell he spent most of his time in the sun.

We all circled up, glancing at each other but trying to maintain focus on what he was saying.

"My name is Matt, should you have any questions, and this is Logan, my assistant." He motioned to the guy Lexi was making eyes with. "Now this is going to be an all day journey. I hope everyone read the memo…?" He paused, giving us the eyebrows as if to ask.

We all nodded in unison, smiles lighting up our faces.

"Great. Does everyone have their bags?" Once again we nodded.

"Okay, then let's head out," he finished with a clap.

"Here we go," I said to Lexi as I picked my bookbag up from off the floor.

The day was a clear sky kind of perfect, tricking our worries about finding the keys away. We spent most of the morning hiking and listening to the tour guide talk about the island and its history.

I wondered what the beanie guy (who introduced himself as Adam) was listening to because, with the way his head was bobbing to and fro, it sure wasn't the tour guide's description of the island's history.

My hands skimmed across the top of the grass that came up to our thighs.

"I love the tall grass on these hills. It's almost as if it's dancing in the wind." The calm surroundings made me believe that there couldn't possibly be any danger after me. That up here, in this peaceful heaven, evil didn't exist. If only.

I pulled my camera out so I could take a few pictures.

It must have been my lucky day. A cloud covered just enough of the sun to reveal what looked like a second sun that seemed to be hidden by the rays.

I snapped a picture quickly and then shook Lexi's shoulders. "I see it," I said, a little too loudly.

"See what?" she asked.

"The second sun! I saw it," I replied, turning to face and point to it. But it was gone. "I swear it was right there," I said, bummed that it had disappeared.

"You can't always see it, Rory, but it's always there. The Fates are all around. They may not be as strong in your realm, but they are present."

"Good to know," I grunted.

We were going up a massive hill, which I'd overheard Matt say was the second highest point on the island, only lower than the volcano.

Lexi smiled and looked ahead at the massive hill that seemed never ending. My legs began to burn in anger.

"This hill is killing me," I whined. Lexi giggled and picked up the pace without even breathing hard.

When we finally made it to the top of the hill everyone sat scattered about, eating packed lunches and drinking an overwhelming amount of water. Matt and Logan were talking in the distance.

"These sandwiches are delicious, Lexi. What's in them?" I had mustard smeared on the side of my mouth, but I didn't care to wipe it. It reminded me of Fenn.

She giggled a little and said, "Salami, mustard, ham, provolone, lettuce, a hero sauce, whatever that means, and some pickles. I felt very creative this morning when I read a sign at the deli in the store that had those ingredients on it. I'd hoped that they would turn out okay with me not knowing, but the lady at the deli was kind enough to let me try a bite of the meats and cheeses." She looked proud of herself.

"You did a great job. They're delicious," I mused taking another bite. I laid back and rested my hands behind my head, creating shapes in the clouds.

"So I've been meaning to ask you…do you know my parents?" I hoped that Lexi would help me find the missing pieces to me. All I wanted to hear was the truth.

"Your mother's name is Eralise, the Draconta Princess."

"Princess? Dragon? But how-"

"Magic, Aurora," she said, cutting me off.

"I know that, and I feel that part of myself wanting to break free. But there's just one part that I can't come to grips with. A part that just can't be right. Lexi…I'm," I looked down, "well, I'm human. And you're telling me my mother is a Draconta Princess. Do all dragons look like humans?"

"Correction, you are part human. Your father, Myrdinn, is a very powerful Mage. You're as much him as you are your mother. Remember the scales? That was a glimpse of your shift. And no, the dragons don't look human. They look like dragons," she snickered.

"My shift?" I asked. "So I'll be able to shift back and forth?"

"That part no one knows because you're the first of your kind. I'm sure it will all be explained in the end."

"I think I saw Myrdinn when Eve gave me the Oraculus, but I can't remember his face. I only paid attention to Zordon." I felt a pang in my stomach.

"Well, once we find these keys you'll get to see him all you want," she replied.

"What if we don't make it?" I said quietly, helping her pack up our stuff.

"Don't think that way," she said with disapproval in her tone. "Although no one had ever thought to turn a dragon into a human, that didn't stop your father from trying. The love your parents felt for each other, combined with their magic, was so strong it gave your mother the ability to morph into a human and inevitably conceive you."

"So she's human now?" I felt even more confused.

"No, she's back in her dragon form. The magic wasn't strong enough to sustain childbirth. Once you were born, the talk of war began and she had to return home to help protect her kind. Save the questions for when we return…for now we have to keep moving." She lightly patted my shoulder and then moved to catch up with the rest of the crowd, leaving me to stand in shocked silence.

"It just keeps getting better and better," I said to myself, following behind as we began our descent downhill.

Lexi bravely walked up to Logan and tapped his arm. He turned to face her. I shook my head.

The grass was still gently swaying, and I could see the ruins not too far off in the distance. A sense of urgency washed over me.

I was so close to the end now. The keys and the cave, it was all so close to being mine. Then it would finally be over. Over enough for things to begin at least.

Chapter 26

~

Not Again...

WHEN THE SUN REACHED THE highest point in the sky, we finally looked upon the ruins. It felt like I was visiting Stonehenge or something. The massive boulders were unexplainably large, making me feel like a tiny ant.

Lexi left Logan's side and made her way back over to me. Although she acted like she was listening to me rant and rave about the beauty of where we stood, I could tell that she was sneaking glances around the two lovebirds to wink at Logan.

Molten lava had spewed from the nearby volcano and onto the ruins creating a grayish rippled river frozen in time, which Matt had explained to us was the original demise of the temple.

"Now everybody, watch your step," called Matt. We descended down the uneven rocky hill, using the car-size boulders as a bracing point while praying our shoes could grip the tiny pebbles that made up the ground.

"This is as physically straining as going uphill," I complained. *I will not fall, I will not fall*, I told myself. But I couldn't get the image of my face smacking into one of the boulders out of my head.

I watched jealously as Lexi moved like a mountain lion, knowing just when to push off of each rock.

At the bottom of the path was a patch of the greenest grass I had ever seen with tiny orchids sprouting up. It was like finding water in a desert to my eyes.

We were surrounded by weathered columns that held glimpses of once being majestic. It was history, and he let us touch each one in an attempt to give us the true meaning of where we stood.

"You're now standing on an ancient piece of history," Matt said with pride. "Lore about dragons and magic says that this very spot was home to Natives who believed in beings more powerful than the imagination."

The girl pried herself off of her boyfriend and asked, "Dragons? There isn't any proof of dragons. Why would a dragon even have a temple? I thought that they lived in caves and ate people."

Matt turned unwillingly towards her. "Well Kathy, some people also don't believe in Santa Claus or the Tooth Fairy. It's a personal preference called imagination," he replied indignantly.

She looked defeated as her boyfriend rubbed her back.

"On that note," he perked up, "let's head out. The altar's not too far from here."

We walked deeper into the ruins, Lexi and I trailing behind to study the columns, and found the group huddling around something. And then I felt the familiar humming vibration.

The second key, I thought with a rush.

Matt's voice carried on the wind as we came up behind them. "...and was carved out of Lapis Lazuli. The altar has been studied by many, the intricate design of the carvings telling a story that many decipher into their own meaning."

Lexi leaned into my ear and whispered, "As soon as they move on, we'll get the key."

I reached around Lexi and traced my fingers along one of the carvings, the missing piece in the picture.

The gouge was definitely big enough to suit a finger. I reached down and twirled the loose-fitting ring, wishing that everyone else would just disappear so I could put it in the missing space.

I eyed Lexi on the other side of the altar and made a motion for her to come near. She wormed her way over and crouched down next to me as the chatter from everyone floated above our heads.

"Here's the gouge."

"Watch this," she said as she balled her hands into two green-glowing fists. She closed her eyes and whispered a chant, slightly rocking back and forth. The green glow trailed up from her hands and into the air, touching each one of the tour members and wrapping around them as she whispered, "Oblivisci."

I had seen this before. After the first altercation with Soothe on the bus. She was bending them to her will like he had, replacing their memory of this moment with something else.

One by one they shook their heads, as if trying to see through a hazy fog. Matt said, "Okay, everyone, this way, follow me," and they all walked off, leaving Lexi and I alone.

"You have to teach me how to do that," I said excitedly-stating, not asking.

"It comes in handy from time to time." She winked. "Now, let's do this," she urged, holding up my hand and looking at the ring.

"Should I leave it on or take it off?"

"Take it off. Don't want to risk you losing a finger," she answered confidently.

I did as she said and held it up, both of us looking at it as if it were the most amazing thing we had ever seen before.

"Put it in," she rushed, pushing my elbow forward.

"Here goes nothing," I said as I leaned in and stuck the stone into the gouge.

For a moment nothing happened and we sat there, our breaths caught in our throats, waiting with fingers crossed.

"Any day now," she said anxiously.

And then the ring moved, twisting and pushing into the altar. Dust flew out of the hole and we jumped back, not sure what was going to happen.

The top of the altar shook and then cracked, a zigzag trail running down the middle. Light seeped through the crack, emphasizing the swirling dust that floated out from the ancient relic.

"What now?" I asked, my heart pounding wildly against my chest.

Then a shimmering light shot up towards the moon intensifying into a beam that was almost blinding.

"The key," I said, bolting forward and shoving my hand inside the crack. "This is the same thing that happened with the first," I quickly told Lexi as she came up beside me.

I reached as far as I could go, my fingertips skimming along a surface inside the altar. I weaved around, trying to feel for a stone but couldn't quite find it.

"I can't feel it anywhere," I said, my arm completely engulfed by the altar.

"Move…let me try something," said Lexi, her hands lit up again with her green energy. Her eyes focused on the altar, and the energy wrapped around the base.

The altar slowly began to open, her magic levitating the top of it into the air. "Quickly," she said, still focusing.

I leaned in and there it sat at the bottom, the beam of light making it hard to see.

"Got it?" she asked, her hands trembling.

"Yeah," I replied as I stepped back, "but we need to put this light out before someone sees it."

"I know. It's a beacon for evil to find us easily." She covered her hands over mine to help shield the light. "What did you do last time?"

"I just wished it would stop and channeled my energy to connect with it, and it disappeared on its own."

"Well, do that again," she instructed, smirking, still holding her hands over mine. I closed my eyes and tapped into the humming energy deep inside me.

The harsh sound of clapping hands broke my connection as it echoed around us.

"Good job,…Progeny," hissed Zane. "Seems like you won't be getting home."

Before I could stop it and before Lexi could register, he hurled an energy ball toward her, shouting, "Immobaltio!"

The spell hit her as her eyes widened in horror, and then she toppled over onto the hard earth with a loud thud.

"Lexi!" I shouted as I ran over to her.

"The key, Progeny, give me the key," Zane demanded, stalking towards us. It was still shining in the palms of my hands, as far as the eye could see.

I risked a glance at Lexi, her eyes wide with fear. I knew what I had to do. I had to protect the key. It was my only way back to Fenn. I shoved it in my pocket, the jean material dimming the radiance.

Zane's pulsating energy was a breaths length away from me. I turned to face him.

"Boo!"

I spun around and ran as fast as I could, searching for something to hide behind. We were surrounded by old, worn columns of stone. As I neared one, I darted to the left watching a whirl of energy whiz by, barely missing my feet.

My chest heaved in and out as I tried to pace myself and think. But there was no time for that. Only time for instinct.

A burly looking man stepped around the column next to me, flashing his snarling yellow teeth as he wove a ball of energy in his hands and threw it at me. I ducked as it zoomed by, shrieking and crawling around the column.

A pair of shoes entered my line of vision. "Hi," Zane snickered as his foot slammed into my face. Stars instantly swarmed my head as I flew backwards, up against a teetering column.

The other guy, with his slicked back black hair, snorted and said, "Look! The Progeny flies." Zane chuckled alongside him as I tried to sit up.

My head throbbed from the collision, a wave of nausea crashing down. I leaned to the side as my lunch resurfaced. This seemed to make them laugh even harder.

"Can you believe this is who's supposed to defeat my father?" Zane denounced as he his lip curled up with disgust.

They stood before me and stared down at my body as if I were nothing more than a defenseless dog left to die. I wiped the bile from my mouth, and tried to focus on their looming figures. When enough sense resurfaced, I scowled up at Zane.

He picked his leg up, his foot digging into my shoulder, pushing me back down. "I will only ask one more time…give me the key." With each word he dug his boot in a little deeper.

I felt the burn of anger building behind the screaming pain of my head and my swollen face. "No!" I said defiantly, the coppery blood pooling in my mouth.

The other guy started laughing again, crouching down to his

knees as he leaned into me and whispered, "You'd better do what he says, Progeny," he spat mockingly. "I don't think you'll like what comes next. We've got the other map."

This might be my last chance, I thought as I grit through the pain and once again met Zane's grim stare.

"No!" I repeated, pushing against his foot and trying my hardest not to wince from the pain it brought. I couldn't show weakness.

His eyes went tight. For a brief moment, I swear I saw Zordon instead of Zane. Then his hands came together as energy pulsed between them. "Good. I'd rather do this the hard way."

Two things happened at once. Lexi's green energy connected with Zane's head, throwing him back, and my own energy surfaced as I directed it towards the other guy.

My energy was infused with fire; the man danced wildly, shrieking in pain. The flames consumed him, slowly shutting off his agonizing cries as his body sizzled and writhed on the ground.

"You okay?" Lexi asked as she rushed over to me. I used her hand for support, my head pounding. Blood pooled in my mouth and I spit it out, trying to pull it together as Zane began to stir.

"I'm okay. We need to move."

She nodded, and threw my arm over her shoulder, pulling me away from the ruins.

"You still have the key?" she asked, letting me lean my weight on her.

"It's the one thing I did right," I weakly jested, running my hand over the outside of my jean pocket, just to be sure. It was still there.

"Okay, you need to merge with it or whatever you did last time so it will be safe." As we slowed to a stop, I held the stone in my hand, and focused my energy on it. In less time, I merged with the stone. "Good, now we need to get to the third. Zane will wake soon.

He must have the other map."

"He does. I heard the other guy with him mention it. Shouldn't we bind him or something?"

She took in a deep breath and then shook her head. "My energy is almost depleted after holding that altar open. I haven't yet mastered conserving it," she said with a weak smile. "We should check the map instead to make sure the other key hasn't been taken."

I agreed. I took the map out of my bookbag and unfolded it, holding it up to the second sun's light. An X appeared over the ruins, a small sliver of light shone through. The only illuminated spot left was the location of the third key. The cave.

"Let's catch back up with the group," she said as I folded the map back up.

A small rush of rocks slid down the hill next to us, a reminder that we were out in the open and alone.

"Zane," I whispered, tucking the map inside my bag and zipping it up.

"Stay here," Lexi mouthed as she slowly crept over to where the rocks had fallen. She came up behind one of the stone pillars, locking eyes with me. "Ready?" she asked as her fist began to glow.

I nodded, prepared for anything, and then she ran around, hands out, ready to attack.

"WHOAH!" Adam cried out. His hands were up in the air. "It's just me, I'm sorry. I saw you guys trail off and wanted to make sure you knew where the group was headed."

I let out a sigh, glad that it wasn't Zane. Lexi's hands fell to her side. "You can't just sneak up on people, you weirdo," she scolded as she shouldered past him.

"I wasn't sneaking. I…I was just going to let you know that we were heading to the woods now. What were you two doing anyway?" he asked as I moved into his line of sight.

"We umm…we saw something cool," I began.

"Oh yeah? What?"

"Yeah, it umm…I think it was an animal or something," I said sheepishly.

"An animal?" he asked distractedly, looking over at Lexi.

"Yeah, it was some kind of strange animal, but we never got a good look. Oh well," she covered, winking in my direction.

"That's odd," he noted, his face puzzled. "I could've sworn I saw a bright light back there. You didn't see that too?"

I stumbled only for a moment, and then said, "Light? No. We didn't see any light, did we Lexi?" I said, searching her eyes for a good answer.

"Nope. No light. We were probably too caught up with trying to find the animal," she said with a laugh, playing it off.

"So is that why her face is all beat up?" he asked Lexi before turning back to me pointedly. "What kind of animal was it? Looks like you've been punched."

More like kicked, I thought bitterly as the forgotten pain pulsed again. I lightly touched it, wincing from the open wound Zane left on my forehead. "I uh…I fell."

"That's quite a fall," he commented, moving to touch it. I turned away before his fingertips made contact.

Lexi started giggling nervously. "Yeah, I barely caught her in time. Can you believe it? She's such a klutz," she quickly threw in.

She started walking again, gesturing for us to follow. I didn't hesitate.

"I'm fine, really," I reassured as we neared the edge of the group.

Logan called out Adam's name. "Glad to hear. Can't risk losing you," Adam added, walking alongside of me. Something strange flickered in his eyes. Like he meant something more than that. Like he knew something. He turned and left.

"What was that all about?" Lexi whispered. "Does he know something?"

"I was going to ask you the same thing," I said under my breath.

"You know…he does look familiar, but for the life of me I can't place him. Oh well," she shrugged, "for now we need to focus on the key. Zane will be waking."

Waking and out for my blood, I thought.

Chapter 27

~

The Full Moon is Coming

WE CAUGHT UP WITH THE group, and tried our best to blend in, but I couldn't shake the anxiety I felt. I felt exhausted after the attack and tried my best to keep up.

I couldn't help the flurry of thoughts that raced through my mind. What if we don't get to the third key in time? What if Zane wakes up? What if he doesn't care if there are witnesses? The questions were never-ending and the answers were becoming fewer and fewer.

I tried to focus as we trailed our way through the forest. But I found myself looking over my shoulder, every sound turning into a possible attack. Time was running out. And Zane was on his way.

Lexi was just as frantic. She whispered, "Inducto," and I saw Matt's eyes light up with her green energy. He looked forward and told us it was time to move on.

"To the cave," he said.

"If something happens and you need to hide, say 'Obscuro.' It's a cloaking spell that will hide you," Lexi instructed.

"But we haven't practiced," I replied franticly.

"Rory, you don't need practice. You are strong." Her confidence bore into me and then she looked around. "Did you feel that?" she asked. She tilted her head. An energy pulsed through the air, one that I had felt before.

"The darkness?" I questioned.

"Yes. It feels like…"

"Zordon," I finished for her. I knew the feeling all too well. It was a feeling that lingered with me ever since I could remember. Only recently had I been able to place its source.

"Do you think he's here?" she asked, the panic unmistakably lacing her voice.

My heart raced in fear as the light from the tree line filtered through the tiny leaves, casting shadows on the ground. I wiped my sweating face onto the end of my shirt as dizziness sent my mind spinning. I was tired, the anxiety of the past week wearing me down.

"I don't know, but I don't feel so well," I replied. My Oraculus was searing through the back of my bookbag. Sharp shooting pains pierced into my brain. I staggered behind everyone, gripping a tree trunk to keep from falling. The bark felt harsh on my skin, scratching and tearing from the pressure of my restraint.

"Aurora," Lexi shouted, reaching for me as I slid down the tree to rest while my brain pulsed and my heart raced. I was hoping that I could just breathe the pain away, but it wasn't letting up.

The pressure behind my eyes felt too strong, and my blood felt on fire. I leaned my head back against the tree, scared of what was happening, keeping my hands gripped tightly onto the straps of my bookbag. He was pulling me to him.

"Aurora, don't worry. I'm here, and I won't let anything happen to you. Just breathe," she coaxed.

Heat was continually beating through my bookbag, causing my shirt to cling to my back in dampness.

"Something's wrong," I said, my hands trembling uncontrollably. It was coming from the Oraculus. "My bag—take the Oraculus out," I said, straining against the sharp pain.

She leaned me forward, pulled it out, and set it on my lap. The book was literally vibrating, a black haze of energy radiating off of it.

"What's happening?" she asked, fear lacing her voice.

"I don't know, Lexi…it's pulling me, whatever's binding us together. I can't fight it…" I admitted, feeling the last bit of grip I had in my realm leaving.

I tilted my head forward, squinting to see through the pain. Lexi's fists were by her side emitting her green energy as she repetitively chanted, "Refutum vehemtia." Then everything went black.

I was back in the Lyceum watching Zordon pace back and forth on a cloud of smoke. There was something different about him this time. He was panicking.

Worry lines were embedded underneath his eyes. His usual oil-slicked hair was a chaotic mess, his hands constantly plunging through, gripping and yanking as if to pull it out. I instantly tucked myself in a shadowed corner, hoping that I wouldn't be spotted.

Just as I was submerging myself into the shadows, his frantic pacing stopped and his back stiffened. He slowly turned in my direction, keeping his face pointed to the ground. And then his eyes lifted toward mine and locked, freezing us both. The blood pumped through my veins so hard my heart echoed in my ears.

He blinked a couple of times, as if trying to determine if I was real, rubbing his eyes and shaking his head in astonishment. In between his blinks, I managed to back completely into the corner and silently chanted, "Obscuro...obscuro...obscuro."

My hands emitted a soft glow of blue, and tiny blue sparkles cascaded around me. I felt them cover me like a shield, a shield from him. The rush of power was momentary.

He gazed towards the spot where I sat, squinting hard, and then huffed angrily before turning his back on me again.

A disgusting smell tainted the air as scurrying footsteps rang through the hull. A scraggly old man with one eye and matted hair ran in and knelt before Zordon.

Zordon's back straightened and he ran his fingers through his hair, quickly pulling himself together as he resumed his demeaning stature.

"The Dark Saar is here, correct, Sayer?" It was his Seer.

"Yes, my Liege. They just arrived," answered Sayer, bowing his head.

"And the meeting has been arranged?"

"Yes, my Liege," repeated Sayer.

"Good...good. This meeting will be my next move forward," Zordon replied, turning his back on Sayer and moving towards the mantelpiece, gripping the edge like it was his only salvation.

"My Liege," Sayer spoke, though barely audible, "I overheard one of them talking about an exchange that is to be made. You never said anything about an exchange. Is this something we should worry about?"

Zordon turned back to face Sayer. "An exchange? Hmmm...I thought the killing of the Draconta was enough. Plenty of souls to go around."

He stared into the distance, pensive, and twisted his cane in slow circles, black sparks shooting out from the tip then fizzling out after hitting the ground.

Then he turned back to Sayer and answered lightly, "No, I will

hear them out. They may have something I want in this exchange."
A smirk peeked at the corners of his mouth.

"But, my Liege, to exchange with the Dark Saar..." Sayer
scrambled, "the only thing they could possibly want is one's soul."
He bent his head down again and backed up a step, careful not to
make eye contact.

"Are you suggesting I'm an imbecile?" Zordon asked quietly.

"My Liege, please don't," but before he could finish, the sparks
that were fizzling out of his cane, shot into Sayers' chest, freezing
him. His body writhed in pain and a gut-wrenching cry left his lips.

"My Liege...I," he bit out as his fingers curled into one another awkwardly and his neck jerked from left to right.

"Liege what, Sayer? You think I'm not a step ahead? How dare
you insult me so," he shouted while striding over to yell in Sayer's
face. Spit flew from his mouth. He plunged his cane into the ground
as he shouted, "Afflictum."

Another uncontrollable cry escaped Sayer. "NEVER doubt me!
Better men than you have died for questioning me."

And then the energy stopped as he turned, moving back to the
mantelpiece. Sayer dropped lifelessly to the ground, desperately trying to collect his breath.

"And what of the Shadows?" asked Zordon as if nothing had
just happened.

"The...the Shadows are here as well, my Liege...residing in
the forest." His voice was hoarse and weak. He straightened out his
back and stood once more but kept his head pointed down.

"I see. Nothing but darkness resides out my window. And that
shall be all the Draconta see as well. It's the beginning of the end for
them," said Zordon, confidently.

"My Liege, I must warn you. It has been heavily rumored that a
Seer is working for the Draconta. A female. I've sent out scouts, try-

ing to find out who she is. Her aura is familiar yet I can't quite read it or place it. There may be some kind of cloaking spell around her."

"A female Seer staying with the Draconta? Of all the things I thought I'd never see," said Zordon in disbelief. "Nevertheless, it won't matter. They cannot defeat my army, and I will not rest until every last dragon is dead." He placed a figurine that looked a lot like him on a map that lay on the table in his room.

"Soon enough I will be standing inside their castle with the Stone of Immortality in my grasp." His hands glowed as black as his deep evil. A fog rose up over the map and spread like a morning mist. I could hear faint, distant cries coming from the paper as figurines of dragons lifted from the corner of the table and flew over the raised castle. The fog reached up to where the dragons were flying and engulfed them, pulling them down into it. Zordon's menacing laugh penetrated the room and my soul.

How could I defeat him?

The fog had taken over the entire map and then a flashing light appeared where the Zordon figurine had stood.

"Yes, it's so close I can taste it. Soon, Sayer, I will be immortal, and then no one, not even The Fates, can stop me from attaining my right."

"The girl, my Liege?" Sayer let the words hang on a whisper.

"What of her? Zane should be back soon with report of her death. And besides, the full moon is tonight. As long as she is kept from the light of the moon, she will remain over there. Now go find Gabe." He twisted his cane and all the figurines dropped back onto the table. Then he turned and left the room.

I waited a moment before creeping out from the shadow of the corner. I felt naked standing in his open room, but I didn't know how to get back.

And what about Zane? If he escaped wherever Lexi put him

and reaches Zordon, then Zordon will know that I'm not dead. He'll do everything in his power to prevent me from reaching the cave. I needed to know what Zordon's next move was, and the only way I could find out was to follow him...and risk getting caught.

Lexi wouldn't approve, or Fenn for that matter, but that didn't matter. I needed to take matters into my own hands. I was, after all, the one chosen to protect. So this had to be my decision.

I heard Gabe's voice carrying down the hall and slowly poked my head around the white-marbled corner. The dimly lit stairs were only wide enough to hold one. The light of the fire holders cast eerie shadows against the wall.

What if I go down and someone comes up at the same time? I wasn't sure if I was visible or not, and Zordon spotting me was the last thing I needed. The murmuring of voices propelled my curiosity so I took a chance and hurried down the steps on my tiptoes.

When light broke at the end of the staircase, I edged up to the archway and slowly peeked out. Goosebumps painted my skin from the cold air that breezed around me.

Zordon, Sayer, and Gabe were facing away from me so I quietly rushed over to the other side of the archway and hid in a small cluster of shadows.

"But, my Liege," said Gabe. His voice was so comforting, like I'd heard it many times before and knew he would protect me. But he was on Zordon's side...right?

"Do I need to express the annoyance I feel when you doubt me?" Zordon threatened, gripping his cane.

"No, my Liege, I'm sorry. I just thought that having Kaede and the leader of the Dark Saar in the same room would push Kaede away from aiding us." He kept his eyes to the ground. "The Dark Saar is the worst kind of dark magic and not everyone wants to be mixed up with that."

"As I've said before, Kaede came all the way from the Orient to help put an end to the Draconta. And I have my motives for bringing him here. He will feel more comfortable if I make him think I am including him in all my plans. A bounty of souls is what I've promised and not just of the dragon kind. Do you understand what I'm saying?" asked Zordon, lifting his brow questioningly. Gabe nodded as realization played over his face. "Good. You may leave."

Gabe bowed and took his exit. I didn't want him to go.

"My Liege," inquired Sayer, who had remained almost invisible throughout their entire conversation. Zordon glanced up as if he hadn't realized Sayer was still there.

"His fate somehow ties into the girl's. I cannot read him, therefore I do not trust him." Sayer wobbled over around the table to stand closer to Zordon.

"He is my second in command, Sayer. That is a high accusation you make against him. One that you should tread carefully with." He tilted his cane towards Sayer's trembling face. "Leave," he motioned, pointing towards the door.

Zane stumbled in a second later, my heart skipping a few beats in fear. He made it back. "Sit," commanded Zordon. He never turned to face his son.

Dirt was smudged all over Zane's face and clothes, blood dripping from his nose and the edge of his mouth.

"Just where have you been?" asked Zordon.

"Well before I found her I was thrown to the Harpy's," Zane said shamefaced, wiping his mouth and smearing blood across his face.

"Harpy's? What in The Fates' names were you doing there?"

He was lying. He already found me. His eyes fell to the floor. "I need more men," Zane half-whispered. He quickly continued as Zordon's energy began to glow around him. "There was an unex-

pected interference. Alexis is with her, the girl that worked in the market and lives with the Draconta."

Zordon began pacing, *fury building in a haze around him. "That's irrelevant. You're saying you failed in killing her, and you let a girl from the market—a mere servant—defeat you? The full moon is tonight. Why are you sitting here in front of me?"* The energy *pulsed around him, quickly growing like a dark storm. It swarmed Zane, picking him up into the air, and Zordon shouted, "Pulsecto!"* Zane's *cry pierced my ears as I braced the wall.*

The energy pulsed *throughout the room, shocking me to the point of dizziness. I tried to hold onto the wall for support to keep from falling and giving myself away, but Zordon's power grew, choking both Zane and me.*

I fell forward, barely able to keep myself from smacking my face against the marbled floor. Zane's eyes shot to mine as he writhed and hollered out in pain. There was nothing I could do to help myself. I felt weak and lost.

"The girl," Zane screamed, *grabbing at his throat in agony as his body twisted in all directions. "The girl...the girl."*

"The girl, what? The girl will find the keys and make it to the cave in time? That's what I foresee," shouted Zordon, *twisting his cane as another cry broke from Zane. "I should kill you right now for failing me and putting a strain on my plans!"*

"Here," Zane choked out. *"She's...here."* I *tried to move but was frozen in place by both fear and the same choking pain as Zane. My hand was at my throat, and I was gasping for air, trying to push away Zordon's magic. But it was too strong.*

"Father...please...don't kill me...Just...just look," he *screamed, pointing with a contorted hand in my direction.*

Zordon's *head followed. His eyes widened when they landed on me and then he smiled, twisting his cane.*

My body flew towards him, propelled into the air next to Zane's, held in the same black cloud of energy. Pain like I'd never felt tore at my limbs, blood trailing from my ears and nose, down my face. I screamed and panicked. This was it. I was going to die, and he was going to live. Zane's body dropped to the ground, but my torture continued. Maybe the prophecy was right. Maybe I was the one who was supposed to die.

"So I did see you back in my room," Zordon said gleefully. "How did you manage to get in here?"

"I...don't know," was all I could squeeze out in between the painful shocks. But I did know. The prophecy...the canvas to your mortal soul...the connection to your immortal enemy. The Oraculus connected us.

"Hmm...something to ponder then," he said as he walked a circle around me, taking all of me in.

"Your name," he demanded from me. I tried to fight the urge to answer but lost control as another shock blasted through me.

"Aurora!" I yelled against my will.

He smiled.

"You're what they prophesied as my downfall...Aurora?" he asked, my name slithering from his mouth. A low chuckle escaped from him. "Too bad," he said, unmercifully sending another electric shock through me. I could feel myself slipping away, falling into nothingness. I was too weak to fight and almost to the point of passing out from the pain.

"I would have preferred if you put up a fight, entertain me even a little bit. But I will settle for killing you instead. This is just too easy." He stalked over to me and stared for a moment as I floated in pain.

"Oh well," he said with a shrug and then slammed his cane into the ground. I braced myself for the last round of pain, for my

death that he'd promised, but there I still remained, floating and alive.

His face fell as he took a step back.

A white light surrounded me, obscuring the black energy. "*Oblitero Mortifico!*" shouted Zordon, slamming his cane back into the ground.

Again nothing happened.

The pain I felt left, now a distant and disturbing memory. In its place I felt the edge of the dream. I was waking up. I wasn't going to die after all. "*My Liege...look,*" cried Zane.

I was disappearing.

"*NO!*" yelled Zordon, trying everything in his power to keep me from leaving. He threw his arms around me in an attempt to pull me back down, but he went through me as if I were transparent.

The sound of his voice grew distant as the light became blindingly bright. "*Go get her and bring her back or it's your death,*" he demanded.

And then I was gone.

Chapter 28

~

The Cave

WITH A GASP I WOKE from my vision clutching my throat. I frantically felt myself all over, making sure everything was still intact. The book was burning against my lap, a pain that I welcomed.

"Aurora, Aurora," Lexi said, shaking my shoulders. "Are you okay? I tried to break the energy, but it was too strong. Then you disappeared, but I could faintly hear you screaming." The words hurried out of her as she stared into my eyes.

I took a calming breath, overwhelmed with gratitude to see her friendly face. I had come so close to losing my life. And now Zordon knew who I was.

"He knows my name," I said, eyes focused on the rotting forest ground. I was still trying to grasp everything that had just happened, my mind scanning through a million mental images.

"Who?" she asked.

"Zordon…he saw me. He wasn't supposed to, but Zane went back and-" I felt panic rising up once again at the pained memory. "And Lexi, he tortured him and it was so much power that it consumed me, and then I fell, and then they both saw me. Lexi, Zane is coming. I don't think he will fail this time."

Her face went white.

"That shouldn't have happened. You should have been protected. Aurora, if something had happened... You should have said something. Your life is my responsibility," she scolded, turning her face away from me.

"Lexi, I'm sorry. It all happened so fast." I stood, brushing the leaves from my pants, not knowing what else to say. The sun was already gone, the moon rising off in the distance. How long had I been gone?

"I know," she said. Her voice was full of regret. "I saw you disappear and had to do a little magic of my own so no one else would notice. You were gone forever. It was the worst few hours of my life," she broke off, staring ahead to where the group was. "And there was nothing I could do to help besides hope that you'd find your way back."

"Why was I gone for so long? It didn't feel that long," I said.

"I don't know, Rory. I guess time runs differently between realms." She looked vacantly around, seeming lost in thought.

"The Dark Saar was with Zordon and someone by the name of Kaede? Do you know him?"

She nodded. "He's one of the four Lieges, like Zordon, but over in the Orient part of the Rebell Islands. They must be planning the war together."

"I'm so sorry, Lexi." We started to move forward. I didn't know what else I could have done to prevent the war.

"It's not your fault. We just really need to find the last key in time for the full moon. I thought we'd have more time than this. And since they know where we're headed...who's to say Zordon won't want to come himself?"

I shook my head confidently. "He won't come. I heard him tell Zane it was his last chance. Besides, he has more important things to worry about."

"Either way, we need to be even more cautious now."

We caught up to the group. Everyone was happily talking in front of a campfire that was close to where we had met Soothe the day before. There were only a few hours left until the full moon.

The forest was lined with many types of trees, the rising moon's glow filtering through. I almost felt protected by the coverage and prayed that it would keep us out of sight.

Lexi and I couldn't help anxiously looking around every few minutes, searching for Zane.

"We have to look relaxed," Lexi said, interrupting the quiet of the forest.

"I'm trying, Lexi," I replied, rolling my eyes in the process. The strain on time was too much.

"Look," she said, holding my arm. "I don't blame you. I blame myself. And you coming face to face with Zordon..." She bit her lip. "That never should have happened, but you got away. You escaped his wrath. You're our only hope."

"I appreciate the pep talk, really, but I don't know what you're hoping for. The only reason why Zordon didn't kill me was because of some mysterious beam of white light," I amended quietly. "The chances of me stopping him are getting slimmer by the minute. His power is too strong." I pulled my arm out of her grip.

"A beam of light? That's odd. And you didn't produce it?"

"No, I didn't. I was preparing for my death," I pointed out bitterly.

She let out a small huff. "Sounds like someone helped you,"

she said thoughtfully, ignoring my attitude. "Someone extremely powerful and all knowing…" she trailed off.

"Lucky me. If only they had shown up sooner. If only someone would just get me to the damn cave so I can at least have my full powers and make it back. And…" I said, trying to level my heightening voice, "if only this whole wild goose chase—finding all the keys before the full moon—weren't happening, then maybe we wouldn't be in this predicament and Zordon wouldn't know my face or my name." I let out a pent-up sigh.

Lexi frowned. "Look, dwelling on the past won't change anything," she said, her tone reproachful. "We have a mission and we need to succeed. Right now we need to get away from this group and get to the cave." She lifted a brow and then moved away from the fire towards the waterfall.

"…Ready to roast marshmallows for the full moon tonight?" Matt congenially chatted with the group. "The waterfall provides a perfect clearing to see the sky away from all the light pollution."

I quickly followed Lexi as we tip-toed away from them, anxious to get this part over with. We stripped down to our underwear, and I shoved our clothes into my backpack, thankful that it was waterproof. I would not be leaving it on the bank, and the only way to the cave was swimming and then climbing up the algae-covered rocks that were continually sprayed from the oncoming rush of water. Could they have made this any more difficult?

I glanced up at the moss-green rocks and winced as a vision of me slipping paraded through my mind. But not even fear could keep the shadow of the cave behind the falls from calling my name. I ran towards the water and dove in.

After the initial gnawing chill of the water, tiny voices sprang to life underneath, humming something that I couldn't quite understand. I looked for Lexi and found her to my right. I motioned to my ear, asking her if she could hear it too. She shook her head no.

I hesitated, listening more closely, and then surfaced for air. She popped up next to me, shouting above the waterfall, "What'd you hear?"

"A humming sound but not from the waterfall. More like a choir?" I shouted back, treading water.

"Could be the spirit of the Natives, follow it." She went back under. I took a deep breath and followed her, swimming towards the rocks that would lead us to the cave.

Moments later I swam up to the surface near a rock and took in a huge gulp of air. Lexi surfaced as well.

"This is it," I shouted, ready for the next step, trying to find a grip against the slime on the rocks.

I noticed her face tilt up, sniffing the air as her eyes moved back and forth, scanning the area.

"He's here, isn't he?" I stated more than asked.

"It's only a matter of time until he finds us," she answered. "His energy is strong, like he's laced with something."

"Drugs?" I asked, not sure what he could be laced with.

"A potion," she replied. She quickly found her grip and pulled up, extending her hand for me.

"Oh right, a potion," I muttered darkly as she pulled me up and helped me find my footing. Being so close made it real. I definitely did not want to die before my time.

The humming picked up as we carefully climbed each rock, in constant danger of slipping from the heavy spray of water.

I could now make out what was being said. "Come, Aurora. Your fate awaits you."

We were as high up as we could go, pulling ourselves up onto a thin ledge. "We have to scoot towards the cave. Be careful," Lexi stressed. "Pay attention, and do not lose your footing. My magic can only do so much."

I nodded and kept my back as far against the rock wall as possible, gripping the sides with my hands. Inch by inch we made our way until we were behind the falls, the water plummeting serenely away.

"Wow," my voice echoed off the cave walls as we came around the corner. It was full of giant sparkling crystals that hung from the ceiling. I had never seen anything like it, besides in my dreams.

"Keep moving," commanded Lexi as she came up beside me. "The key is in here somewhere."

It was so enchanting, like a small piece of heaven. The distant drips of water, falling from the ceiling, played like an orchestra.

There was a hole somewhere near the back where a small beam of the moon's light shined through, illuminating the crystals into millions of tiny jeweled stars.

I moved closer to the middle where Lexi stood. I couldn't feel the vibration like I had with the other two keys. The annoying humming sound was missing.

"What?" she asked, noticing the puzzled look on my face.

"Are you sure it's supposed to be in here?" I asked, moving slowly about the cave.

"Yes, Rory, you saw the map. This was the last marked spot," she replied.

"But I don't feel it," I admitted, trying to push down the dread. "Lexi," I began, turning to face her, "there is another map out there… what if…" I broke off.

"No. Don't think like that. It's here. It has to be," she went on, but her tone was skeptical.

I wasn't convinced. I knew that it was gone. I slowly slunk to my knees, sitting in a heap on the damp floor.

"That's it, Lex, no going back for me," I said ruefully. I reached into my bag to pull out my clothes. Suddenly I felt cold with despair.

"Here," I said, tossing Lexi her clothes as well. She was still walking around, searching for the key.

"Aurora, just take a deep breath. We have at least an hour until the full moon is at its peak. That gives us plenty of time," she tried to encourage, but there was a transparent sadness in her voice.

"You know you're just as annoyingly optimistic as Fenn was," I said, feeling a tantrum come on, "This whole thing was a joke. To think that I, Aurora, could actually be useful...what was I thinking? You know I might as well..." I broke off as footsteps echoed off the walls.

"Hide," Lexi whispered, shoving me behind a crystal. Her hands instantly lit up. "Who's there?" she called out. "Show yourself."

We both waited, my mind racing with possibilities. I peeked around the crystal, anxious to know who was in here with us.

Soothe stepped out. Lexi and I both exhaled at the same time.

"Soothe, what are you doing? Are you crazy?" asked Lexi in a weak voice. "Don't answer that, we all know you are," she threw in with a wink in my direction.

"Troubled?" he asked, staring directly at me.

My head dropped in defeat. "The key is gone," I admitted.

"Is it?" he asked dubiously.

"Umm...yeah...that's what I said. I don't feel it here. Now we're screwed," I replied harshly.

"I wouldn't be so sure," he countered. "Your Oraculus?"

"In my bag." I pulled it out and noticed the quiet hum it was giving off. To my left, a reflection of light caught my eye.

"What was that?" asked Lexi, noticing it as well.

"Maybe a doorway or something," said Soothe, casually resting against a crystal.

"But we need the keys to unlock it, Sea Brain," said Lexi.

"Yes, but there may be something more for our savior to find besides her way back home," he sneered. "I am after all the one who foresaw her future."

I glanced back down at my Oraculus and suddenly knew what he was talking about, as if he had planted the very thought in my mind. I smiled back at him and stepped towards the answer.

"Fire," I whispered.

Chapter 29

The Shift

THE TIPS OF MY FINGERS lit up with the heavenly flame, energy pulsing out of me. I held my hand out towards the cave wall where I had seen the glint of a reflection. The flames jumped off my fingers and onto the wall, instantly engulfing the surface.

My fingertips sizzled, purple sparks shooting off as lettering inscribed itself into the wall. Lexi came up beside me, her face flickering in the firelight, her amazement mirroring my own.

"Good job," said Soothe from behind us, clapping sarcastically. "So the Progeny isn't such a disappointment after all."

I ignored his criticism as the flames died off, leaving tiny trails of smoke and a glowing message.

"I smell it," I said looking back to Lexi.

"The magic?" she asked. I nodded. "Everyone's magic has a different scent," she explained.

"It smells like pine needles and a cold winter's day if that makes any sense." I leaned in and took a deep whiff, scrunching my nose at the dust.

Then I stepped back to read.

My Little Flame,

　　I'm so proud that you've made it this far. Life, I'm sure, hasn't been easy for you but has strength-ened and protected you.

　　By now you should have all the keys and will seal your fate inside this cave. This must be your choice. That is all I have wanted and now ask from you—that you choose your own destiny. I have planted all these steps to give you ample time to de-cide if this is what you really want.

　　To cross back over, the keys must be placed in-side the port key which is in the doorway below. But in order to do that you must first reunite with your powers. Great pain will come with this.

　　Be brave.

I stammered back a step before plopping onto the ground. *Great pain?* Lexi walked up behind me, reading the words on the wall, and then sat down next to me.

"That's the only thing Astral wanted."

"What's that?" I asked blankly.

"For this all to be your choice. He made it very clear that you need to choose and not be forced into anything…no matter what." She turned and stared at the side of my face.

It was the only way back to Fenn. But great pain? I took in a brave breath. It didn't matter. I would suffer anything if it meant I would have the chance to tell Fenn my true feelings.

"Take a chance," said Soothe, still standing off in the distance. "What have you got to lose?"

"But we *don't* have all the keys and barely any time to find the last one," I reminded.

"Do you think I would have come here if I thought you wouldn't make it? The key will come," he said certainly.

"Our people are waiting for you, Aurora, waiting for liberation," Lexi added, trying to take the edge off.

I took in a deep breath and then gave her a reassuring smile. "Thanks, Lexi. Thanks for being here with me."

I walked past her to the wall and placed my hand on the hexagon etched in an ancient pattern. This must be the doorway. It had appeared from the fire, just below Astral's message.

My hand felt hot, and I watched as the etchings burned and sunk deeper and deeper into the rock, opening like a door going inward and then sideways, revealing a tiny hole. I bent down and stared into the hole, squinting to see what was inside. A small box. On the lid were two dragons intertwined at the neck and tail.

"That's your father's family crest," said Lexi, hovering over my shoulder. "Open it!"

The discovery was exhilarating and scary as my hands trembled in anticipation. I un-clasped the lid and braced myself for the great pain to come as a white light peeked out at me.

So far no pain. So I opened it all the way.

Suddenly the box became as heavy as weighted lead, falling from my hands. It crashed onto the cavern floor as the wood splintered into thousands of pieces and revealed an orb. The orb shot into the air—a sphere of light hovering before me, illuminating the cave walls.

A high-pitched screeching pierced my ears as my hands shot up to cover them. I couldn't make out what it was. I'm not sure I even wanted to.

I turned to Lexi. "Do you hear that?"

"Hear what?" she asked.

"The voices? I can't make out what they're saying."

"No, I don't hear anything. Soothe?" Her face turned back to where Soothe was, but he was gone.

"I knew we couldn't rely on him. Look, either grab it or don't, we don't have time. Zane is close, I can feel him. This is it…make a choice."

I reached out and grabbed the orb, instantly swarmed by a multitude of heavenly voices all combined into one. The awful screeching ceased. A voice spoke, a woman's voice that sounded as heavenly as a thousand angels singing all at once.

"Two fates merged by a deceitful brother, creating Immortality's revenge is how you came to be.
A mask of evil hides your other half's true intentions, intentions that you must find and see.
A journey you must take, overcoming your biggest fears. Choices you must make which will bring heady tears.
The all-knowing has planted the seed of a dangerous trade. The trade can't be made or hope will fade.
Go home to find me, hidden by a mother's love when He disappears.
Or fight alone and live in fear."

The illuminated orb slowly floated down and into my hands. I looked to Lexi, but before I could say anything, an overwhelming affliction shot throughout me as the orb floated a few inches away. I fell to the ground.

"What are you guys doing in here?" asked Logan as he came around the corner of the ledge. I twitched and moaned, unable to speak as Lexi moved to stand protectively in front of me. I couldn't make out the words of their exchange. Suddenly the amulet lit up and seared into my chest.

"Get it off, get it off!" I shrieked while trying to pull the amulet off, but it wouldn't budge. My chest was glowing red along with the stone, black markings were inscribed into my skin. A low growl left my lips as the dragon in me acknowledged the amulet's power.

The cave rumbled, the crystals rattling and the ground shaking. My body shook with the earth, vibrating and making the pain worse. I bit the inside of my cheek, the coppery taste glazing my tongue.

"Oh no," said Lexi, turning away from Logan and kneeling beside me.

I felt my insides ignite causing me to curl into myself. My bones began cracking and realigning, a scream ripped from my throat.

Lexi whispered, "Mendaro," as the pain consumed every piece of my experience. Her spell wasn't working, her green energy unable to penetrate what was happening to me. For the second time, I really felt as if I was dying.

Flames surged throughout my blood, but this time it wasn't comforting. My fingers dug into the palms of my hands while my mind deliriously spun.

"Jesus, what is wrong with her?" asked Logan, taking a drag from a cigarette. I could barely make him out between the spasms of pain and bone shifting. Then I started convulsing, my body slamming against the rock floor, adding to my misery. My skin stretched over my back as something grew beneath my shoulder blades.

Lexi could only watch as I flailed uncontrollably. Her hands hesitated, reaching out to me like she was afraid, and then she plunged them forward but was hindered by an unforeseen protective barrier.

Then everything went blurry. My head pounded, preventing me from thinking rationally. I felt everything slip away. I was dying.

"Eww," I heard Logan comment as my eyes glazed over, searing like liquid fire. "Her eyes are changing to red."

"Just shut the hell up and GO!" screamed Lexi. As my bones moved beneath my skin, she could actually see what I felt.

Logan let out a girly scream and added, "Holy Shit! She's a flipping alien!"

"It…hurts…help," was all I could muster as another surge of bones cracking and fire burning waved over me. I felt the scales once again rushing up my arms. I wanted it to stop, but the dragon stirred inside me. It wanted out. It wanted to take over.

"I wasn't prepared for this," whispered Lexi in my ear.

The cave was still shaking, the earth shifting beneath us. My hearing was fading, the pounding behind my eyes so intense I thought my head would explode. I could make out Lexi and Logan moving back and forth, but I had no idea what they were saying. I looked up to the cave ceiling and screamed in agony as the scales finished covering my entire body. Another gut-wrenching scream left me as the skin on my back ripped apart. Wings popped out, and I rolled over on all fours, trying to give them the space they required. A rush of hot tears stung my cheeks. I pleaded and screamed for the unbearable pain to end.

And then I heard a man's voice. It was deep and raspy. "Aurora," it called sagely. It was faint, but it was there.

"Please," I barely stammered out, squinting at the massive form that was standing in the distance. I reached my hand out, knowing that the person behind the voice would make the pain go away. "Aurora, my youngling, you are reborn. You are my child," said the raspy voice.

"It hurts," I cried as my body grew in size. Muscles that had never been now sculpted my thighs.

"One's birth usually doesn't feel good," the voice said sensibly. The form moved towards me. The cave shook with each gigantic step he took. Whoever he was, he wasn't human. His shape was that of a dragon and it reflected off the giant crystals, creating a herd of him. "Who are you?" I asked, trying to hold back a scream as more bones shifted and aligned.

"I am the fifth brother. I am your creator," he said soothingly.

"You're a dragon?" I asked, my voice quivering.

He chuckled deeply. "I appear how you wish to see me. I am here to bless you, my child. You are my only hope at restoring the balance." He moved closer, each step rattling the cave's floor. His voice was soothing, easing the ache from the constant pain.

"Will it always hurt?" I asked, trying to gain control of my mind.

The Fate laughed, causing a few crystals to fall and crash into a thousand pieces. "Not always. You are my greatest creation yet. You are a Draconta hybrid. You are the only one to ever control the flame."

As he bent his snout towards me, I smelled the fumes leaving his nostrils. Then he opened his mouth and roared, flames encompassing my entire body.

I heard Lexi scream as my body was lifted into the air, surrounded by a cocoon of fire. The flames licked my skin and sealed my change. Surprisingly, it didn't hurt. Instead, it felt cleansing. And through all of it, the one face that stayed present in my mind was Zordon's. His hollow laugh echoed through my brain as if encouraging the pain to swell deeper. But I wasn't going to let that happen. I was of Draconta now.

"I don't know what to do," Lexi cried, her green glow flowing towards my body without helping in the slightest. "Astral didn't say this would happen."

I didn't understand how my senses could suddenly be so acute. I was almost aware of things a moment before they happened. I was coming into my powers.

I saw Zane flash before my eyes. Danger was coming.

"The key!" I yelled as the flames died down around me, glad that my voice remained the same.

The moon was now visible through the hole in the cave ceiling. It was huge, illuminating the entire cave like a sparkling treasure. I looked back for the Fate, but he had vanished.

"We don't have it," Lexi shouted back.

"No, I can hear it," I confirmed, the humming rattling my eardrums. I tried to get up, the pain slowly fading away.

"Aurora, that's imposs-"

"Looking for this?" interrupted Zane's voice, his hand holding the third key out in front of him.

Chapter 30

~

The Return

LEXI JUMPED IN ANGER AND shouted, "Immoblatio," throwing an energy ball that caught him off guard. He was too busy staring wide-eyed at me to notice what she was doing.

I was on all fours in a heap on the ground. Without clothes and covered in gleaming red scales. Far more reptilian than human. I barely had time to note that my fingers had become claws.

Zane's body flew towards the back of the cave, the echo of the slam reverberating around us. He quickly regained his footing and threw the same spell at Logan, causing him to fall face flat, unconscious but hopefully alive.

Lexi screamed. She screamed at Zane calling him every name in the book and then shouted, "Afflictum," which he deflected as easily as he had in the forest.

Her attempt to make him focus on her instead of me failed. He ran towards me, but she was just as quick, standing in between the two of us just as the moon ray touched the orb that remained hovering over me.

"You're too late. What's done is done. She has the powers now, Zane, so go back to daddy and whine. Better yet, die because you know better than I do that he will not be pleased when he finds out you failed. Something I'm sure he's used to you doing."

I caught the paling look he gave as she struck a nerve. "But you don't have the last key," he replied, his tone brittle.

"Think again," she said, pointing to the three keys that were floating towards the orb. A void had opened up behind the orb, showing a blip from the other realm. Only it wasn't the Lyceum. A line of bookshelves as tall and as far as the eye could see hovered inside the void. Two blinding lights shot towards us and connected to the orb. It was the purest white I'd ever seen before. *The Hall of Knowledge*, I thought in awe. Just seeing it made me feel cleansed.

Zane growled, summoning more energy, and then hurled a ball towards Lexi. She ducked in time and swiped his legs with her right foot, knocking him onto the ground.

"You won't stop this, Zane. This is The Fates' work."

But he caught her off guard as he tripped her with his hands and then jumped on top of her, punching her in the face. Her head rebounded off the ground, and then she went unconscious as well.

"NOooooooo!" I yelled as flames shot from my mouth and hands. I felt the strength and the anger inside of me build. Something clicked. The old me shut off as the dragon took over, reveling in the emotions I felt.

Zane ducked, but wasn't quick enough as the flames caught the edge of his cloak. He stumbled amongst the broken shards of crystals, rushing backwards on his bloodied hands. Then he noticed the flames as they scorched up his back. He quickly took it off, moving away from it.

I let out a large roar, the entire cave vibrating as everything I had kept pent up for the past two weeks was released.

"This fight has always been about me, not Lexi and not Logan. Now you're going to pay." My voice sounded different, more powerful. I leapt into the air, spreading my wings. I couldn't control the urge to hurt him. He needed to pay for what he did to my friend.

"What?" I asked as he stood frozen in shock. "Cat got your tongue? Or shall I say dragon?"

He didn't reply as he continued to scurry away from me. The orb was swirling now, a light shining through the portal that was opening.

I noticed Lexi waking. It looked like she was going to say something, but the portal sucked her through. She had disappeared.

"What's going on?" asked Logan in a daze, rubbing his forehead.

Then Zane was also pulled through the portal, screaming bloody murder the whole way.

I landed, suddenly realizing the mistake I was about to make. It wasn't like me to kill someone. And I would have gladly killed Zane in that moment.

The scales on my body began to disappear, and my wings retracted into me. My amulet was lit up, searing my chest as my body shifted back to my human form. The only problem was…I was naked. I grabbed my bookbag and quickly slid on shorts and an oversized t-shirt from the day before. Then I started to feel the pull of the portal, sucking me towards it like a massive vacuum. I could not have run from it even if I'd wanted to. It was calling me, telling me that this was it. I let go of everything, of my fears, of the island, of who I thought I was and who I may never be, and ran towards it with the hope of finding Fenn.

But of course, right as I jumped in, Logan grabbed onto my ankle in a state of idiocy. I felt myself floating through space and knew that I was porting.

"Get off of me, you idiot!" I yelled, kicking my foot into his face and accidentally knocking him out. I had to grab his arm so he wouldn't float away. I turned my head and found myself back in the same cave.

Okay?

Lexi came running over to me and pulled me into a bear hug. "Welcome home," she said.

My body roared to life, screaming for my conscious mind to catch up with the change. I knew in my core that this was home. I had finally found myself.

I looked around and noticed Zane, in the corner, bound in some sort of magical trance and looking defeated.

"Aurora," spoke a familiar deep voice. I turned and came face-to-face with my father.

Chapter 31

~

Home Again

HE EXTENDED HIS ARMS WITH a twinkle in his sparkling lavender eyes. I ran, not thinking twice about hugging a complete stranger. Finally things fell into place for me; finally I found the missing pieces to my puzzle. My mind flooded with childhood memories.

"I remember everything," I admitted excitedly. My Oraculus was lying in front of me, closed. I quickly grabbed it and shoved it into my bookbag that was next to me.

My father cleared his throat and then said, "Astral's anxiously waiting for us. I've missed you, Little Flame." He leaned in and kissed my forehead. It felt so natural, so right. I closed my eyes and savored the moment I'd waited so long for. I wanted to freeze time.

"I want to meet, well, reunite with him. I need to actually. I have so many questions about what I'm capable of. I feel different...stronger," I said excitedly, flexing my fists and reveling in the muscle tone that had replaced my previously lanky stature. There was an unfamiliar urge there as well. The urge to fly. Something lived inside of me, an entity striving to break free. My dragon side.

My dad smiled and said, "I agree. We all have questions about what you're truly capable of. It's something your mother and I have waited a long time to see."

My mother...where was she?

"Where is she?" I asked, pushing off him to look around. He stood an inch taller than I, dusting off his robes. "I need to see her too. This isn't a true reunion without her."

His eyes frowned a little. "She's been with her family ever since we left you with Astral. I can't turn her back into a human with a war on the brink. She needs to fight alongside her family. It's her duty as heir to the throne." I felt the sadness I saw on his face, and my heart skipped a beat with knowing that I would now be able to build a relationship with my dad. "We will open a port at Astral's so you can talk to her." He tilted up my chin to stare into my eyes. "So don't worry." He winked, but something in the way his eyes shadowed told me he was hiding something. I let it go for the moment. I had so many things to worry about.

"What are we going to do about Logan?" I turned to Lexi. She was still kneeling next to him, keeping him under some sort of sleeping spell. Her fingers were absentmindedly playing with his hair.

"I, um...I haven't quite figured that out yet," she said on the edge of a nervous giggle. "I...uh, I think until we decide what we're going to do with Zane, we should keep him here." Her eyes darted over to my father and then shot to the ground. "Zane has seen him, and I don't think it's wise to send Logan back unprotected." She looked up with a slight nod as if willing us to agree.

Obviously I would agree with her. I knew her situation with the marriage arrangement, and I knew she really liked Logan. I had promised myself that if I made it home, I would have her back no matter what.

My father's eyes rolled to the ceiling as he let out a sigh. Lexi started to say something, but my father's hand shot out, silencing her. Then he bridged his nose with his fingers and walked over to where Zane sat. I followed him. My father stared at Zane for a moment as if deciding, weighing the pros and cons.

"Zordon will be expecting him back, which creates a problem. We need to figure out what to do with him," I announced. I was taking charge. This was a new, vaguely familiar side of me. A confident side. I liked it. I had missed it.

"Well..." Lexi let hang.

"Well, Alexis, then you're responsible for him and his actions. Though I don't think your mother," my father turned to face her, tipping his head forward, "or Brohm for that matter will be happy about this." He finished his scolding, sounding just like a dad would sound. I smiled at that thought. Then I looked over and shared a secret smile with Lexi as we laughed on the inside. It was amazing the way some friendships are forged.

"Sounds like a fair deal to me," she chimed, jumping to her feet. "About this whole Brohm thing, couldn't you just put a good word in to my mother? I really think it's unnecessary that my marriage be planned for me. I'm completely capable of making my own life-changing decisions." She glanced down at Logan, confusion clouding her eyes.

My father let out a whole-hearted laugh. "I see the other realm has taken an effect on your point of view," he commented dryly.

She shot back with a bit of feistiness. "For your information I've always been like this. This experience has helped me shed my outer shell, and it was your amazing daughter who showed me that there's more to life." She strode over to me and threw her arm over my shoulder. A gesture of sisterhood. I placed my arm on the small of her back, supporting her, and we both stared back at my dad defiantly.

"And so it begins," he muttered under his breath, shaking his head and smiling.

"In that case…" said Lexi moving back to Logan. She grabbed his arm and threw it over her shoulder, picking him up fireman style. "I guess we can get a move on it now that we've decided," she finished.

Laughter bubbled up out of me. Girl rescuing guy… I loved it.

I felt my own strength stirring deep inside my aching bones and was reminded about the new tattoo-like markings on my chest. The pain was a distant memory now, like it had never happened.

I pulled the neck of my shirt down just enough to see the black markings. From one side of my shoulder to the other, swirling lines in the form of dragon wings spread themselves out across the front of my chest. When I traced my finger along the markings, a fiery glow followed. I felt a tinge of heat on the ends of my fingers. "Cool," was the best comment I could think of. I ran my fingers over them once again.

"Those are the dragon wings of the family crest, dear," said my father. "I see you have been blessed to wear them." He moved his robe aside, revealing similar markings along his chest. "It takes years before a young Mageling like you is granted the right to wear their family crest. Your power must be stronger than I thought."

I glanced back down at them.

Lexi huffed from behind us. "Umm…he's not exactly as light as a feather. Can we go?" she asked, annoyed.

I hoped it wasn't because of my markings.

Myrdinn waved his hand, and the port opened to take us back to Astral. Lexi jumped in without waiting for him to get out the sentence he had started.

He turned to me with a smile and said, "I'm going to grab Zane. You go on through. I'll meet you on the other side." Then he kissed my forehead and stepped around me.

Again the feeling of drifting through space pulled me until I was standing in a sunny field. Knee-high grass was swaying softly in the midday breeze.

I looked all around me and up to the skies, closing my eyes and breathing deep as the feeling of home washed over me. This was where I played as a little girl. I could picture my former self running through the grass, chasing after the butterflies.

"Hey, you," said Lexi. She had laid Logan down on the grass next to her and was sitting with her legs crossed. She always managed to make herself comfortable wherever she was.

"This is amazingly beautiful," I replied tracing one of the sun's rays with my fingers. I picked a purple flower that swayed with the grass and sat down next to her.

We both lay back and looked up, watching the clouds. It was nice to have a quiet moment with her. Was this what it would have been like had I not been born to fight Zordon? All peaceful and cozy.

The sun felt delicious on my skin. A tingling burn blazed behind my new tattoo.

"I see you earned your markings," she said, a hint of jealousy in her voice. She sighed. "You deserve it though."

"I didn't even know this would happen," I admitted.

"Yeah. I have a few more years before I can earn mine. Unless something crazy happens and the energy I use impresses the Counsel."

"Counsel?"

"You have a lot to catch up on."

I was sure of that.

After a brief moment of awkward silence, I said, "This was where I was raised, where Astral taught me everything." I twirled the flower that I'd picked and put it in my hair, reaching for another to play with.

"Really? I've only been here once before. My mother and I had to stay for a few days while the Draconta left the castle. It was all hush-hush, but Astral was very kind to us. I was taught a lot about magic in the few days that I was here."

I felt slightly jealous. Although I now remembered a lot of my time with Astral, I couldn't remember how I learned the things he had taught me. The magic that I had then and the magic that I have now were different. I was stronger than before.

My father came through the port with Zane on his back and found us lying in the grass. He looked angry, alerting me.

"Let's keep moving," he griped. We both got up and followed behind his hurried steps. Were we in danger? Had Zordon found out about Zane already?

"This house is completely protected. You will feel it the moment we step through the enchantment he has put up. It will feel like a stinging sensation. It's to keep out unwanted visitors." I nodded and felt the energy ripple through me as we stepped through the shield. Magic was going to be something I really enjoyed, especially if I could do things like this.

"What about Zane?" I asked, confused as to why he was allowed in. He was definitely not wanted here.

"He's with me under my magic. The shield recognizes me."

Even though he was my father and I didn't really know him, I could definitely sense aggravation in the way he shorted each word and practically spat them out. I looked over to Lexi and discovered a confused look on her as well.

An enormous invisible bubble rippled around us and then Astral's house appeared. It looked exactly as I remembered it. A giant-sized country cottage resting on the top of a hill. It was painted yellow with a large wooden door that had incredible detailing of animals and creatures mixed in with flowers. A picture of a fairy tale came to mind. I went to touch it, feeling like the animals may have been moving, but my fingers never made it to the wood. Astral stepped out from behind the front door, as colossal as ever. His smile was contagious, and I felt my heart swell. A part of me felt that he was a stranger, but the new memories that filled my mind told me otherwise.

"Aurora Jay Megalos, my-my you certainly have grown up." He wrapped his large arms around me with a deep-bellied chuckle as he shrunk down to a more manageable size. He was still several feet taller than I was so my arms could only reach around his sides. I got a face full of pale skin from his arms.

He pulled my face into his hands and said, "You've got your mother's eyes but your father's face. You've sure grown into a beauty, Aurora Megalos." I blushed uncontrollably.

The smell of the fireplace crept out from behind him and teased my nose, making me feel even more comfortable. I suddenly remembered that he burned special logs that kept a feeling of comfort for his guests and that he liked to put orange peel into the fire. "Come inside, I've got something for you." I followed him into the cottage forgetting all about my father and Lexi. I was too excited to care about the issue my father seemed to have. That is, until he brought it up.

"We've got a major problem, Astral," called Myrdinn as he slammed the door shut behind us. He dropped Zane onto the wooden floor like a pile of wood. I flinched at the sound.

Lexi quickly walked in and set Logan on one of the cozy chairs by the fire. He stirred a little as green energy once again pulsed from her hands. She managed to keep him sleeping.

I turned to listen to my father. "Zordon will be expecting Zane anytime now. I found this in his pocket." He held up a round object. I wasn't quite sure what it was so I stepped a little closer hoping to figure it out.

I'd never seen anything like it before. It was the size of a compass and had a tiny dial like you'd find on a pocket watch. There were etchings on the outside that looked similar to hieroglyphics. As the dial moved in the light, the etchings lit up and then returned to their dull color.

Thankfully Astral came to my rescue by explaining it out loud. "A spectol?" He looked over to me. "It's a magical device that can recreate the time and place of anything going on with the person who holds it." He took it from Myrdinn and brought it up close to his glowing eyes.

"Thankfully we have it. We won't have to worry about Zordon seeing it," I said with relief. But the look on my father's face took that relief away.

"There are two parts to this device, Aurora. They feed into each other. This part takes the images and the other part plays them out." My stomach sank to my feet. This was not good. "Now you see the problem. He knows everything that has just transpired, including your name and what you look like." Myrdinn frowned and looked up to Astral. Astral closed his eyes. I couldn't tell if there was disappointment or worry there.

Should I tell them that I already had a run in with Zordon? I looked back at Lexi who shook her head no. *Keep it to myself, I agree,* I thought.

"It will only be a matter of time before he finds this place," finished Myrdinn. He looked defeated. "How could I be so stupid?" I went to him and hugged him. This was a huge burden to carry. How could he have known?

Astral took control of the situation. "Let's focus on fixing this. Call on Gabe. He may be able to help." Myrdinn nodded and left the room. "Now back to where we were. Follow me, Aurora, I have something to show you."

The gentleness of his nature was pleasing. Even in a time of panic, he remained calm. But I felt defeated. I had no idea how to fix the situation and could not believe that I was supposed to defeat Zordon.

Astral began to laugh. "You can't expect to be able to fix everything, my dear. At least not right away. You've only been your true self for a small amount of time. Give yourself some time to adjust... to remember." His ancient eyes held so much knowledge. I couldn't begin to understand it all.

"I just expect a lot out of myself I guess. I don't want to be a burden to anyone and that's what I feel like."

He patted me on the back and opened a door in a hallway that we had approached.

"Yes, you do expect too much, but that's a good thing. It will keep you persistent. As for being a burden, I'm sure that in just a few days you'll have enough of your powers under control to take that feeling away."

He moved out of the doorway so that I could look in to a room full of knick-knacks. Things I had never seen before. A desk sat in the far corner, surrounded by shelves. There was another small fireplace and a chair that sat in front of the desk.

"What is this place?" I asked, confused as to why he was showing me this.

"My room."

It reminded me of the Lyceum the way everything floated on air. I grabbed onto something that was similar to what my father had pulled from Zane's pocket.

"Ah, that is an earlier version of a spectol," Astral explained. I let it go expecting it to fall, but it only floated past me. Then everything zoomed towards the walls and landed on the many shelves that were built there. I noticed how bright Astral's blue eyes went when he used his magic.

"Wow," I said, amazed at how easy the cleanup was.

"That's the advantage of having magic. You can bend things to your will. But that is another lesson. I wanted to talk to you about something." He stopped moving and turned to me. "That amulet you wear is extremely important and must remain protected. It is what binds you to your dragon side."

"How?"

"On the day of your birth, I forged this amulet and cast a binding spell that I found in the Hall of Knowledge. No one knew exactly how your human side would mesh with the dragon blood that runs through your vein. Your mother and I thought it best that we take precautions. By binding your dragon to this amulet, you are able to keep your human form and shift into your dragon form safely," he said softly.

"So the dragon isn't in me, it's in the amulet?" I was confused. I know I had felt the stir of the dragon before.

"No, the amulet is the anchor for what's inside of you. When you fully merge with your dragon side, you will need this amulet in order to remain alive, otherwise the shift would kill you," he said gravely. "That's why it is so important that you keep it on at all costs. It's as important as your Oraculus. That book is your life, Aurora." His tone was serious, and his eyes stared deeply at the amulet lying on top of my tattoo.

"I know. I feel it every time I have it in my hands. This feeling of protection takes over. I don't want anyone touching it, not even people I love. It's like—I know that without it, I would be nothing."

"That's because it is your lifeline. You *wouldn't* be anything without it. It is the beating of your heart." I knew exactly what he was talking about because I had felt that deep down before.

"About Zordon, umm…" I wasn't exactly sure how to begin telling him about my previous encounter. He stopped walking around the room and turned to face me, his eyes intently probing my thoughts.

I stammered, trying to sound positive. "Well, the Oraculus... sometimes I'm thrown into his world. Zordon's world, I mean." My hands were flying a mile a minute as I tried to explain. When I looked to his face, his brows were furrowed.

"And...the last time that happened, he, umm...well...he kind of saw me."

"And what happened?" he asked calmly.

"Nothing good. He tried to kill me. Zane was there, and it's all his fault that I was even spotted because I was trying to hide, but yeah, he put me in this bubble thing and I knew that I was about to die, but then this white light clouded the bubble and saved me." I exhaled loudly with a half-hearted smile.

Astral stood quietly. A moment later he spoke. "I thought so, but I wasn't sure. The Oraculus is a link between you and Zordon. A very dangerous link that I didn't see coming. It makes sense though. Your Oraculus and Zordon's are one and the same, only split in half. It all ties in with the prophecy." I stood still, hoping he would continue with his explanation. This was what I had been waiting to hear.

He began pacing back and forth, a nervous habit of his that I remembered. "One of The Fates tried to hide the creation of Zordon. It upset the balance. Rather than exiling him like their previous fifth brother who broke the law, they decided to try something different. They decided to take Zordon's unfinished Oraculus and have me rip it in half, intending to create an ultimate rival." He looked me dead in the eyes as if trying to etch that sentence into me.

"Wait, you wrote our Oraculus? How?" I asked.

He smiled and said, "I am an Ancient, Aurora. I was chosen. As far as the white light that you saw, I would say you were saved by a higher power. A Fate is on your side. But that, my dear, is another lesson. I have much to think on, and you should get settled in before we delve deeper into this discussion. There is a lot to talk about."

I huffed but didn't push it, remembering that it wouldn't help anyway. When he chose not to say something, well, that was it. There was no persuading him. So I changed subjects.

"Will the whole seeing Zordon thing keep happening?"

"I have to research this anomaly more. Nothing like this has ever occurred, and I can't tell you exactly how deep the connection is. This is why we must consider precautions." He braced my shoulders, his eyes glowing a bit brighter. "And I don't want you doing anything with your Oraculus until I say otherwise. You could not only put yourself, but everyone you love in danger by continuing to toy with it. Especially now that he has seen you, and we have confirmation that the connection is a physical one."

I silently nodded. He squeezed my shoulders and then let go, walking over to his desk.

"I have a question about the prophecy," I said quietly. "The last line talks about a death to He that breaks the barrier. Do you know what that means?"

"Not without the missing piece. Soothe insisted on keeping it to himself. Did he tell you?"

I shook my head no. "He didn't tell me much of anything actually. Don't you think it's important that we find out the missing piece?" I boldly questioned.

He smiled brightly. "Yes I do. I think it would help. But then one's faced with knowing the truth, good or bad. Which leaves me questioning if we really should know. Soothe may not seem all there, but he knows what he's doing. If you are meant to know, you will…one day."

One day can't come soon enough. I'll have to go back and find him, I thought, tucking the idea away for a later day. I didn't know if he was in my head or not, but if he heard what I was thinking, then he must have agreed or he would've said otherwise. I hoped.

I had one last question. "What happened after I left that night?" The sound of Gabe's cry and the image of Astral's worried faced was the most prominent memory.

"The other two Fates were on their brother's tail. They stopped them before they could go any further."

"What about you and Gabe?"

Instead of answering, he smiled coyly. "There will be time to discuss these things, Aurora. For now we need to plan what we're going to do with Zane and get you settled in."

I followed him out of the room and back into the living room. Gabe and Myrdinn were huddled with their backs to us, whispering something I couldn't understand. Myrdinn looked up at my arrival, and I caught him mouthing "…We'll talk about this later."

What couldn't they say in front of me?

Gabe turned around to face me. It was strange seeing his face, knowing that I was wide-awake. "Aurora," he said as he walked slowly towards me. He stopped right in front of me, and as I reached out to hug him I wound up hugging the air.

I opened my eyes and found him kneeling in front of me. I tried to recover myself as quickly as possible without anyone noticing, but of course nothing got past Astral. He chuckled from behind me.

"It's so good to see you alive and all grown up. The last time I saw you, you were…"

I cut him off by finishing, "…a little girl. The night I left."

He stood back up, now looking down at me. "Yes, the night you went into hiding. Though we didn't protect you as well as we should have." His eyes shot to Myrdinn and then to the ground.

Astral stepped in before I could ask what he meant. "Myrdinn, there was nothing anyone could have done to prevent the connection from happening. You have to accept what The Fates have planned." Gabe must have told my father about my near death experience.

"Honestly, it's okay Myr…I mean, Dad. I'm fine. And we have bigger problems to worry about right now."

"As in dealing with Zane, I assume you mean," he replied.

Lexi walked in. "He's chained up downstairs," she announced, answering everyone's question.

"I don't think it's a good idea that we keep him here," said Gabe. "We shouldn't take the chance of Zordon tracking him."

Astral rubbed his chin as he paced back and forth.

"He shouldn't be able to track this house. Astral has enough enchantments to hide it from anyone," said Myrdinn.

"Except The Fates," added Astral.

"But they wouldn't…" replied Myrdinn. Lexi grabbed my hand and pulled me away from the conversation to stand by the fire.

"Your father heard about Zordon meeting with the Dark Saar. That is really why he is so upset." I should have known. It's not like I was going to come back to a perfect life. I was returning to fight a war.

"How do you know?" I asked.

"I overheard them talking while you were with Astral." She looked as nervous as I felt.

"My mother?" I asked, hoping that she would be okay.

"That's the thing. Myrdinn can't get in touch with her. Gabe wants to keep that from you thinking it's in your best interest, but I feel like you should know. This is, after all, about you."

She's right, I should know. They want me to fight for them, to be their savior, so they should keep me in the loop. At least I think they should. And how could my mom defeat the Dark Saar alone?

"Thank you for telling me, Lexi." My aggravation was growing and I could feel an outburst brewing. It was well overdue. "Although I appreciate them looking out for me, I think they should know that I'm not a little girl." I tilted my eyebrows, hoping for her permission to confront them about what she just told me.

She threw her hands up in front of her face and said, "By all means feel free. We are friends of honesty, my dear." Her smile made me feel a little bit better. Then she tilted her head towards the hall and perked her ear up "Got to go…good luck." And with a pat on my arm she was gone.

I sucked in a deep breath hoping to find some courage, but it didn't seem to help. So I stood there for a minute and had a mental debate with myself. This was my fight. I had to take ownership of that. Zordon and I were connected, and it was up to me to end him. I needed to know exactly what was going on at all times, right? I blocked the weaker side of my brain and stormed up to Gabe and my dad. It was now or never.

"Is there something you'd like to tell me?" I demanded in my most authoritative tone. Any spectator would have laughed but I kept my game face on, determined to walk away with an understanding between us. If we were all going to coexist and get through this mess together, then we needed to go into it on the same page.

"What do you mean?" asked my father in an innocent voice. I intertwined my fingers and gazed at them, waiting. They both exchanged glances. "Lexi!" yelled Myrdinn. She poked her head out of a door in the hallway and smiled before shutting it again. *I'm glad I can handle things on my own*, I thought as I tried to hide a smile.

"I swear that girl has issues," said Gabe under his breath. He ran his hands through his black, medium-length hair.

"This is not about her. You know what this is about. Now before you explain everything in detail, I want you two to understand something. I'm a grown woman. I've been on my own for the past eight years and I know how to take care of myself. I've accepted all of this," I spread my arms out in front of me, "with open arms. The least of what I deserve is to be told the truth. Especially if I'm supposed to save everyone somehow."

I don't know where the boost of confidence came from, but I was glad it came when it did. The look on their faces was priceless. My heart pounded with excitement.

I waited for what seemed like forever for one of them to say something when finally my father spoke up. "You have a lot of your mother in you. It makes me proud." His smile was genuine.

If only I knew her and could see that for myself.

"Everything you've heard is true. We are on the brink of war, but your mother is safe," he interjected seeing the look on my face. "I'm sure she will contact me as soon as she is able. Your safety is important above everything else." His lavender eyes seemed dull.

Gabe spoke up and added, "Rest assured, Progeny. My people will engage when it is time. We won't let anything happen to your mother or the royal family."

But what about all the others? What would they do to fight the Dark Saar? I couldn't just sit by and let innocent people...well... Draconta get hurt or killed. This was what my life had become— mystical creatures that needed protection from other mystical and magical things.

Astral chimed in. "Now that that is all settled, we do have things to deal with. I need you to get settled in your room, Aurora."

I tried to get out a "but," but Astral saw it coming and put up his hand to stop me from speaking.

"No buts. You have proven your point valiantly, and you will be included in everything from now on. For now, please do as I ask so we can get everything in place. You need your rest if we are to train." He used what he knew would shut me up.

My room was where I remembered it, and it actually felt like my room, not like a new place. I knocked lightly and heard Lexi.

"Come in," she said with an odd tone in her voice. I opened it. Shock replaced all other emotions and thoughts.

The moment I caught my breath and registered just who exactly he was, I was able to speak again.

"Fenn! I made it back to you," I declared, rushing in for a kiss. Our lips met, the world disappearing around us. He squeezed me tightly in return, his familiar scent warming my soul. Time suspended as everything rushed to the surface, the fears, the love, the doubt.

"Excuse me," whispered Lexi as she quietly tip-toed around us and out of my room.

I let myself revel in the feel of his mouth while his fingers passionately twisted in my hair. This is what I had waited for-to go for what I wanted rather than letting fear control me. I opened my eyes, gazing at his squeezed tight with a hungry yearning and smiled, gently leaning my forehead against his.

My mind raced as it searched for the right words. There was so much to say, so much that had happened that I wanted to share with him. And there were so many questions.

But there would be time for that later. Right now I just wanted to be with him, touch him, and feel that he is alive and safe.

I looked up at him and smiled, finally okay with how I felt and said, "Love you."

He grinned from ear to ear, chuckling in satisfaction.

"Love you, too."

THE END...
For now...

About the Author

Candace Knoebel is the award-winning author of *Born in Flames*-a young adult fantasy trilogy. Published by 48fourteen in 2012, *Born in Flames* went on to win Turning the Pages Book of the Year award in February of 2013.

Candace Knoebel dreamed of being a dancer ever since she could remember. With a love of all things art, she saw herself moving to New York and pursuing her passion as an artist. But all that changed on October 10, 2002 when she met the love of her life. Her dreams diverged. After marrying her high school sweetheart and having two beautiful children, she realized she missed her creative side. Through lunch breaks and late nights after putting her kids to bed, she built a world where she could escape the ever-pressing days of an eight to five Purgatory. Since then, she crawled out of Purgatory and has devoted her time to writing and sometimes heelying.

Born in Flames Trilogy
Coming Soon

~

Embracing the Flames, Book II
From the Embers, Book III

CPSIA information can be obtained at www.ICGtesting.com
Printed in the USA
LVOW06s0323220713

343859LV00004B/160/P